RAVEN'S GATE

BOOK ONE OF THE GATEKEEPERS

ANTHONY HOROWITZ

Scholastic Inc.

New York   Toronto   London   Auckland   Sydney
Mexico City   New Delhi   Hong Kong   Buenos Aires

ISBN 0-439-85629-9

12 11 10 9 8 7 6 5 4 3 2 1   6 7 8 9 10 11/0

Printed in the U.S.A.   40

First Scholastic paperback printing, May 2006

Text design by Steve Scott

Text was set in New Baskerville.

before the beginning was the gate.

And

five gatekeepers

children.

Four boys. One girl.

it has been written

The night of everlasting darkness is

drawing in

The gate is about to open

The gatekeepers must return

ONE
The Warehouse

Matt Freeman knew he was making a mistake.

He was sitting on a low wall outside Ipswich Station, wearing a gray hooded sweatshirt, shapeless faded jeans, and sneakers with frayed laces. It was six o'clock in the evening and the London train had just pulled in. Behind him, commuters were fighting their way out of the station. The concourse was a tangle of cars, taxis, and pedestrians, all of them trying to find their way home. A traffic light blinked from red to green, but nothing moved. Somebody leaned on their horn and the noise blared out, cutting through the damp evening air. Matt heard it and looked up briefly. But the crowd meant nothing to him. He wasn't part of it. He never had been — and he sometimes thought he never would be.

Two men carrying umbrellas walked past and glanced at him disapprovingly. They probably thought he was up to no good. The way he was sitting — hunched forward with his knees apart — made him look somehow dangerous and older than fourteen. He had broad shoulders, a well-developed, muscular body, and bright blue, intelligent eyes. His hair was black, cut very short. Give him another five years and he could be a footballer or a model or — like plenty of others — both.

His first name was Matthew, but he always called himself Matt. As the troubles had begun to pile up in his life, he had begun to use his last name less and less until it was no longer a part of him. Freeman was the name on the registry at school. It was the name on the truancy list and it was a name well known to the local social services. But Matthew never wrote it down and seldom spoke it. Matt was enough. The name suited him. After all, for as long as he could remember, people had been walking all over him.

He watched the two men with umbrellas cross the bridge and disappear in the direction of the city center. Matt hadn't been born in Ipswich. He had been brought here and he hated everything about the place. For a start, it wasn't a city. It was too small. But it had none of the charm of a village or a market town. It was really just an oversize shopping center with the same shops and supermarkets that you saw everywhere else. It didn't even have a decent football team. You could swim in the Crown Pool or you could see movies at the multiplex — or, if you could afford it, there was an artificial ski slope and go-karting. But that was about it.

Matt had just three pounds in his pocket, saved up from his newspaper round. There was another twenty pounds at home, hidden in a box under his bed. He needed money for the same reason every other teenager in Ipswich did. It wasn't just because his sneakers were falling apart and the games on his Xbox were six months out-of-date. Money was power. Money was independence. He didn't have any and he was here tonight because he wanted some.

But already he was wishing he hadn't come. It was wrong. It was stupid. Why had he ever agreed?

4

He glanced at his watch. Ten past six. They had arranged to meet at a quarter to. Well, that was excuse enough. He swung himself off the wall and started forward, heading across the station front. But he hadn't taken more than a couple of steps before another, older boy appeared out of nowhere, blocking his path.

"You off then, Matt?" the boy asked.

"I thought you weren't coming," Matt said.

"Oh yes? And why did you think that?"

"Because you're twenty-five minutes late. Because I'm cold. Because you're about as reliable as a local bus." That was what Matt wanted to say. But the words didn't come. He just shrugged.

The other boy smiled. His name was Kelvin and he was seventeen, tall and scrawny, with fair hair, pale skin, and acne. He was dressed expensively . . . designer jeans and a soft leather jacket. Even back when he still went to school, Kelvin had always had the best gear.

"I got held up," he said.

Matt said nothing.

"You haven't had second thoughts, have you?"

"No."

"You've got nothing to worry about, Matt, mate. It's going to be easy. Charlie told me . . ."

Charlie was Kelvin's older brother. Matt had never met him, which wasn't surprising. Charlie was in prison, in a young offenders' institution just outside Manchester. Kelvin didn't talk about him often. But it was Charlie who had first heard about the warehouse.

It was fifteen minutes away from Ipswich Station, in an industrial zone. A warehouse stacked with computer games,

DVDs, and compact discs. Amazingly, it had no alarm systems and only one security guard, a retired policeman who was half-asleep most of the time, with his feet up and his head buried in a newspaper. Charlie knew all this because a friend of his had done some electrical work there. According to Charlie, you could break in with a bent paper clip and you could probably walk out with a lot of valuable equipment. It was easy. Just waiting to be taken.

And that was why the two of them had arranged to meet here. Matt had agreed to the idea when they were talking about it, but half of him had thought Kelvin wasn't being serious. The two of them had done plenty of things together. Under Kelvin's guidance, they'd stolen stuff from supermarkets. Once they'd even driven off in someone's car. But Matt knew this was much worse. This was serious. It was breaking and entering. Burglary. Real crime.

"Are you sure about this?" he asked now.

"Sure I'm sure. What's the problem?"

"If we get caught . . ."

"We won't. Charlie says they don't even have security cameras." Kelvin rested a foot on the wall. Matt noticed he was wearing a pair of brand-new Nikes. He often wondered how Kelvin could afford his clothes. Now, he supposed, he knew. "Come on, Matt," Kelvin went on. "If you're going to be such a wuss, I don't want to hang out with you. What's the big deal?"

A look of exasperation had crept into Kelvin's face, and in that moment Matt knew he would have to go. If he didn't, he would lose his only friend. When Matt had first started at St. Edmund's comprehensive in Ipswich, Kelvin had taken him under his wing. There had been kids who thought Matt was weird. Other kids who tried to bully him. Kelvin fended them off. And it helped having Kelvin just a few doors away on Eastfield Terrace, where Matt lived with his aunt and her boyfriend. When things were really bad, there was always somewhere to go. And he had to admit that it was flattering, hanging out with someone three years older than him.

"There's no big deal," he said. "I'll come."

And that was it. The decision had been made. Matt tried to damp down the sense of rising fear. Kelvin slapped him on the back. The two of them set off together.

Darkness came very quickly. It was the end of March, but there was little sign of spring. It had rained heavily all month and the night still seemed to arrive before it was meant to. As they reached the industrial zone, the street lamps flickered on, throwing pools of ugly orange light onto the ground. The zone was fenced off with signs warning that this was private property, but the fence was rusty and full of holes and the only other barrier was the wild grass and thistles that sprouted all around where the pavement ended. Railway lines stretched out overhead, high up on a series of brick supports. As the two boys approached quietly, flitting through the shadows, a train rattled past, on its way to London.

There were about a dozen buildings in all. Some of them had advertisements painted on the side. L for Leather, office furniture. J. B. Stryker Auto Engineering. Spit & Polish Industrial Cleaning. Kelvin's warehouse was unmarked. It was a long, rectangular block with corrugated iron walls and a sloping tiled roof. It had been built slightly apart from its neighbors, separated from them by a row of bottle banks and a junk heap of cartons and old tires. There was nobody in sight. The whole area seemed deserted and forgotten.

The main entrance to the warehouse — a large sliding door — was at the front. There were no windows, but Kelvin led Matt around to a second door at the side. The two of them were crouching now, hurrying through the darkness on tiptoe. Matt tried to relax, to enjoy what they were doing. This was an adventure, wasn't it? An hour from now they'd be laughing about it with their pockets full of cash. But he was sick at heart, and when Kelvin reached into his pocket and produced a knife his stomach tightened and he felt even worse.

"What's that for?" he whispered.

"Don't worry. It's just to get us in."

Kelvin inserted the point of the blade into the crack between the door and its frame and began to play with the bolt. Matt watched him without saying anything, secretly hoping that the door wouldn't open. The lock looked secure enough and it seemed somehow improbable that the seventeen year old would be able to unfasten it with anything as cumbersome as a knife. But then there was a click and light spilled out as the door swung open. Kelvin stepped back and Matt saw that he was equally surprised, although he was trying not to show it.

"We're in," he said.

Matt nodded. For a moment he wondered if Charlie might have been right after all. Perhaps this was going to be as easy as Kelvin had said.

They went through the door.

The warehouse was huge — much bigger than Matt had expected. When Kelvin had talked about the place, he had imagined nothing more than a few racks of DVDs and the rest of it an otherwise empty space. But it seemed to go on forever, with hundreds and hundreds of shelves, numbered and divided into corridors that formed a complex grid system, the whole thing lit by vast industrial lights hanging on chains. And as well as the games and the DVDs there were boxes of computer equipment, Game Boys, MP3 players, and even mobile phones, all wrapped in plastic, ready for the stores.

Matt looked up. There were no security cameras. Just like Kelvin had said.

"You go that way." Kelvin pointed. "Go for the small, expensive stuff. I'll meet you back here."

"Why don't we stick together?"

"Don't you worry, Matty. I won't leave without you!"

The two of them split up. Matt found himself in a narrow corridor with DVDs on both sides. Tom Cruise, Johnny Depp, Brad Pitt . . . all the familiar faces in all the most recent feature films were there. He reached out and took a handful, not even looking at what he'd chosen. He was sure there were more expensive things in the warehouse, but he didn't care. He just wanted to get out.

Everything went wrong at once.

It began with a smell that was suddenly in his nostrils, everywhere, coming from nowhere.

The smell of burnt toast.

And a voice. *"Come on, Matthew. We're going to be late."*

A flash of color. A bright yellow wall. Pine cupboards. A teapot shaped like a teddy bear.

The smell told him that something was wrong in the same way that a dog will often bark before danger actually appears. Matt knew that it was odd, but he had never really questioned it. It was a knack . . . a sort of instinct. A warning. But this time it had come too late. Before he knew what was happening, a heavy hand had clamped down on his shoulder, spinning him around. A voice exclaimed, "What do you think you're doing?"

Matt felt his arms go weak, and the DVDs cascaded to the floor, clattering around his feet. He found himself looking into the face of a security guard and knew at once that this wasn't the old codger Kelvin had described. This was a tall, serious man in a black and silver uniform with a radio transmitter attached to some sort of holster on his chest. The man was in his fifties but looked fit, built like a rugby player.

"The police are already on their way," he said. "You set off the alarm when you opened that door. So don't try anything funny. . . ."

Matt couldn't move. He was too shocked by the appearance of the guard. His heart was hammering in his chest, making it difficult to breathe. He was suddenly feeling very young again.

"What's your name?" the guard demanded.

Matt said nothing.

"Are you here on your own?" This time, his voice was a little kinder. He must have seen that Matt was no threat to him. "How many of you are there?"

Matt drew a breath. "I . . ."

10

And then, as if a switch had been thrown and the whole world sent into a spin, the real horror began.

The security guard jerked upright, his eyes widening, his mouth falling open. He released Matt and fell sideways. Matt looked past him and saw Kelvin standing there, a dazed smile on his face. At first he didn't understand what had happened. Then he saw the hilt of the knife, sticking out of the guard's back, just above his waist. The security guard didn't look hurt at first. He just looked surprised. Then he folded slowly downward, rested on his knees, pitched forward onto the floor, and lay still.

A whole eternity seemed to pass by. Matt was frozen. He felt he was being sucked into some sort of black hole. Then Kelvin grabbed hold of him.

"We've got to move," he said.

"Kelvin . . . ?" Matt fought for control. "What have you done?" he whispered. "Why did you have to do that?"

"What else could I do?" Kelvin demanded. "He'd seen you."

"I know he'd seen me. But you didn't have to stab him! Do you know what you've done? Do you know what you are —"

The words wouldn't come. Matt was horrified, and before he knew what he was doing he had thrown himself at Kelvin, hurling him into one of the shelves. Kelvin recovered quickly. He was bigger and stronger than Matt. He coiled forward, then lashed out with a fist, catching Matt on the side of the head. Matt fell back, dazed.

"What's the matter with you, Matt?" Kelvin snarled. "What's your problem?"

"You are! You didn't have to do that! You must be out of

your mind!" Matt's head was spinning. He didn't know what to say.

"I was only thinking of you, mate." Kelvin jabbed forward with a finger. "I only did it for you."

The security guard groaned. Matt forced himself to look down. The man was still alive. But he was lying in a pool of blood that seemed to be widening with every second.

"Let's go!" Kelvin hissed.

"No. We can't leave him."

"What?"

"Where's your phone? We have to call for help. . . ."

"Forget that!" Kelvin ran a tongue over his lips. "You stay if you want to. I'm out of here."

"You can't!"

"Watch me!"

And then he was gone, disappearing down the corridor. Matt ignored him. The security guard groaned a second time and tried to say something. Feeling sick, Matt crouched down beside him and placed a hand on his arm. "Don't move," he said. "I'm going to get help."

But help was already here. Matt heard the sirens seconds before the screech of tires announced that the police had arrived. They must have begun their journey to the warehouse the moment Kelvin forced open the door. Leaving the guard, Matt stood up and walked out into the open. A whole section of the wall suddenly slid aside. Matt could see all the way down the warehouse and out into the darkness, which was flashing black blue black blue. There were three cars parked across the entrance. A set of headlamps came on and a dazzling beam of light shot through the darkness and hammered into his eyes. At the same time, half a dozen figures — no more than silhouettes — moved toward him. He could see that they were all dressed in protective clothing. Some of them were carrying guns.

They had already caught Kelvin. Matt saw him being led across the entrance by two armored men a great deal bigger than he was. Kelvin was squealing and crying. Seeing Matt, he suddenly turned and pointed.

"It wasn't me!" he shouted in a whining high-pitched voice. "It was him! He made me come! And he killed the guard!"

"Don't move!" Somebody shouted the words as two more men came running toward Matt.

Matt stood where he was. Slowly, he raised his arms. The palms of his hands were caught in the light from the cars and now he saw that they were glistening red, covered in blood.

"He did it! He did it! He did it!" Kelvin screamed.

The two police officers reached Matt and fell on him. His hands were twisted behind his back and cuffed. He heard the click of the metal and knew there was nothing he could do. Then he was jerked off his feet and dragged, silent and unresisting, out into the night.

TWO
Broken Glass

They took Matt to a building that wasn't a prison and wasn't a hospital but was something in between. The car drove into a rectangular, pavement-covered area with high walls all around. As they drew to a halt, a steel door slid across, blocking the way out. The door closed with a loud electric buzz. Matt heard the locks engage. They seemed to echo inside his head. He wondered if he would ever see the world on the other side of the door again.

"Out!" The voice didn't seem to belong to anyone. It told him what to do and he obeyed. It was drizzling and for a few moments he felt the cold water against his face and was almost grateful for it. He wanted to wash. He could still feel the blood on his hands, behind his back. It had dried and gone sticky.

He passed through a set of double doors into a corridor with harsh lighting, tiles, and the smell of urine and disinfectant. People in uniforms passed him by. Two policemen, then a nurse. He was still handcuffed. He had seen people being arrested on television, but he had never realized what it really felt like, to have his freedom taken away like this. He could feel his arms pinned behind his back. He was utterly defenseless.

There were two policemen with him and they stopped in front of a desk where a third, older man made some entries in a book. He asked a few questions, but Matt didn't hear what he was saying. He could see the man's mouth moving. He heard the words. But they seemed far away and made no sense.

And then he was on the move again, escorted into an elevator that needed a key to be operated. He was taken up to the second floor and down a corridor. Matt kept his head bowed, his eyes fixed on his feet. He didn't want to look around. He didn't want to know where he was.

They stopped again in an open-plan area, a meeting place of several corridors, painted green, with police information posters on the walls. There was an office with a window that had been wired off and, in front of it, a table with a computer and two chairs. The handcuffs were unlocked and he brought his arms forward with a sense of relief. His shoulders were aching.

"Sit down," one of the policemen said.

Matt did as he was told.

About five minutes passed. Then a door opened and a man in a suit and a brightly colored open-neck shirt appeared. He was black, with a slim figure and kind, intelligent eyes. He looked a bit more friendly than the others. He was also younger. Matt didn't think he could be out of his twenties.

"My name is Detective Superintendent Mallory," he said. He had a pleasant, cultivated voice, like a news anchor on TV. "Are you all right?"

"I'm all right." Matt was surprised by the question.

Mallory had sat down at the table opposite him. He pressed a few keys on the computer. "What's your name?" he asked.

"Matt."

Mallory's fingers hovered over the keyboard. "I'm afraid you're going to have to tell me your full name. I need it for the report."

Matt hesitated. But he knew he had to cooperate. "Matthew Freeman," he said.

The detective tapped the letters in and pressed ENTER, then watched as a dozen lines of information scrolled up on the screen. "You seem to have made quite a name for yourself," Mallory said. "You live at 27 Eastfield Terrace?"

"Yes." Matt nodded.

"With a guardian. A Ms. Davis?"

"She's my aunt."

"You're fourteen."

"Yes."

Mallory looked up from the computer screen. "You're in a lot of trouble," he said.

Matt took a breath. "I know," he said. He was almost afraid to ask, but he still had to know. "Is he dead?"

"The guard has a name. Mark Adams. He's married, with two kids." Mallory couldn't conceal his anger. "Right now he's in the hospital. He's going to be there for a while. But he won't die."

"I didn't stab him," Matt said. "I didn't know anyone was going to get hurt. That wasn't the idea."

"That's not what your friend Kelvin told us. He said it was your knife and your plan and it was you who panicked when you were caught."

16

"He's lying."

Mallory sighed. "I know. I've already spoken to the guard and he's told us what happened. He heard the two of you argue and he knows that you wanted to stay. But you're still responsible, Matthew. I have to tell you that you're going to be charged as an accessory. Do you know what that means?"

"Are you going to send me to prison?"

"You're fourteen. You're too young for prison. But it's quite possible you will be facing a custodial sentence." Mallory stopped. He had faced dozens of kids in this room. Many of them had been thugs. They had ranged from openly defiant to snivelling and pathetic. But he was puzzled by the good-looking, quiet boy who sat opposite him now. Matt was somehow different, and Mallory found himself wondering what had brought him here. "Look, it's too late to talk about this now," he said. "Are you hungry?"

"No." Matt shook his head.

"Is there anything you need?"

"No."

"Try not to be too scared. We'll look after you tonight, and tomorrow morning we'll try to make sense of all this. Right now, you'd better get out of those clothes. I'm afraid someone will have to stay with you while you undress. Your clothes are evidence. You can have a shower and then a doctor will look at you."

"I'm not sick. I don't need a doctor."

"It's just routine. He'll give you a quick examination and maybe something to help you sleep." Mallory glanced at one of the policemen. "All right. . . ."

Matt stood up. "Will you tell him I'm sorry?" he said.

"The security guard. Mark Adams. I know it doesn't make any difference and you probably don't believe me anyway. But I am."

Mallory nodded. The policeman took Matt's arm and led him back down the corridor.

He was taken to a changing room — bare wooden benches and white tiles. His clothes went into a plastic bag that was stapled shut and labeled. Then he showered. He had no privacy, just as he had been warned. There was a policeman in the room with him the whole time, but he still managed to enjoy the shower, the rush of water, scalding hot, shuddering down on his head and his shoulders, washing away the blood and the horror of the last hours. It was over all too quickly. He dried himself, then pulled on a gray T-shirt, pajama pants, and underwear that had been laundered and pressed as flat as paper. Finally, he was led to a room that could have been a ward in a hospital with four metal beds, four identical tables, and nothing else. The room felt as if it had been cleaned fifty times. Even the air felt clean. It seemed he was going to be the only occupant.

He climbed into bed and, before any doctor could arrive, he was asleep. Sleep came as quickly as a train plunging into a tunnel. He simply lay back and kept on falling.

• • •

Meanwhile, in a room downstairs, Stephen Mallory was sitting opposite a crumpled, sullen-looking woman who was managing both to scowl and to yawn at the same time. The woman was Gwenda Davis, Matt's aunt and legal guardian. She was short and drab, with mousy hair and a pinched, forgettable face. She wore no makeup and there were heavy bags under her eyes. She was dressed in an old, shapeless coat. It might have been expensive once, but now it was frayed at the edges. Like the woman who was wearing it, Mallory thought. He guessed that she was about forty-five. She seemed nervous, as if it were she, not her nephew, who had been accused of something.

"So where is he?" Gwenda asked. She had a thin, whiny voice that made every question sound like a complaint.

"He's upstairs," Mallory said. "He fell asleep before the doctor could see him, but we gave him a tranquilizer anyway. It's possible he's in shock."

"*He's* in shock?" Gwenda laughed very briefly. "I'm the one who's in shock, I can tell you. Getting a call in the middle of the night like this! Having to come down here. I'm a respectable person. All this business with knives and burglary. I've never heard of such a thing."

"I understand you share your house with your boyfriend."

"Brian." Gwenda noticed Mallory had taken out a pen. "Brian Conran," she continued, and watched as the detective wrote it down. "He's in bed. He's not any relation to the boy. Why should he come out in the middle of the night? He's got to be up first thing in the morning."

"What's his job?"

"What's it to you?" Gwenda shrugged. "He's a milkman."

Mallory pulled a sheet of paper out of a file. "I see from his record that Matthew's parents are dead," he said.

"A car crash." Gwenda swallowed. "He was eight years old. The family was living in London then. His mother and father were killed. But he'd stayed behind."

"He was an only child?"

19

"He didn't have any brothers or sisters. He didn't have any relatives, either. Nobody knew what to do with him."

"You were related to his mother."

"I was her half sister. I'd only met them a few times." Gwenda drew herself up, crossing her hands in front of her. "If you want the truth, they were never very friendly. It was all right for them, wasn't it. A nice house in a nice neighborhood. A nice car. Nice everything. They didn't have any time for me. And when they died in that stupid accident . . . well, I don't know what would have happened to Matthew if it hadn't been for me and Brian. We took him in. We had to bring him up all on our own. And what did we get for it? Nothing but trouble!"

Mallory glanced again at the report. "He had never been in trouble before," he said. "He started missing school a year after he came to Ipswich. From there it was downhill all the way."

"Are you blaming me?" Two pinpricks of red had appeared in Gwenda's cheeks. "It was nothing to do with me! It was that boy, Kelvin Johnson . . . he lives just down the road. He's to blame!"

It was eleven o'clock at night. It had been a long day and Mallory had heard enough. He closed the file and stood up. "Thank you for coming in, Ms. Davis," he said. "Would you like to see Matthew?"

"There's hardly any point seeing him if he's asleep, is there?"

"Maybe you'd like to come back in the morning, then. The social services will be here. He'll also need legal representation. But if you're here at nine o'clock . . ."

"I can't come at nine o'clock. I have to make Brian his breakfast when he gets in from his rounds. I'll come in after that."

"Right."

Gwenda Davis picked herself up and left the room. Mallory watched her go. He felt nothing for her. But he couldn't avoid a sense of great sadness for the boy who was asleep upstairs.

●　　●　　●

Matt woke up.

It was still dark. The room with its four metal beds was deserted. No sound came from anywhere in the building. He could feel a pillow cradling the back of his head. He wondered how long he had been here. The walls were bare and there was no sign of a clock. It was pitch-dark outside — he could see the night sky through a barred window. The room was softly lit. They probably never turned the lights off completely.

He tried to go back to sleep, but now he was wide awake. Suddenly he was seeing it all again, the events of the evening. The images flickered in front of him like cards caught in the wind. There was Kelvin, outside the railway station. Then the warehouse, the DVDs, the guard, the knife, Kelvin again with that stupid smile, the police cars, and his own hands, stained with blood. Matt squeezed his eyes shut, trying to force the memories out of his mind.

It was very warm in the building. All the windows were closed and the radiators were on. He could feel the heat shimmering around him. He was suddenly thirsty and looked around, wondering if he could call someone. But there was no bell to press and nobody in sight.

And yet there was a jug of water and a glass on a table on the other side of the room. All he had to do was get out of bed and he could help himself. He lifted a hand to move the bedcovers, but they were too heavy. No. That wasn't possible. He flexed his muscles and tried to lift himself. He could hardly move. And then he realized that a doctor must have seen him while he was asleep. He had been injected with something, tranquilized. He couldn't move.

He almost cried out. He felt the panic, suffocating him. What were they going to do to him? Why had he gone to the warehouse? How had he allowed all this to happen? He sank back into the pillow, fighting the wave of despair that had risen over him. He couldn't believe that a man had almost died for the sake of a handful of DVDs. How could he have been stupid enough to think of Kelvin as a friend? *"He did it! He did it!"* Kelvin was pathetic. He always had been.

The water . . .

The room seemed to be getting hotter and hotter, as if the police had turned up the radiators just to torment him. Matt found his whole concentration focused on the jug. He could see the perfect circle made by the water where it touched the edge of the glass. He willed himself to get up and, when that failed, found himself willing the jug of water to come to him. He ran a tongue over his lips. His mouth was parched. For a moment, he thought he smelled something burning. The jug was so close to him, only five meters away. He reached out to it, pulling it toward him with his mind.

The jug smashed.

It seemed to explode outward, almost in slow motion. For a single split second, the water hung in the air, its tentacles sprawling. Then it splashed down onto the table, onto the pieces of glass.

Matt was stunned. He had no idea what had happened. He hadn't broken the jug. It had broken itself. It was as if it had been hit by a bullet. Was that what had happened? But he hadn't heard a shot. He hadn't heard anything. Matt stared at the glass fragments scattered over the table with the water pooling around, dripping onto the floor. Had the heat in the room caused it? Or was it him? Had his thirst, somehow, in some inexplicable way, smashed the jug?

Exhaustion finally overcame him a second time and he fell into a deep, suffocating sleep. When he woke up the next morning, the broken pieces weren't there. Nor was the spilled water. A single jug and a glass stood on the table, exactly where they had been the night before. Matt decided that the whole experience must have been nothing more than a weird sort of dream.

THREE
The LEAF Project

Matt, dressed in his own clothes, sat in a chair facing the four people who were examining him from the other side of a long wooden table. This was the sort of room where people got married ... or perhaps divorced. Not uncomfortable but spare and official, with wood paneling on the walls and portraits of officials — probably all dead by now — in gold frames. He was in London, although he wasn't exactly sure where. It had been raining too hard to see much out of the car windows, and he had been driven straight to the door, shown up a flight of a stairs and into this modern, unattractive building. There had been no time for sightseeing.

A week had passed since Matt's arrest, and in that time he had been interviewed, examined, assessed, and, for many hours, left on his own. He had filled in papers that were like exams except that they didn't seem to have any point. *2, 8, 14, 20 . . . what is the next number in the sequence? How many spelling misteaks are their in this sentence?* Different men and women — doctors, psychologists — had asked him to talk about himself. He had been shown blobs on pieces of paper. *"What do you see, Matthew? What does the shape make you think about?"* And there had been games. Word association. Stuff like that.

Finally they had told him he was leaving. A suitcase had appeared, packed with clothes that Gwenda must have sent from home. A three-hour journey in an ordinary car — not even a police car — and he had found himself here. The rain was still lashing against the windows, obscuring the view. He could hear it hammering against the glass, as if demanding to be let in. It seemed that the whole outside world had dissolved and all that was left was the five people, here, in this room.

On the far left was his aunt, Gwenda Davis. She was dabbing at her eyes with a paper tissue, and this had made her mascara run. There was a dirty brown streak all the way down one side of her face. Detective Superintendent Stephen Mallory sat next to her, looking the other way. The third person was the magistrate. Matt had only met her for the first time today. She was about sixty, smartly dressed, a little severe. She had gold-rimmed spectacles and a look of disapproval that had, over the years, become permanent. The fourth person was Matt's social worker, an untidy gray-haired woman about ten years younger than the magistrate. Her name was Jill Hughes and she had been assigned to Matt when he was eleven. She had worked with him ever since and privately thought of him as her greatest failure.

It was the magistrate who was talking.

"Matthew, you have to understand that this was a very cowardly crime and one that involved violence," she was saying. The magistrate had a very precise, clipped manner of speaking, as if every word were of the utmost importance. "Your associate, Kelvin Johnson, will be sent to the

Crown Court and he will almost certainly be sentenced to imprisonment in a young offenders' institution. He is seventeen. You, of course, are younger. But even so, you are above the age of criminal responsibility. If you went before the court, I suspect you might well be given a Section 91. This means you would be locked up for perhaps three years in either a Secure Training Center or a Local Authority Secure Children's Home."

She paused and opened a file that was on the table in front of her. The sound of the pages turning seemed very loud in the sudden silence.

"You are an intelligent boy," she went on. "These are the results of the tests you have been given during the past week. Although your school results have never done you any credit, you seem to have a good grasp of the basic skills . . . maths and literacy. Your psychological report suggests that you have a positive and a creative mind. It seems very strange that you should have chosen to drift into truancy and petty crime.

"But then, of course, we have to take into account your unfortunate background. You lost your parents suddenly and at a very early age — and this must have caused you enormous distress. I think it's fairly clear to all of us that the problems in your young life may have resulted from this one tragic event. Even so, Matthew, you must find the strength to overcome these problems. If you continue down the path you have been following, there is a very real chance that you will end up in prison."

Matt wasn't listening. He was trying to, but the words sounded distant and irrelevant . . . like a train announcer in a station where he didn't want to catch a train. He couldn't believe that this woman was talking to him. Instead, he listened to the rain beating against the windows. The rain seemed to tell him more.

"There is a new government program that has been designed specifically for people like you," the magistrate went on. "The truth is, Matthew, that nobody wants to see young people sent into care. It's expensive and, anyway, we don't have enough places. That is why the government recently created the LEAF Project. Liberty and Education Achieved through Fostering. You can think of it, if you like, as turning over a new leaf."

"I've already been fostered once," Matt said. He glanced at Gwenda, who twitched in her seat. "And it wasn't exactly a success."

"That's certainly true," the magistrate said. "And I'm afraid Ms. Davis no longer feels able to look after you. She's had enough."

"Really?" Matt said scornfully.

"I did what I could!" Gwenda cried. She twisted the tissue into her eye. "You were never grateful. You were never nice. You never even tried. . . ."

The magistrate coughed and Gwenda fell silent before the magistrate continued. "And I'm afraid your social worker, Miss Hughes, feels much the same. I have to tell you, Matthew, that you've left us with no other alternative. LEAF is your last chance to redeem yourself."

"What is LEAF?" Matt asked. He suddenly wanted to get out of this room. He didn't care where they sent him.

"LEAF is a fostering program," Jill Hughes took over.

She was a small woman, half-hidden by the table against which she was sitting. In fact, she was the wrong size for her job. She had spent her whole life dealing with aggressive criminals, most of whom were much bigger than she was. "We have a number of volunteers living in remote parts of the country —"

"There are fewer temptations in the countryside," the magistrate cut in.

"— all of them are well away from urban areas. They take on young people like yourself and offer an old-fashioned home environment. They provide food, clothes, companionship, and, most important of all, discipline. The *L* in *LEAF* stands for *Liberty* — but it has to be earned."

"Your new foster parent may ask you to help with light manual labor," the magistrate said.

"You mean . . . I have to work?" Matt said, his voice full of contempt.

"There's nothing wrong with that!" The magistrate bristled. "Working in the countryside is good for your health and many children would be delighted to be out there with the animals and the crops on a farm. Nobody can force you to join the LEAF Project, Matthew. You have to volunteer. But I have to say, this is a real opportunity for you. And I'm sure you'll find it preferable to the alternative."

Locked up for three years. That was what she had said.

"How long will I have to stay there?" he asked.

"A minimum of one year. After that, we'll reassess the situation."

"You may like it," Stephen Mallory said. He was trying to sound upbeat. "It's a whole new start, Matt. A chance to make new friends."

28

But Matt had his doubts. "What happens if I don't like it?" he asked.

"We'll be in constant touch with the foster parent," the magistrate explained. "The parent has to make a weekly report to the police, and your aunt will visit you as soon as you feel ready. There'll be a settling-in period of three months. But after that she'll see you every month."

"She'll provide an interface between the foster parent and the social services," Jill Hughes said.

"I don't know how I'll afford it," Gwenda muttered. "I mean, if there are going to be traveling expenses. And who's going to look after Brian while I'm away? I have responsibilities, you know. . . ."

Her voice trailed away. The room was suddenly silent, apart from the sound of the traffic and the rain hitting the windows.

"All right." Matt shrugged. "You can send me wherever you want to. I don't really care. Anything would be better than staying with her and Brian."

Gwenda flushed. Mallory cut in before she could speak. "We won't abandon you," he promised. "We'll make sure you're looked after."

But the magistrate was annoyed. "You have absolutely nothing to complain about," she snapped. She looked at Matt over the top of her glasses. "Quite frankly, you should be grateful you're being given this opportunity. And I should warn you. If your foster parent is unhappy with your progress, if you abuse the kindness you're being shown in any way, then you will be returned to us. And then you will find yourself in an institution. You won't be given a second chance. Do you understand?"

"Yes. I understand." Matt glanced at the windows. The light was almost lost behind the gray, endlessly moving curtain of water. "So when do I get to meet my foster parent?"

"Her name is Jayne Deverill," the social worker said. "And she should be here any minute now."

· · ·

They were mending the escalators at Holborn Station, and as the woman rose up to street level, sparks from the oxyacetylene torches flashed and flickered behind her. But Jayne Deverill didn't notice them. She was standing completely still, clutching a leather handbag under her arm, staring at a point a few meters in front of her, as if she were disgusted by her surroundings.

She fed her ticket into the barrier and watched as it sprang open. Someone knocked into her and for a second something dark flashed in her eyes. But she forced herself to keep control. She was wearing ugly old-fashioned leather shoes and she walked awkwardly. There was, perhaps, something wrong with her legs.

Mrs. Deverill was a small woman, at least fifty years old, with white hair, cut short. Her skin was not yet withered, but it was strangely lifeless. She had very hard, ice-cold eyes and cheekbones that formed two slashes across her face. It was hard to imagine her gray lips ever smiling. She was smartly dressed in a brown skirt and matching jacket with a shirt buttoned to her neck. She had a silver necklace and a silver brooch on her lapel. The brooch was shaped like a lizard.

Her progress from Holborn Station had been observed.

Mrs. Deverill didn't realize she was being followed as she made her way down Kingsway, heading for the offices behind Lincoln's Inn. But the man in the hooded anorak was never more than ten steps behind. He was twenty years old, ratlike, with greasy blond hair and a thin, unhealthy-looking face. He had recognized the woman as an out-of-towner the moment he had spotted her coming through the barriers. He had no idea who she was and he didn't care. Just two things about her had interested him: the handbag and the jewelry.

He didn't know where she was going but hoped that she would leave the main road with its many pedestrians and occasional police officers and follow one of the quieter streets that twisted away behind. Anyway, it was worth a few minutes of his time to see. He was still with her as she paused at a corner and then turned left next to a pub. He smiled. It couldn't have worked out better. Now there was just the two of them, walking down a street that was little more than an alleyway, but cut through to the legal offices — solicitors' firms and council buildings — that existed in their own, quite separate world. He took one quick look around, checking there was nobody in sight, then dug into the pocket of the dirty anorak he was wearing. He took out a jagged knife and turned it in his hand, enjoying the sense of power that it gave him. Then he ran forward.

"You!" he shouted.

The woman stopped, her back toward him.

"Give me the bag. Now! And I want the necklace. . . ."

There was a pause.

Jayne Deverill turned around.

•   •   •

The office of the Family Proceedings and Youth Court, which was where Matt was being held, was on Cowburne Street, about ten minutes away. Jayne Deverill was a little breathless, holding a cup of tea that she had been offered.

"I'm very sorry I'm late," she was saying. She had a deep, rather throaty voice — the voice of someone who had smoked too many cigarettes. "It's very rude of me — and I deplore rudeness. Punctuality is the first sign of good breeding. That's what I always say."

"You had trouble getting here?" Mallory asked.

"The coach was late. I would have called you from the station, but I'm afraid I don't carry a phone. We're not as up-to-date in the Yorkshire countryside as you are down here in London. In fact, there's no signal where I live, so a mobile telephone would be something of a waste of time." She turned to Matt. "I'm very glad to meet you, my dear. I have, of course, heard so much about you."

Matt looked at the woman who had volunteered to be his foster parent in the LEAF Project. He didn't like what he saw.

Jayne Deverill could have stepped out of another century — a time when teachers were allowed to beat children and there were Bible readings before breakfast and tea. He had never met anyone more severe. Jill Hughes had greeted the woman like an old friend although it turned out that the two had never met. They had only spoken on the telephone. Stephen Mallory looked more uncomfortable. He was also meeting Mrs. Deverill for the first time, and although he had shaken her hand, he had lapsed into silence and seemed to be lost in his own thoughts. The magistrate was more interested in the paperwork than anything else, in a hurry to get this whole thing over with. Matt examined Mrs. Deverill again. She was sipping her tea, but her eyes never left him. They were devouring him.

"Do you know Yorkshire at all?" she asked.

It took a moment for Matt to realize that she was talking to him. "No," he said. "I've never been there."

"Lesser Malling is the name of the village. It's a bit out-of-the-way. The nearest town is Greater Malling and nobody's heard of that, either. And why should they have? There's nothing there. We're very down-to-earth in Yorkshire. We look after the land and the land looks after us. I'm sure you'll find it very quiet after the city. But you'll get used to it in time." She glanced at the magistrate. "I can really take him with me today?"

The magistrate nodded.

Mrs. Deverill smiled. "And when will you make your first visit?"

"Six weeks from now. We want to give Matthew time to settle in."

"Well, after six weeks with me, I can assure you, you won't recognize him." She turned to Gwenda Davis. "You won't need to worry about him, Ms. Davis. You can telephone him any time you want and, of course, we'll both look forward to you coming up to visit."

"Well, I don't know about that." Gwenda was still worried. "It's a long way. and I'm not sure Brian . . ." She fell silent.

"There are some final forms you have to fill in, Mrs. Deverill," the magistrate said. "But then the two of you can be on your way. Ms. Davis brought a suitcase with some of Matthew's clothes and things." She turned to Matt. "I expect you'd like a few minutes on your own to say good-bye to your aunt."

"No." Matt shook his head. "I've got nothing to say to her."

"It wasn't my fault," Gwenda said, and suddenly she was angry. "I never had anything to do with your family. I never had anything to do with you. I didn't even want to take you in after what happened to your parents. But I did and you were never grateful. You were nothing but trouble. You've got nobody to blame but yourself."

"There's no need for this," Mallory cut in. "Good luck, Matt," he said. "I really hope this works out for you." He held out a hand. Matt hesitated, then shook it. This wasn't Mallory's fault. That much he knew.

"Time to go!" Mrs. Deverill said. "We don't want to miss the coach!"

Matt stood up. Mallory watched him with thoughtful, anxious eyes as he left the room.

• • •

Two hours later, Matt walked across Victoria Coach Station, carrying the suitcase that Gwenda had packed for him. He looked around him at the coaches, thundering in and out, the crowds of travelers, the snack and magazine stalls behind the plate glass windows. It was an unpleasant place, cold and damp, with air that smelled of diesel. He could hardly believe he was here. He was free . . . finally out of police custody. No. Not free, he reminded himself. He had been handed over to this woman who called herself his foster mother.

But not for long. That was one decision he had already made.

"That's our bus," she said, and pointed to a coach with YORK written — white letters on black — across the front.

Matt handed his case to a man who slid it into the luggage compartment, then climbed on board. They had reserved seats at the very back. Mrs. Deverill allowed Matt to take the seat next to the window and then sat down next to him. Soon the coach was full. At one o'clock exactly, the doors hissed shut, the engine started up, and they began to move. Matt sat with his forehead pressed against the glass and he watched as they emerged from the coach station and out into the streets of Victoria. It was still raining. The raindrops chased in front of his eyes. Next to him, Mrs. Deverill sat with her eyes half-closed, breathing heavily.

He tried to concentrate, tried to work out what he was feeling. But then he realized he felt nothing. He had been sucked into the system. Evaluated. Approved for the LEAF Project. And sent on his way. At least he wasn't going back to Ipswich. That was something to be thankful for. It was the end of six years with Gwenda and Brian. Whatever lay ahead couldn't possibly be worse.

Meanwhile, about five miles away, an alleyway in Holborn was being sealed off by two police cars and an ambulance. A dead body had been found, a young man in a hooded anorak.

The forensic team had only just arrived, but already the photographers and police scientists knew they had stumbled onto something completely bizarre. The man was well known to them. His name was Will Scott and he was a drug addict who had been involved in many muggings in central London. There was a kitchen knife clutched in his hand and it was this that had killed him. But nobody had attacked him. There were no fingerprints. No sign that anyone had come close.

The dead man's mouth was stretched in a hideous smile and there was a look of sheer terror in his eyes. He was holding the knife very tightly. He had taken it and pushed it, inch by inch, into his own heart. It was unclear how he had done it or why, but the forensic people had no doubt at all.

For some reason, Will Scott had killed himself.

FOUR
Lesser Malling

There were two hundred miles of dreary motorway between London and York, and the journey took more than four hours. The coach stopped twice at service stations, but neither Matt nor Mrs. Deverill left their seats. She had brought sandwiches with her. They were in her handbag, wrapped in brown paper. She took them out and offered one to Matt.

"Are you hungry, Matthew?"

"No, thank you."

"In Yorkshire, I'll expect you to eat what you're given. We don't waste food in my house."

She unwrapped one of the bundles and Matt saw two slabs of white bread filled with cold liver. He was glad he hadn't accepted her offer.

"I expect you're wondering about me," Mrs. Deverill said as she began her lunch. She took small mouthfuls and chewed the food carefully. When she swallowed, her throat twisted painfully. It seemed she had difficulty getting the food down. "I am now your legal guardian," she went on. "You are a thief and a delinquent and the government has given you to me. But I'm willing to forget your past, Matthew. I can assure you that it is your future that is of much more concern to me. If you do as you're told, we'll get on. If you disobey me, if you try to defy me, let me assure you that you will be more miserable than you can imagine. Do you understand?"

"Yes," Matt said.

Her eyes slid over him and he shivered. "You have to remember that nobody cares about you. You have no parents. No family. You have little education and no prospects. I don't want to be cruel to you, my dear, but I'm really all you have left."

She turned away from him and continued eating her sandwiches. After that, she took out a farming magazine and began to read. It was as if she had completely forgotten him.

The motorway stretched on. There was nothing to look at out of the window and Matt found himself hypnotized by the white lines and the median flashing endlessly past. Almost without knowing it, he found himself drifting away, neither awake nor asleep but somewhere in between.

He was back again in the terraced house in Dulwich, a leafy, friendly suburb of London. This was where he lived with his mother and father. It had been six years since he had seen them, but, staring out of the window, he saw them now.

There was his mother, rushing around the kitchen that was always a mess, even when it had just been cleaned. She was wearing the clothes she had been dressed in that last day: a pink dress with a white linen jacket. Whenever he remembered her, she was always wearing the same clothes. It was a brand-new dress, which she had bought especially for the wedding. And there was his father, Mark, looking uncomfortable in a suit and tie. He was a doctor and he normally went to work in whatever he could find. Jeans, a sweater. He didn't like dressing up. But it was one of the other doctors at his practice who was getting married and it was going to be a swank affair. First the service, then an expensive hotel. Mark Freeman was sitting at the table, eating his breakfast. Then he turned around, tossing his dark hair in the way he always did, and asked, *"Where's Matthew?"*

And then Matthew arrived. Of course, he was still Matthew then. Six years later, sitting on a coach headed toward a place he had never heard of, Matt pictured himself as he had been at that time — a short, slightly plump, dark-haired boy coming into the bright yellow kitchen. His father at the table. His mother holding a teapot shaped like a teddy bear. And he heard it all again.

"Come on, Matthew. We're going to be late."

"I don't want to go."

"What? What are you talking about?"

"Matthew . . . ?"

"I don't feel well. I don't want to go."

On the coach, Matt put a hand over his eyes. He didn't want to remember any more. Remembering only hurt him . . . every time.

"What do you mean, you don't want to go?"

"Please, Dad. Please don't make me. . . ."

They had argued, but not very much. His parents only had one child and they spoiled him. They had thought he would enjoy the wedding because they had been told there would be other children there and a special marquee with a magician and balloons. And now this! His father made a quick phone call. It wasn't really a big problem. Rosemary Green — their friendly, always helpful neighbor — agreed to take him for the rest of the day. His parents left without him.

And that was why he wasn't in the car when they had their accident. That was why they had died and he had lived.

Matt lowered his hand and looked out again. The coach had slowed down. He realized he wasn't feeling very well. He was hot and cold and there was a dull pounding in his head.

"We're here," Mrs. Deverill said.

Matt looked out of the window. They had arrived in another coach station, this one more modern and smaller than Victoria. The coach stopped and they jostled forward with the other passengers. It was colder outside than it had been in London, but at least it had stopped raining. Matt collected his case, then followed Mrs. Deverill across the concourse.

A man was waiting for them, standing next to an old, beaten-up Land Rover that only seemed to be held together by the mud that covered it. The man was short and very fat, with yellow greasy hair, watery eyes, and a face that seemed to be slowly slipping off his head. He was wearing dirty jeans and a shirt that was too small for him. Matt could see the buttons straining. The man was about forty. He had flabby lips that parted in a wet, unpleasant smile.

"Good afternoon, Mrs. Deverill," he said.

Mrs. Deverill ignored him. She turned to Matt. "This is Noah," she said.

40

Matt said nothing. Noah was examining him in a way that made him feel uneasy. "Welcome to Yorkshire," Noah said. "I'm very pleased to meet you." He held out a hand. The fingers were fat and stubby, the nails encrusted with mud. Matt shook it quickly.

"Noah works for me on the farm," Mrs. Deverill explained. "He makes very little conversation, so I wouldn't bother talking to him."

The farmhand was still staring. His mouth was open and there was saliva on his chin. Matt turned away.

"Get in the car," Mrs. Deverill said. "It's time you saw your new home."

• • •

They drove for an hour, first on a dual carriageway, then on a B-road, then on a twisting country lane. The farther they went, the bleaker the landscape became. Lesser Malling seemed to be hidden somewhere on the edge of the Yorkshire moors, but Matt didn't see a single sign. He was feeling even sicker than before and he wondered if it was Noah's driving or some sort of virus that he had picked up.

They came to an intersection, a meeting of five roads — all of them identical. They were surrounded by trees. Matt hadn't noticed them entering the wood, but now it surrounded them, totally enclosing them. The wood had obviously been planted recently. All the trees were the same sort of pine. They were the same height, the same color, and they had been set in dead-straight lines with an identical amount of space between them. No matter which direction Matt looked, the view was exactly the same. He remembered what his social worker in London had told him. The LEAF Project wanted to keep him out of urban areas, away from temptation. They certainly couldn't have chosen anywhere more remote than here.

A single signpost stood at the intersection, but the top had been broken off. A splintered pole was all that remained.

"Lesser Malling is a mile up the road," Mrs. Deverill said, gesturing to the left. "I'll show it to you when you've settled in a little more. We live the other way."

Noah twisted the steering wheel and they turned left, following one of the other lanes for about fifty meters, until they came to a gateway. Matt just had time to see a name, written in dull brown paint. HIVE HALL. Then they were following a gravel drive between two barbed-wire fences that ran down to a courtyard and a complex of barns and buildings. The car stopped. They had arrived.

Matt got out.

It was a miserable place. The bad weather didn't help. But even in the sunshine there would have been little to recommend Hive Hall. The main farmhouse was made out of great stone slabs with a slate roof that was buckling under the weight of a single large chimney. The barns had been built with wooden planks that were so old and sodden that they were rotting where they stood, with dark green moss spreading across them like a disease. The farmyard itself was an irregular square of land that was as much water as earth and gravel. Chickens limped to and fro. They had scarcely moved to avoid the wheels of the Land Rover. Six pigs stood in the mud, shivering.

"This is it," Mrs. Deverill said as she got out of the car and stretched her legs. "It may not look like much, but it's my home and it does well enough for me. Of course, there's no PlayStation here. There's no television. But once you start working, you'll find you're too tired for these things. We go to bed early in the country. You'll get used to our ways in time."

They went into the farmhouse. The front door opened into a long kitchen with a flagstone floor and an Aga stove at one end, pots and pans hanging from the ceiling, and dozens of jars and bottles on wooden shelves. From here, Mrs. Deverill led him into a living room with old and battered furniture, shelves full of books, and, above a massive fireplace, a portrait of herself. It must have been painted five hundred years ago but it looked just like her. It had the same cruel eyes, the same sunken cheeks. Only the hair was different, running loose as if caught in the wind.

"My ancestor," Mrs. Deverill explained.

Matt looked past the figure in the canvas. She was standing in front of a village. He could see a few desolate buildings behind her. He looked back at the face. And shivered. Nothing had moved, but he could have sworn she had been looking toward the frame, over to the left. Now her eyes were fixed on him. He swallowed hard. His imagination was playing tricks on him. He turned around and saw that Mrs. Deverill was staring at him, too. He was trapped between the two of them.

Mrs. Deverill smiled thinly. "She looks like me, doesn't she?" she said. "She was also a Deverill. There have been Deverills in this part of Yorkshire for three hundred years. Her name was Jayne, like mine. She burned to death. They say that when the wind blows in the right direction, you can still hear the screams. Let me show you upstairs. . . ."

Matt followed Mrs. Deverill up a twisting staircase to the second floor and into a room at the end of the corridor. This was to be his bedroom . . . and it was the one room he most wanted to see. His headache had gotten worse. He wondered if he was going to be sick.

The room had a low ceiling, exposed beams, and a bare wooden floor with a small rug in the center. It looked over the back of the farm, across a field to the wood. The windows were small, set in walls that were at least a meter thick. There was a sagging bed, made up not with a quilt but with blankets and sheets. Opposite the bed was a washbasin and a chest of drawers with a vase of dried flowers on top. The pictures on the walls showed views of Lesser Malling, painted in watercolors.

"They made me decorate for you," Mrs. Deverill remarked sourly. Of course, the LEAF Project would have visited the farm. They would have insisted that the room was clean and comfortable. "I dried the flowers myself. Belladonna, oleander, and mistletoe. Three of my favorites. All of them poisonous . . . but such lovely colors."

Matt put his case on the bed. At the same time, he noticed something sitting between the pillows.

"And this is Asmodeus," Mrs. Deverill said. "My cat."

It was a huge black cat with yellow eyes. Its stomach was bulging as if it had recently eaten, and Matt noticed a patch of gray where some of the fur had worn away. It was stretched out on the bed, purring lazily. Matt reached out his hand to stroke it. The cat purred louder. Slowly, it turned its head and looked Matt in the eyes. Then it sank its teeth into his flesh.

With a cry, Matt pulled his hand back. Bright red blood welled out of a jagged bite in his thumb. A drop fell onto the floor. Mrs. Deverill took a step back. Matt saw that her eyes had widened and now, for the first time, she was smiling. All her attention was fixed on the blood on the floor.

It was too much for him.

The room twisted. Matt swayed on his feet. He tried to say something, but the words refused to come. The walls were spinning around him. He heard a door boom open. He looked through it and saw — or thought he saw — a circle of huge granite stones. Someone was holding a knife. He could see it hovering over his head, the pointed blade curving toward his eye. The floor seemed to shake and then, one after another, the wooden planks cracked open, splinters exploding all around. Brilliant light streamed through and in the light he thought he saw something like a giant inhuman hand.

A voice echoed in his ears.

"One of the five!" it whispered.

The light engulfed him. He felt it sweeping through his body, burning the inside of his head. He slammed the heels of his hands into his eyes, trying to block it out. Then he was falling backward — unconscious long before he hit the floor.

FIVE

A Warning

"What's wrong with him?"

"He has pneumonia."

"What?"

"He may die."

"He can't! You must cure him, Mrs. Deverill. It's your responsibility. See that he lives!"

Matt heard the voices, but he wasn't sure who they belonged to. He was lying in bed. He could feel a pillow against the back of his head. But as for the rest of it, he wasn't sure if he was asleep or awake. He propped himself up and half-opened his eyes. Sweat trickled down the side of his face. The single movement had taken all his strength.

The door had just closed. Someone — the last person who had spoken — had left. It was a man, but Matt had been unable to see his face. Mrs. Deverill was still in the room with him, standing next to another woman, also white-haired but with some sort of bright red mark on the side of her face. Noah was lingering in the background, rubbing his hands.

Then the room shimmered and suddenly the curtains were closed. There were flames leaping up, right next to the bed. Was the building on fire? No. They had set up some sort of metal tripod with a brazier filled with coals. The two women were speaking in a language that he didn't understand, whispering to each other as they fed the flames with black-and-green-colored crystals. Matt saw the crystals melt and bubble and at once the room was filled with yellow smoke. The smell of sulphur crept into his nostrils. Matt choked and his eyes watered. He tried to lick his lips, but his mouth was too dry.

Noah came forward, holding a dish. The second woman — the one Matt didn't know — was holding a snake. Where had it come from? It was an ugly brown, half a meter long, writhing in front of her. A viper? She had produced a scalpel, the sort of thing a surgeon might use. Matt saw her hold the snake by the head and then slit it open. Dark red liquid oozed out, dripping down into a metal cup. The snake became rigid and still.

Mrs. Deverill pulled back the bedcovers. Matt was only wearing underpants and he shrank back as she leaned over him. She dipped a finger in the snake's blood, then drew a line down his chest and onto his stomach. The liquid was warm and sticky against his skin. He tried to move, but his body would no longer obey him. He could only watch as Mrs. Deverill reached up and made some sort of mark on his forehead.

"Open your mouth," she commanded.

"No. . . ." Matt tried to say the word. He tried to stop himself. But suddenly his mouth was open and Mrs. Deverill was feeding him from the cup. He knew that he was drinking blood. It tasted bitter, more horrible than anything in the world. He was going to be sick. He wanted to get it out of his system, but instead it slithered into his stomach like the ghost of the snake it had come from. And at the same time, he was sucked backward, into the mattress, into the floor, buried alive until . . .

He opened his eyes.

Mrs. Deverill was in the room, reading a book. There was nobody with her. The window was open, allowing the breeze to come in. Matt swallowed. He was feeling lightheaded but otherwise fine.

"So you've woken up at last," Mrs. Deverill muttered, closing the book.

"What happened?" Matt asked.

"You've been ill. Nothing very serious. Pneumonia. A touch of pleurisy. But it's all behind you now."

"You gave me something to drink. . . ." Matt tried to remember even though he didn't want to. The very thought of what had happened repulsed him. "There was a snake," he said.

"A snake? What are you talking about? You've been having bad dreams, Matthew. I would imagine it comes from watching too much television."

"I'm hungry," Matt said.

"I expect you are. You haven't eaten for three days."

"Three days!"

"That's how long you were unconscious." She got up and shuffled over to the door. "I'll bring you up some tea," she said. "You can rest tomorrow, but after that I want you up on your feet. The fresh air will do you good. And anyway, it's time you began work."

She took one last look at him, nodded to herself, and closed the door.

Two days later, Matt stood in the pigsty with stinking mud and filth reaching up to his knees. Mrs. Deverill had spoken of fresh air, but the stench here was so bad he could barely breathe. Noah had provided him with boots and gloves, but he had no other protective clothes. His jeans and shirt were soon dripping with black slime. The disinfectant he had been given burned his throat and made his eyes water.

He reached down with the spade and scooped up another bucketful of muck. It would be lunch soon and he was looking forward to it. Mrs. Deverill was, despite everything, a good cook. When Matt was living with Gwenda Davis, all his meals had come out of the freezer and into the microwave. He preferred the food here: home-baked bread, rich stews, and fruit pies with thick pastry crusts.

He had changed. He knew that something had happened to him during his illness, even if he had no idea what it was. It was as if a switch had been thrown inside him. He couldn't explain it, but he felt stronger and more confident than he ever had before.

And that was good, because he had already decided he was going to run away. He still found it incredible that the LEAF Project could have sent him to this godforsaken place and made him the slave of a grim, unsmiling woman. Matt disliked Mrs. Deverill, but it was Noah, the farmhand, who really made his skin crawl. Noah was usually out in the fields, bouncing along in an ancient tractor that belched black smoke. But when he was close, he couldn't keep his eyes off Matt. Noah was always leering at him, as if he knew something that Matt didn't. Matt wondered if he was brain-damaged. He didn't seem to be quite human.

Matt didn't care what happened to him, but he knew he couldn't stay at Hive Hall. Not for a year. Not even for another week. He had no money, but he was sure he would be able to find some if he looked hard enough. Then he would either hitchhike or take a train to London. He would lose himself in the capital, and although he'd heard plenty of horror stories, he was sure that somehow he would be able to survive. In just two years he would be sixteen and independent. Never again would any adult tell him what he had to do.

Mrs. Deverill appeared at the door of the farmhouse and called out to him. Matt wasn't wearing his watch but guessed it must be one o'clock. She was always punctual. He threw down the spade and climbed out of the sty. In the distance, Noah appeared, carrying two buckets of animal feed. He never ate in the farmhouse. He had a room on the second floor of the barn and that was where he cooked, slept, and presumably washed . . . although not often as, Matt knew, he smelled worse than the pigs.

Matt took his boots off outside the front door, then went into the kitchen and washed his hands in the sink. Mrs. Deverill was already serving vegetable soup. There was bread, butter, and cheese on the table. Asmodeus was sitting on the sideboard and Matt shivered. He disliked the cat even more than he disliked Noah — and it wasn't just because of the jagged scar on his hand. Like Noah, the cat was always watching him. It had a way of appearing out of nowhere. Matt would turn his head and there it would be . . . in the branch of a tree, on a windowsill or a chair, always with its ugly yellow eyes fixed on him. Normally he would ignore it, but if he came close, the cat would arch its back and hiss.

"Out of the kitchen, please, Asmodeus," Mrs. Deverill said. The cat understood her perfectly. It leaped out of a window and was gone.

Matt sat down and began to eat.

"There's something I want you to do for me this afternoon, Matthew," Mrs. Deverill said.

"I'm cleaning the pigs."

"I know what you're doing. One day you'll learn that being rude to people who are older and wiser than you won't do you any good. In fact, I have a task for you which you might enjoy. I'd like you to pick up something for me from the chemist in Lesser Malling."

"What do you want me to pick up?"

"It's a package. It's addressed to me. You can go in after lunch." She held a spoonful of soup to her lips. Steam rose up in front of her unsmiling face. "There's an old bicycle in the barn you can use. It belonged to my husband."

"You were married?" That was news to Matt. He couldn't imagine anyone sharing a life with this woman.

"For a short time."

"What happened to your husband?"

"Young people shouldn't ask questions. It's not good for them. However . . ." She sighed and lowered the spoon. "Henry disappeared. That was his name. Henry Lutterworth. We'd only been married a few months when he went for a walk in the woods and never came back. It's possible that

51

he simply got lost and starved to death. Let that be a lesson to you, Matthew. The woods are very thick around here and you can easily get swallowed up. It's quite possible that he stumbled into a bog. That's my guess. It would have been a very unpleasant way to die. He'd have tried to swim, but of course the more he struggled, the faster he'd have gone down. The water and the mud would have risen up over his nostrils, and that would have been the end of him."

"If his name was Lutterworth, how come you call your-self Deverill?" Matt asked.

"I prefer my own name. The name of my ancestors. There have always been Deverills in Lesser Malling. Mar-ried or unmarried, we keep our own name." She sniffed. "Henry left me Hive Hall in his will," she explained. "We used to have bees, but they all went away. They often do that, when their owner dies. I inherited all his money. But the point of all this is, my dear, that if I were you, I'd steer well clear of the woods."

"I'll do that," Matt said.

"Remember now. The chemist. Just tell them it's for me."

• • •

After lunch, Matt crossed the farmyard and went into the barn. He found the bicycle parked behind an old plow. It obviously hadn't been used for years. But he pulled it out, oiled the chain, and pumped up the tires. A few min-utes later he was able to pedal out of the farm. It felt good, passing through the rusting gates. He was still doing chores for Mrs. Deverill. But anything was better than the pigs.

As he went, a car came the other way and for a moment it seemed they were going to collide. The car was a black Jaguar with tinted windows. Everything happened so quickly that Matt didn't even see who was driving. He jerked the handlebar and the bike veered up a bank of nettles before curving back onto the lane. He came to a halt and twisted around. The Jaguar had driven into the farmyard. He saw the red glow of its brake lights, but then it disappeared behind the farmhouse. He was tempted to go back. It was the first modern car he had seen since he'd come to Hive Hall, and he wondered if it had come on account of him. Could it be someone from London, from the social services? He hesitated, then continued on his way. It was the first time he had left the farm. His first taste of freedom. He wasn't going back yet.

It was a mile to the village. Matt quickly arrived at the broken sign where the five roads met. The wood was all around him and he was glad that Mrs. Deverill had shown him which road to take, since they all looked the same. No cars passed. Nothing moved. Matt had never felt more alone as he pedaled on. The last part of the road was uphill and Matt had to work to get the bike to the top. Despite the oil, he could hear the chain groaning beneath him. But ahead of him he could see the outer buildings of Lesser Malling, and a few moments later he pulled into the village square.

Mrs. Deverill had already warned him that there wasn't much to Lesser Malling, and she was certainly right. The village was small and self-contained, with a dull, half-dilapidated church at one end and two rows of shops and houses facing each other across an empty cobbled area. A war memorial stood in the middle, a slab of gray stone engraved with twenty or thirty names. One of the shops sold sweets, the next general groceries, another antiques. All of them looked fifty years out-of-date. There was a pub — it was called The Goat — and next to it a butcher's. Matt could see chickens hanging by their feet, their necks broken. Slabs of meat, gray and sweating, lay spread out on the counter. A large man with a beard and a blood-splattered apron chopped down with an ax. Matt heard the metal as it sliced through bone.

There were quite a few people around, and as he rested the bicycle against the war memorial more of them appeared, coming from all sides of the square. Matt sensed that they had been drawn here because of him. Their faces were more curious than welcoming. He saw them stop some distance away and whisper among themselves. It was unnerving, being the center of attention in this forgotten community. He had no doubt that they all knew exactly who he was and why he was here.

A woman walked toward him and he thought he recognized her. She had long white hair, a tiny head, and black eyes that could have belonged to a doll. As she turned toward him, he saw that she had been disfigured by a birthmark. One side of her face was an ugly mauve blotch. He thought back to when he was ill. Had this woman been in his room at Hive Hall?

She came right up to him. "How nice to see you back on your feet, Matthew," she said. She had a squeaky, rasping voice. She seemed to strangle the words at the back of her throat. "My name is Claire Deverill. You're staying with my sister."

So he was right. He *had* seen her before.

"I am the head teacher at the primary school here in Lesser Malling," she went on. "You may be joining us soon."

"I'm too old for primary school," Matt said.

"But too stupid, I'm afraid, for secondary school. I've seen your reports. You've done no work. You know very little. Not a good example for the other children."

Another woman — tall and thin — had appeared, pushing an antique pram. The wheels squeaked as they turned. "Is this the boy?" she demanded.

"It is indeed, Miss Creevy." Claire Deverill smiled.

Matt glanced down at the pram. There was no baby. Miss Creevy was nursing a large china doll. It looked up at Matt with a frozen smile and wide, empty eyes.

"I'm looking for the chemist," Matt said. Suddenly he wanted to be out of here. He was beginning to wish he hadn't come.

"It's over there." Claire Deverill pointed. "Next to the sweetshop."

Two more women had appeared on the far side of the village, in front of the church. They looked like ragged scarecrows, their black coats flapping in the breeze. They were identical twins. At the same time, a short, fat man with blue and green tattoos on his arms, face, and head stepped out of the pub. He was smoking a clay pipe. He saw Matt and began to laugh. Matt walked away before he could get too close.

It was no surprise really that everyone in Lesser Malling seemed to be a little mad. You'd have to be, to live in a place as forlorn as this. There was a pond near the church and

Matt noticed a group of children feeding the ducks. He went over to them, but as soon as he was close he realized he was going to find no friends here. There was a ten-year-old boy with strange greenish hair and fat legs bulging out of short trousers. A couple of girls, apparently sisters, stood together in identical old-fashioned dresses and pigtails. The last boy was about seven and crippled, one of his legs enclosed in a metal calliper. Matt would have felt sorry for him, but as he approached, the boy pulled out a BB gun and, smiling, took aim at the ducks. Quickly Matt kicked out, sending loose gravel into the water. The ducks flew away. The boy fired at them and missed.

"What did you do that for?" one of the girls demanded sulkily.

"What are you doing?" Matt asked.

"We feed the ducks and then Freddy kills them," the other girl explained. "It's a game!"

"A game?"

"Sitting ducks!" both girls chorused.

Freddy reloaded the gun. Matt shook his head in disgust. He left the children and walked back to the chemist.

The shop was like nothing he had ever seen before — a dark, evil-smelling place with rows of wooden shelves. There were a few boxes of headache pills. A few packets of soap. But for the most part, the shelves were stacked with old bottles. Some of these were filled with powders, some with dried herbs. Others contained strange, lumpy objects, floating in murky water. Matt read some of the handwritten labels. Nox vomica. Aconite. Wormwood. They meant nothing to him. He found a flask filled with yellow liquid and turned it around, then almost cried out as a severed eye floated to the surface, kissing the edge of the glass. The eye had been taken from a sheep or a cow. It was trailing tissue behind it. Matt felt sick.

"Can I help you?" a voice asked.

It was the chemist — a short ginger-haired man in a shabby white coat. The hair continued down his neck. There was more of it on the backs of his hands. He was wearing heavy black spectacles that had sunk into his nose in such a way that Matt wondered if he ever took them off.

"What is this?" Matt demanded.

"An eye."

"Why is it here?"

The chemist turned the jar around and examined the specimen, his own eyes magnified by the lenses. "The vet requested it," he said. He sounded irritated. "He was doing tests."

"I've come to collect something for Mrs. Deverill," Matt said.

"Oh, yes. You must be Matthew, then. We've all been looking forward to meeting you. We've all been looking forward to it very much."

The chemist produced a small package, wrapped in brown paper and tied with string. "My name is Barker," he said. "I hope I'll be seeing more of you. In a village like this, it's always nice to have new blood." He handed the packet over. "Do drop in again anytime."

Matt came back out of the shop, noticing that more of the villagers had arrived in the square. There were at least a dozen of them, talking among themselves. He hurried over to the bike. There was a bag behind the saddle and he thrust the package in. He just wanted to get back on the road, away from the village. But it wasn't to be. As he wheeled the bicycle around, a hand suddenly appeared, grabbing hold of the handlebar. Matt followed the arm it belonged to and found himself looking up at a man in his thirties with straw-colored hair and a round, ruddy face. The man was dressed in a baggy jersey and jeans. He was strong. Matt could tell that from the ease with which he held the bike.

"Let me go!"

Matt tried to pull the bike away, but the man held on to it. "That's not very friendly," he said. "What's your name?"

"Why do you want to know?"

"You're Matthew Freeman?"

Matt said nothing. They were both still holding the bike. It had become a barrier between them.

"They sent you here on this project?"

"That's right. Yes. You all know that — so why ask?"

"Listen to me, Matthew Freeman," the man said suddenly. "You don't want to be hanging around this village. You don't want to be anywhere near here. Do you understand me? I shouldn't be talking to you like this. But if you know what's good for you, you'll get away. You'll go as far away as you can and you won't come back. Do you hear me? You need to . . ."

He broke off. The chemist had come out of his shop and was watching the two of them from the doorway. The fair-haired man let go of Matt's bike and hurried away. He didn't look back.

Matt got onto the bicycle and pedaled out of the village. Ahead of him, the pine trees waited, black and ominous. Already it was growing dark.

SIX
Whispers

Matt was standing on a tower of glistening stone. It was pitch-dark, but somehow he could still see. Far beneath him, the waves rolled forward as if in slow motion, thick and oily. There were rocks slanting outward, each one razor sharp. The waves hovered, then threw themselves forward, tearing themselves apart. The wind howled. There was a storm raging. Jagged spears of lightning crashed down — but the lightning was black, not white — and now he realized that the entire world had been turned inside out, like the negative of a photograph.

In the distance, he could see four people standing on a gray, deserted beach. Three boys and a girl, all of them about his own age. They were too far away for him to be able to see their faces, but somehow he recognized them and knew they were waiting for him. He had to reach them, but there was no way. He was trapped on his tower of rock. The storm was growing and now there was something dark and terrible stretching out across the sea. A giant wing that was folding around him. The girl was calling to him.

"Matthew! Matthew!"

The wind caught the two words and tossed them aside. The girl pleaded with him, but time was running out for her, too. The beach cracked and began to break up. Dark crevices appeared, the sand spilling into them. The waves were rushing in. The four of them were trapped, unable to move.

"I'm coming!" Matt called.

He took a step toward them and stumbled, then twisted forward and fell. He cried out. But there was nothing to stop him. Everything spun as he plummeted through the night sky, down toward the sea.

He woke up with a start.

He was lying in bed at Hive Hall. He could make out the wooden beams on the ceiling, the dried flowers in their vase on the chest of drawers. There was a full moon, the pale light washing through the room. For a moment, he lay still, thinking about his dream. He had dreamed it many times, not just at Hive Hall but before. It was always the same apart from two things. Each time the presence he had felt forming itself . . . the folding wing . . . whatever it was . . . had come a little closer to taking shape. And each time he woke up a few seconds later, a few centimeters nearer to the end of his fall. He wondered what would happen if he didn't wake up in time.

He looked at his watch, turning it to the window to check the time. It was almost midnight. It had been ten o'clock when he went to bed. What had woken him up? he wondered. He had been exhausted by the day's work and should have slept through.

And then he heard it.

It was faint and far away and yet still quite clear, carried on the stillness of the night. It came from the wood, sliding over the silver tips of the trees, under the moonlight.

Whispering.

At first Matt thought it was nothing more than the wind rustling through the branches . . . but there was no wind. And as he threw back the cover and sat up in bed, he heard another sound. It was underneath the whispers, constant and unchanging. A soft, electronic hum. The whispers stopped, then started again. The hum went on.

Despite himself, Matt felt the hairs on the back of his neck begin to prickle. The sounds were far away, but the horrible thing was that they could have been coming from somewhere inside the building. They were all around him. Everywhere and nowhere. He got out of bed and went over to the window.

The moon slid behind a cloud and for a moment everything was dark. But there was a light. In the surrounding darkness, somewhere not far from the edge of the wood, he could see a faint glow. The light was being swallowed up by the trees, hemmed in on all sides. However, some of it had escaped through gaps in the branches and had spread out, the cold white shafts evaporating in the air. It was electric, not the light of a fire. And it seemed to be coming from the same source as the sound.

Who was there? What could be happening in the middle of a Yorkshire wood — and could it have something to do with the warning he had been given only that afternoon?

"You don't want to be anywhere near here. Do you understand me?"

Suddenly Matt wanted to know — and almost before he had worked out what he was doing he had put on his clothes, opened the door, and slipped into the hall. He paused for a moment, listening for any sound within the farmhouse. Mrs. Deverill's room was at the end of the corridor. The door was closed. Matt had never seen inside her room and guessed she would be sound asleep. She always went to bed at exactly half past nine. The last thing he wanted to do was wake her up. Moving more carefully now, he tiptoed down the stairs and into the living room. The portrait of Mrs. Deverill's ancestor watched him as he made for the front door. Its eyes almost seemed to follow him. The face was dark and secretive.

It was cold in the yard. Nothing moved. Matt could hear the whispers more clearly now. They seemed not only louder but closer. He could even make out some of the words . . . not that they made any sense.

"NODEB . . . TE MOCMOD . . . EMANY . . . NEVAEH . . . NITRA . . .

The strange sounds danced around him as he stood there, alone in the night. They were human whispers, he realized. Human and yet at the same time unworldly. He wondered what to do. Part of him wanted to get out the bicycle and try to get nearer. Part of him wanted to go back to bed and forget the whole thing. And then he noticed something that he should have seen straightaway.

Mrs. Deverill's car wasn't there.

The Land Rover was always parked in the same place, next to the barn. It had been there at dinnertime. It wasn't there now. Could it be that she had left Hive Hall, that she was herself somewhere in the wood, part of whatever it was that was going on? Was Matt alone at the farm?

He went back into the living room. The portrait was the first thing he noticed and this time he knew it wasn't his imagination. It had definitely changed a second time. The figure had raised a hand. Matt was certain it hadn't been painted that way. But a skeletal finger was pointing upward, as if ordering him to bed.

Upstairs, he found himself looking into a cold, empty room with bare floorboards and an iron bed. There was a wardrobe and a chest of drawers but little else. The bed was empty. He was right. Mrs. Deverill wasn't here. At last he'd been given the opportunity he needed.

Matt had already decided he was going back to London. Now he knew it was going to happen tonight. By daybreak he would have reached the motorway and he would hitch-hike south. He had no doubt that Mrs. Deverill would call the police, but the farther away he managed to get, the harder it would be for them to find him. Once he reached London, he would be safe. But he needed cash. Money was the difference between survival and constant danger. He would have to buy food. He'd need to find a room. There had to be money in the house. He would find it and steal it now.

He began in the kitchen. No longer caring how much noise he made, he rifled through the drawers and cup-boards, opened jars and boxes, trying to work out where Mrs. Deverill kept her housekeeping funds. He could still hear the whispering, but more intermittent now. Was it coming to an end? He glanced at his watch. It was a quarter past one. He moved more quickly, afraid the woman could return at any time. There was no money in the room. He looked for her handbag. A handbag would mean cash and possibly credit cards. But she must have taken it with her.

He tried the living room. The portrait seemed to watch angrily as he searched, looking behind the books and under the chairs in the hope that Mrs. Deverill might have tucked her purse away. Matt hadn't turned on the lights. Noah might still be in the barn and he was afraid of giving himself away. He was crossing over to look around the fireplace when something screamed at him, sending him back, his heart pounding. It was Asmodeus, Mrs. Deverill's cat. It had been asleep on one of the chairs, but now it was standing up as if electrocuted, its hair bristling, its eyes ablaze. It opened its mouth and hissed, revealing a set of white fangs. Matt stood still. The cat was going to attack him. He was sure of it. It was already bracing itself, the claws of its two front paws ripping at the material, practicing what it was going to do to his throat.

Matt looked around. There was a poker next to the fire, a heavy antique thing. He thought of snatching it up but wasn't sure he could bring himself to use it. The cat's tail whipped briefly. Its eyes had never left him. He had dared to abuse Mrs. Deverill's hospitality and now he was going to pay. The cat hissed a second time and leaped.

But Matt was ready for it. There was a large basket beside the poker. Normally it would contain logs, but for once it was empty. Matt grabbed it and threw it down over the cat as it left the chair. He heard a terrible screaming and yowling, felt the claws battering desperately at the straw cage. Matt slammed the basket down onto the chair, imprisoning the cat inside. Holding the basket with one hand, he reached out with the other. Mrs. Deverill had an old-fashioned sewing machine on the floor beside the chair. Using all his strength, Matt picked it up and dropped it on top of the basket. The straw creaked. The cat hurled itself against the side. But the basket held. Asmodeus wasn't going anywhere.

Matt straightened up. He was trembling from the shock of what had just happened. And he was suddenly aware of something else. There was no sound coming from the wood. The whispering had stopped. So far he had found nothing and he was running out of time.

There was just one room left.

He went back upstairs and into Mrs. Deverill's bedroom. Surely he would find money here. He opened the wardrobe. Mrs. Deverill's clothes hovered in the darkness, suspended from wire hangers with her shoes underneath. Matt was about to close the door when he noticed a cardboard box in the back corner. He leaned down and opened it. There was something inside. Not money. Photographs.

He took one of them out and found himself looking at a cemetery. The photograph was black-and-white, taken with a telephoto lens. There was a crowd of people, dressed in the usual somber clothes, and in the middle of them a boy who was eight years old. Matt recognized him instantly. With a sense of horror and sickness, he realized he was looking at a picture of himself.

This was his parents' funeral.

Six years ago.

But it was impossible. Nobody had taken any photographs. And even if they had, even if a journalist or someone had been there, what was this picture doing here? How had Mrs. Deverill got hold of it?

There were two sheets of paper attached to the photograph by a clip. With his heart pounding, Matt slipped them loose, then turned them around so he could read them. An official police report. Each page was marked CONFIDENTIAL in red letters. Matt tried to concentrate on the words in the half-light.

. . . THE WITNESS STATEMENT OF MRS. ROSEMARY GREEN IN RELATION TO THIS CASE IS NOT TO BE RELEASED AND WE RECOMMEND A COMPLETE MEDIA BLACKOUT. THE CHILD, MATTHEW FREEMAN, IS ONLY EIGHT YEARS OLD AND HAS DEMONSTRATED PRECOGNITIVE ABILITIES WHICH WOULD SEEM TO BE BEYOND . . .

Precognitive abilities. Matt didn't want to put the words into simple English. Nor did he want to read any more of the report. In that second, he made his decision. He thrust the box back into the corner, closed the wardrobe doors, and left. In the living room, the portrait watched silently. Asmodeus slammed himself again and again against the sides of the basket, trying to escape. Matt didn't notice either of them. He threw open the door and ran across the yard.

He hadn't found any money, but he would just have to do without it.

It was definitely time to leave.

It took him just a few minutes to cycle up to the cross-roads. The night had grown colder and his breath frosted as he paused by the broken sign, taking his bearings. He had a choice of five country lanes, each one cutting through the wood in a different direction. One, he knew, led to Lesser Malling. He had just taken one from the farm. That left only three. He chose the middle path and set off, grateful for the moon showing him the way. There was no sound coming from the wood. The electric light had been turned off. His greatest fear was that he would run into Mrs. Deverill, returning from wherever she had been. He listened out for the sound of her Land Rover, but there was nothing. He was utterly alone.

He tried to concentrate on what he was doing. He didn't want to look at the woodland, but he couldn't stop himself being aware of it as it surrounded him on all sides. The trunks of the trees, arranged in their dead-straight lines, were silhouetted against the moon. They were like the solid bars of a huge open-air jail. The branches, swaying slightly, cast a thousand shadows over the ground. The pine needles rustled together and seemed almost to be whispering to themselves as he pedaled past.

Matt kept his eyes fixed on the road in front of him. He intended to cycle all night. The discovery of the photograph had decided it. He was just going to have to chance it in London. Without money. Without anywhere to live. The police would probably find him in the end, but that didn't matter. They could put him in a Secure Training

Center for as long as they liked . . . anything so long as it didn't involve Mrs. Deverill or Lesser Malling.

Why did she have a photograph of him in her wardrobe? How had she gotten her hands on a secret police report? And what did the death of his parents mean to her? It was a horrible thought but he wondered if Mrs. Deverill had known about him *before* he had been introduced to her by the LEAF Project. In which case, could she have in some way chosen him? But that would suggest that she had been planning whatever was going on in Lesser Malling for years and years, and that he had always somehow been part of it.

But he had decided. He was going to forget the whole lot of them. His aunt, his social worker, Mallory . . . he had been pushed around far too long. It was time to start looking after himself. He might be able to get a job in a kitchen or a bed-and-breakfast. He looked old for his age. Grimly he pushed down, urging the old bike forward. It must be two o'clock in the morning. How many minutes had passed since he left the farm?

There was an intersection coming up ahead of him. Matt slowed down, coasting the last few meters. He looked around him. There was a choice of five directions and a broken signpost without any names. It took him half a minute to realize where he was. Somehow, the lane he had chosen had brought him around in a big circle. He was back exactly where he had begun.

He was angry with himself. He had wasted time and precious energy. Mrs. Deverill might have gotten back to Hive Hall. She would have found the cat under the basket and would have checked Matt's room. She might have already called the police.

Gritting his teeth, Matt chose one of the other lanes and pedaled forward again. He was beginning to wish he had waited until the morning. No. He would have been set to work on the farm, and between them, Noah and Mrs. Deverill always had him in their sight. He concentrated on his rhythm, left foot then right foot, listening to the bicycle chain as it groaned and creaked underneath him. The trees rolled past endlessly. About another twenty minutes passed. Matt was strong and he was fit again after his illness. There was a dull ache in his legs, but otherwise he was fine. The road turned a corner.

He stopped.

He was back at the intersection. It was impossible. The lane he had been following had run straight and he must have covered at least two miles. He gazed at the broken signpost with disbelief. It was the same signpost. There could be no doubt of it.

Now he was angry. For this to happen once was unfortunate. But twice! It was stupid. He jerked the bike around and set off down the fifth lane, the one farthest away. He cycled more quickly this time, forcing the pedals down, using his anger to lend himself strength. The night breeze rushed over his shoulders, cooling the sweat on the side of his head. A cloud covered the moon and suddenly everything was very dark. Matt didn't slow down. The cloud separated. Matt lurched to a halt, unable to believe what was happening.

The fifth lane had somehow turned into the first lane.

They had looped him back to the start. The broken sign-post stood there, mocking him.

Very well. He set off back the way he had come, passing Hive Hall. This lane had to go somewhere different. He cycled past the gate as quickly as he could. There were no lights visible at the end of the drive, so maybe Mrs. Deverill wasn't back yet after all. The lane climbed steeply uphill — but that was good. A hill was something different. None of the other lanes had gone up or down. Matt no longer really cared where he was going. He just wanted to find a main road. He was fed up with the wood, fed up with country lanes.

He reached the top of the hill and stopped. For the first time he was really afraid. He has been cycling for the best part of an hour, but he still hadn't gone anywhere.

He was back at the crossroads where he had begun.

Matt was breathing heavily. His hands were clutching the handlebar so hard that the blood couldn't reach his fingers. He stood there for a moment, considering his options. He didn't really have any. Either the darkness was playing tricks on him or something was happening that he didn't understand. But he knew now that even if he cycled all night, he wasn't going anywhere.

He would just have to take his chances with Mrs. Deverill. He turned the bike around and pedaled slowly back to the farm.

SEVEN

Omega One

"He was in my room last night," Mrs. Deverill said. She was talking on the telephone. The receiver was old-fashioned and heavy, made of black plastic. A thick wire coiled out of her hand. "I think he found the photographs."

"It was a mistake keeping them there."

"Perhaps. But there's something else I'm worried about. Matthew is stronger than he was when he first came here. I think he may be starting to work things out. I don't like having him here. If you ask me, we've got a tiger by the tail. We should deal with him before it's too late."

It was a man's voice at the other end of the phone. He spoke in a way that was very cold and deliberate. It was an educated voice. A headmaster, perhaps, in an old-fashioned private school. "What do you mean?" he demanded.

"Lock him up. There's a crypt in the church. We could put him in there, underground, somewhere nobody would find him. It's only for a few more weeks. And then we'll be done with him."

"No." The single word was final. "Right now the boy thinks he's ordinary. He has no idea of who or what he is. Bury him alive and you could actually help him discover himself. And what happens if the police or his social worker comes calling? How will you explain where he is?"

"Suppose he escapes. . . ."

"You know he can't escape. We have him contained. There's nothing he can do. And very soon now we'll be ready for him. All you have to do is watch him. Where is he now?"

"I don't know. Somewhere in the yard. . . ."

"Watch him, Mrs. Deverill. Don't let him out of your sight."

There was a click and the line went dead. Mrs. Deverill weighed the phone in one hand, then lowered it. "Asmodeus!" she called.

The cat, sitting on the arm of a chair on the other side of the room, opened one eye and looked at her.

"You heard what he said," she snapped. "The boy . . ."

The cat leaped off the chair. With no effort, it sprang up onto a windowsill and then out of the window. Outside, Noah walked past, pushing a wheelbarrow piled high with manure. The cat ran past him and continued up the lane. A moment later, it had disappeared from sight.

● ● ●

Matt stood at the edge of the wood, looking down a tunnel of trees. The bicycle lay on its side on a grassy verge beside the road. Five minutes had passed since he had slipped past Noah and made his way out of Hive Hall. But he still couldn't make up his mind.

He was tempted once again to find his way to London.

He must have been confused the night before. He was unable to see where he was going and had somehow missed his way. But part of him warned him not to try navigating the lanes a second time. He didn't want to spend any more time going round in circles and, anyway, there was another way out of this. The LEAF Project was supposed to be voluntary. A single phone call to Detective Superintendent Mallory was all it would take.

But before he did that, he wanted to know more. What were the sounds he had heard the night before? What was going on in the wood? There was only one way to find out.

He had pinpointed the spot he thought he saw the light coming from. It had to be somewhere in front of him now. And yet he was unwilling to step off the road. It wasn't the story Mrs. Deverill had told him . . . he doubted there was any chance of wandering into a bog. It was the wood itself that scared him — its unnaturalness, the straightness of its lines. Nature wasn't meant to grow like this. How could he possibly find his way when every pine tree looked the same, when there were no hillocks, plants, or streams to act as landmarks? And there was something else. The corridors between the trees seemed to go on forever, stretching into a dark universe of their own. The darkness was waiting for him. He was like an insect on the edge of a huge web.

He made a decision, stepped off the road, and took twenty paces forward, following a single path. The pine needles crunched underneath his feet. Provided he didn't turn left or right, he would be fine. He would let the trees guide him. And if he thought he was getting lost, he would simply follow the same path back to the road.

And yet. He stopped to catch his breath. It really was extraordinary. He felt as if he had stepped through a mirror between two dimensions. On the road it had been a cool, bright spring morning. The atmosphere in the wood was strangely warm and sluggish. Shafts of sunlight, a deep, intense green, slanted in different directions. On the road, he had heard the twitter of birds and the lowing of a cow. In the wood, everything was silent . . . as if sound was forbidden to enter.

Already he saw that he should have brought a compass with him. At the very least he could have brought something to help him find his way back: a knife or a tin of paint. He remembered a story he'd been told at school. Some Greek guy — Theseus or someone — had gone into a maze to fight a creature that was half man, half bull. The Minotaur. He'd been given a ball of wool that he'd unraveled, and that was how he'd found his way out. Matt should have done the same.

He turned around and, counting out loud, he retraced the twenty paces he had taken.

The road wasn't there.

It was impossible. He turned around. The trees stretched on endlessly. He looked left and right. The same. He took another five steps. More trees, all of them identical, running as far as the eye could see . . . and farther. The road had disappeared as if it had never been there. Either that, or somehow the trees had grown. That was what it felt like. The artificial wood was all around him. It had captured him and would never let him go.

He took a deep breath, counted twenty paces forward, then turned left and walked another ten. Still no road. It didn't matter what direction he looked in. Everywhere he saw the same thing. Tall, narrow trunks and dark green needles. Gloomy corridors between them. A hundred different directions but no real choice. Matt stood still, hoping that he would hear a car on its way to Lesser Malling. That would help him find the road. But no car passed. A single crow cawed, somewhere high above. Otherwise, the silence was as thick as fog.

"Great!"

He shouted out the single word, because he wanted to hear the sound of his own voice. But it didn't even sound like him. His voice was small and weak, muffled by the unmoving trees all around him.

He walked on. What else could he do? His footfall was soft on the bed of needles, measuring out his progress into nowhere. Looking up, he could barely see the sky through the dark green canopy. He was suddenly angry with himself. The roads had played exactly the same trick on him the night before. But at least they were roads. This was much, much worse.

A glimmer of silver caught his eye, quite unexpected in the middle of so much green. The sun was reflecting off something behind a wall of trees a short distance away. With a surge of relief, Matt turned toward it, leaving one path and following another. But if he thought he had discovered the way out, he was mistaken. There was no way forward. He found himself up against a tall, rusting fence. The silver he had seen was the wire. The fence was at least six meters high. The top was barbed with steel spikes. It ran to the left and to the right, curving in what must be a huge circle.

There was a clearing behind the fence and, in the center of the clearing, a large building that was at once out-of-date and yet futuristic. The building was divided into two parts. The main part was rectangular, built of gray bricks, two stories high, with windows — half of them broken — running the full length. Some of the brickwork was cracked, with weeds and ivy eating their way in. It had obviously been there for a long time. Matt reckoned the building must be thirty or forty meters long. It would have fitted neatly onto a football field.

But it was the second part of the building that drew his attention. This was nothing more nor less than a giant golf ball, at least thirty meters high, sitting on the ground as if it had rolled there. The outside was white. Was it an observatory? No. There was no slit in the dome for a telescope. In fact, it didn't have any windows at all. The ball had also been stained by time and the weather. The white paint was discolored and in places it looked as if it had caught some sort of disease. But it was still impressive. It was the last thing he would have expected to find in the middle of a wood.

A brick rectangle — some sort of passageway — connected the two parts. He could see an oversize door set right in the middle. The main entrance? He wondered if he could get closer. He had no idea what he was looking at. It would be good to find out.

Matt turned right and followed the fence for about fifty meters. After a while the wood fell back and he came to a pair of gates, firmly locked together with a heavy padlock on a thick, discolored chain. On one of the gates was a sign, the words painted in faded red paint on a peeling wooden square:

OMEGA ONE
Property of HM Government
Trespassers will be prosecuted

Omega One. The building had reminded Matt of an observatory, but looking at it again, he wondered if it might have some military use. The sign said that it was government property. The Ministry of Defense? Briefly he examined the gates. They were old, but the padlock was new, meaning someone had been here recently. There was no way he was going to get it open. He looked up and saw the razor wire twisted round the top. So much for that.

With growing curiosity, he continued walking, following the fence, wondering if he might find a tree he could climb over. Instead he found something better. There was a hole in the wire where several strands had rusted loose. The hole was just about big enough to allow him to squeeze through. He glanced at his watch. The afternoon was wearing on and already the light was fading. But there was still time.

He had leaned over and was about to squeeze through when someone grabbed hold of him and spun him around.

"What are you doing here?" a voice demanded.

Matt's heart lurched. After his time alone in the wood he hadn't dreamed for a minute that there would be anyone else here. His fist was already curled in self-defense, but then he recognized the fair hair and unhappy face of the man who had approached him in Lesser Malling. It was the man who had warned him to leave.

"I got lost," Matt said, relaxing slightly. "What is this place?" He gestured at the building on the other side of the fence.

"It's a power station," the man told him.

Matt examined the man more closely, noticing now that he was carrying a shotgun, the two barrels broken over his arm. He was still wearing jeans, this time with an open-neck shirt.

"You shouldn't be here," the man said.

"I told you. I got lost. I was looking for . . ."

"What were you looking for?"

"I saw lights in the forest. Last night. I wondered what they were."

"Lights?"

"And I heard something. Strange noises — a sort of humming. Why don't you tell me what's going on around here? You warned me to go away."

"Why didn't you?" the man asked.

"I tried." Matt left it at that. He was in no mood to explain what had happened to him on the moonlit roads. "What were you warning me about?" he demanded. "Why is everyone in Lesser Malling so weird? Who are you?"

The man seemed to relax a little — but his eyes remained watchful. He rested a hand on the barrel of his gun. "My name is Burgess," he said. "Tom Burgess. I'm a farmer. I own Glendale Farm. It's a short way down the Greater Malling Road."

"And what are you doing here? Are you guarding this place?"

"No. I'm hunting. These woods are full of foxes. They come for my chickens in the night. I'm out to get a few of them." He patted the gun.

"I didn't hear any shots."

"I didn't see any foxes."

Matt looked back at the building. "You said this place was a power station," he began. Suddenly the shape was more familiar. He had seen pictures at school. "Is it a nuclear power station?"

Burgess nodded.

"What is it doing here?"

"It's nothing." The farmer shrugged. "It was experimental. The government put it here a long, long time ago. It was before they started building the real things. They were looking into alternative sources of energy, so they built Omega One, and when they'd finished all their experiments they shut it down again. It's empty now. There's nothing there. Nobody's been anywhere near it for years."

"They were here last night," Matt said. "I saw lights. And I heard them."

"Maybe you were imagining things."

"I don't have that much imagination." Matt was angry. "Why won't you tell me the truth?" he went on. "You warned me I was in some sort of danger. You told me to run away. But I can't run away unless I know what it is I'm running from. Why don't you tell me what you know? We're safe here. Nobody can overhear us."

The farmer was clearly struggling with himself. On the one hand, Matt could see that he wanted to talk. But strong though he was, and armed as well, he was still afraid. "How could you begin to understand?" he said at last. "How old are you?"

"Fourteen."

"You shouldn't be here. Listen to me. I only came to this place a year ago. I got left money. I always wanted to have my own place. If I'd known. If I'd even had the faintest idea . . ."

"If you'd only known *what*?"

"Mrs. Deverill and the rest of them . . ."

"What about them? What are they doing?"

There was a rustle in the undergrowth, followed by an angry snarl. Matt turned and saw an animal appear, stepping out of a patch of fern a couple of meters away. It was a cat, its eyes ablaze, its mouth wide open to reveal its fangs. But it wasn't just any cat. He recognized the yellow eyes, the mangy fur. . . .

He relaxed. "It's all right," he said. "It's only the cat. It must have followed me here."

But the farmer's face had gone white. All at once he had snapped the barrel of his gun shut and raised the whole thing to his shoulder. Before Matt could stop him, he pulled the trigger. There was an explosion. The cat had no chance. Tom Burgess had emptied both barrels, and lead pellets tore into its fur, spinning it in a horrible somersault over the grass, a ball of black that spit red.

"What did you do that for?" Matt exclaimed. "It wasn't a fox. It was just a farm cat."

"Just a cat?" The farmer shook his head. "It was Asmodeus. Mrs. Deverill's cat."

"But . . ."

"We can't talk. Not here. Not now."

"Why not?"

"There are things happening . . . things you wouldn't believe." The color hadn't returned to the farmer's face. His hands were trembling. "Listen!" he whispered. "Come to my farm. Tomorrow morning — at ten o'clock. Glenwood Farm. It's on the Greater Malling Road. Turn left when you come out of Hive Hall. Can you find it?"

"Yes." Then Matt remembered. "No. I've tried finding my way around these lanes, but they don't seem to lead anywhere. I just end up where I began."

"That's right. You can only go where they want you."

"What do you mean?"

"It's too difficult to explain." Burgess thought for a moment. Then he suddenly reached up and grabbed hold of a leather cord around his neck. Matt watched as he drew it over his head. He held it out and Matt saw there was a small, round stone — a talisman — dangling from it. There was a symbol in the stone, engraved in gold. The outline of a key.

"Wear this," Burgess said. "Don't ask me to explain it, but you won't get lost if you're wearing it. Come to my house tomorrow. I'll tell you everything you want to know."

"Why not now?" Matt demanded.

"Because it's not safe — not for either of us. I have a car. You come to my house and we'll leave together."

Tom Burgess strode away, heading for the line of trees.

"Wait a minute!" Matt called after him. "I don't know how to get out of the wood!"

Burgess stopped, turned around, and pointed. "Look under your feet," he shouted. "You're standing on the road." Then he was gone.

Matt examined the ground around him. There was a line of black pavement, barely visible beneath the weeds and the pine needles. He would have to follow it carefully, but at least it would lead him out. The stone talisman was still in his hand. He ran a finger along the key, wondering if it was real gold. Then he slipped it around his neck, making sure it was hidden under his shirt.

Ten minutes later, Matt found himself back on the main road. He examined the entrance to Omega One carefully. It was nothing more than a gap between two trees in a line of five hundred. He had pedaled past it without even knowing it was there, and it would be almost impossible to find it again. Matt took off his jacket. He tore a strip of material from the shirt, then tied it in a knot around a branch. He stepped back and examined his handiwork. He had created a tiny pale blue flag. It would show him the way back if he ever needed it. Satisfied, he put his jacket back on and set off to retrieve his bike.

He got back to Hive Hall about forty minutes later. It was almost midday. Noah was working on the side of the barn, painting it with creosote. Matt could smell the chemical in the air. Mrs. Deverill would be in the farmhouse, making lunch.

Brushing a few needles off his jacket, Matt walked up to

the front door. He was just reaching for the handle when he stopped and stepped back with a shiver of disbelief.

Asmodeus was there, sitting on the windowsill, licking one of its paws. Seeing him, it purred menacingly. Asmodeus was there! The cat wasn't dead. It wasn't even hurt.

EIGHT
Wet Paint

Matt didn't sleep well that night. He had too many unan-
swered questions in his head, and the fact that Tom
Burgess had promised to answer them made him tense and
restless. He couldn't wait to find out the truth. But that was
exactly what he had to do, tossing around in his narrow
bed as the sky became gray, then silver, then finally blue.
Mornings on the farm normally began with breakfast at
seven o'clock. Mrs. Deverill was already in the kitchen
when he came down.

"So what happened to you yesterday?" she demanded.
She was wearing a pale blue cardigan, a shapeless gray dress,
and Wellington boots. All the clothes that she wore at Hive
Hall looked as if they had come out of a charity shop.

"I went for a walk," Matt said.

"A walk? Where?"

"Just around."

Mrs. Deverill took a pan off the Aga and spooned thick
porridge into two bowls. "I don't remember you asking per-
mission," she said.

"I don't remember you telling me I had to," Matt
replied.

Mrs. Deverill's eyes narrowed. "I can't say I'm used to

being spoken to in that way," she muttered. Then she shrugged as if it didn't matter anyway. "I was only thinking of you, Matthew," she went on. "If you look at the booklets provided by the LEAF Project, you'll see quite clearly that I'm supposed to know where you are at all times. I'd hate to have to report that you've broken the rules."

"You can report what you like," Matt said.

She placed the two bowls on the table and sat down opposite him. "There's a lot of work to be done today," she said. "The tractor needs hosing down. And we could do with some firewood being chopped."

"Whatever you say, Mrs. Deverill."

"Exactly." The gray lips pressed together in something like a smile. "Whatever I say."

• • •

It was nine o'clock, an hour before Matt had arranged to meet Tom Burgess. Matt was working on the tractor, washing it down as he had been told. For the fiftieth time he looked around and realized he was alone. Noah was on the other side of the barn, mending some pipes. Mrs. Deverill was feeding the pigs. Neither of them was watching him, nor was there any sign of Asmodeus. Matt dropped the hose, then went over to the tap and turned it off. He waited until the last jet of water had splashed itself onto the ground. Nobody came. He had left the old bicycle in the yard, close at hand. He stole over to it now and, taking hold of the handlebar, pushed it out of the farm. Pedaling would have made too much noise.

Nobody tried to stop him. Nobody seemed to have noticed he had gone. A minute later he was through the gate and onto the lane. He looked back with a sense of relief. It had all been much easier than he had thought.

Too easy? He remembered the way Mrs. Deverill had smiled at him in the kitchen. He had wondered then if she knew more than she was letting on. All the time he got the feeling she was playing with him, and the photograph and police report he had found in her bedroom cupboard had only confirmed it. She knew who he was. He was more sure of it than ever. He had been chosen on purpose.

He got onto the bike and began to pedal, turning left as Tom Burgess had told him. The last time he had attempted this journey, the lane had simply looped him back to where he had started. But this time was different. He was wearing the talisman that the farmer had given him. He reached up and felt it against his chest. Why a stone with a picture of a key should make any difference was beyond him. That was just one of the many questions he intended to ask.

The lane led uphill, but there was no intersection at the top. Instead the road continued past a series of fields. A low stone wall rose and dipped ahead. He came to a signpost — and this time it wasn't broken. It read: GREATER MALLING 4 MILES. Matt stared at it. It was the first reminder he'd had that there was an actual world outside. He had no idea how he'd managed to miss it when he made the journey two nights before.

He found Glendale Farm easily enough. There was a turning about a quarter of a mile farther along with the name printed in bright blue letters on a white gate. Even as

Matt cycled down the flower-bordered drive that led from the main road he thought how much more welcoming it was than Hive Hall. The barns and stables were clean and ordered, standing next to a pretty pond. A swan glided on the water, its reflection shimmering in the morning sunlight. A family of ducks waddled across the lawn. A cow chewed grass, lowing contentedly in a nearby paddock.

The farmhouse itself was redbrick, with neat white shutters and a gray slate roof. One part of the roof was covered in plastic sheeting where the farmer had been working on repairs. An old weather vane stood at one corner, a wrought-iron rooster looking out over the four points of the compass. Today it was facing south.

Matt got off the bike, crossed the farmyard to the front door, and pulled a metal chain to ring a bell in the porch. He was early. It was half past nine. He waited, then rang again. No answer. Perhaps Tom Burgess was working in the barn. Matt walked over and looked inside. There was a tractor and an assortment of tools, a pile of sacks, a few bales of hay . . . but no sign of the farmer.

"Mr. Burgess?" he called.

Silence. Nothing moved.

But the farmer had to be there. His car, a Peugeot, was parked in the drive. Matt went back to the front door and turned the handle. The door opened.

"Mr. Burgess?" he called again.

There was no answer. Matt went in.

The front door led straight into the main room. There was a large fireplace to one side with a gleaming pair of bronze tongs and a small shovel leaning against the grate. The fire had evidently burned during the night, for the ashes were still scattered in the hearth. The room was a mess. Tables had been overturned and books and papers scattered on the floor. All the shutters were hanging open, some of them broken in half. Matt's foot caught a loose can of paint. He picked it up and put it to one side.

The kitchen was worse. All the drawers were open and their contents seemed to have been thrown everywhere. There were broken plates and glasses and, in the middle of the kitchen table, a half-empty bottle of whiskey lying on its side. Matt glanced up. A huge carving knife had been thrust into a kitchen cupboard. Half the blade had penetrated the wood. The handle slanted toward him. It looked odd and rather menacing.

Every fiber of his being was telling him to get out, but Matt couldn't leave yet. He found himself drawn to the stairs. Narrow and twisting, they led up from the kitchen. Before he knew what he was doing, Matt was halfway up, dreading what he would find at the top but still unable to stop himself. He wasn't expected for another half an hour. Maybe Tom Burgess was still asleep. That was what he told himself. But somehow he didn't believe it.

The stairs led to a landing with three doors. Gently he opened the one nearest to him.

It led into a bedroom — and this room was worse than anything he had seen downstairs. It looked as though a whirlwind had hit it. The bedclothes were crumpled and torn, spread out over the carpet. The curtains had been ripped down from the window and a pane of glass was smashed, the glass scattered over the floor. A bedside table had been turned over, throwing a lamp, an alarm clock, and a pile of paperbacks onto the floor. The wardrobe had been flung open, all the clothes pulled off their hangers and thrown into a heap in one corner. A tin of green paint had toppled over, spilling its contents into the middle of the mess.

Then Matt saw Tom Burgess.

The farmer was lying on the floor on the other side of the bed, partly covered by a sheet. He was obviously dead. Something — some sort of animal — had torn into his face and neck. There were hideous red gashes in the skin and his fair hair was matted with blood. His eyes were bulging, out of focus, and his mouth was forced open in a last attempt at a scream. His hands were stiff and twisted in a frantic attempt to ward something off. One hand was smeared with green paint that had glued his fingers together. His legs were bent underneath him in such a way that Matt knew the bones must be broken.

Matt backed away, gasping. He thought he was going to be sick. Somehow, he forced his eyes away, and then he saw it, painted on the wall behind the door. In the last moments of his life, the farmer had managed to scrawl two words, using his own hand smeared with paint.

RAVEN'S GATE

Matt read it as he backed out of the room. He shut the door behind him and reeled down the stairs. He remembered seeing a telephone in the kitchen. He snatched up the receiver and dialed for help with a finger that wouldn't stop shaking. There was no answer. The phone had been disconnected.

He threw the receiver down and groped his way out of the house. The moment he reached the yard, he threw up. He had never seen a dead body before. And a twisted, tortured body like Tom Burgess's . . . he hoped he would never see one again. He found that he was shivering. As soon as he felt strong enough, he began to run. He had forgotten the bicycle. He just wanted to get out of there.

He ran back up the lane and onto the main road. He was only four miles away from Greater Malling, and that was the direction he took. He must have run for at least half a mile before he collapsed onto a bed of grass and lay there, the breath rasping in his throat. He didn't have the strength to go on. And what was the point? He had no parents and no friends. Nobody cared about him. He was going to die in Lesser Malling and nobody would remember that he had even been alive.

He didn't know how long he lay there, but at last the sound of an approaching car reached his ears, so he sat up and looked down the road. The car was white, a four-wheel drive with sirens attached to the roof. Matt breathed a sigh of relief. It was a police car. For the first time in his life it was something he actually wanted to see.

He pulled himself to his feet and walked into the center of the road with his arms raised. The police car slowed down and stopped. Two officers got out and walked over to him.

"What's the matter?" the first one asked. He was plump and middle-aged, with a high forehead and thinning black hair.

"Shouldn't you be at school?" the second one said. He

was the younger of the two, thin and boyish, with short-cut brown hair.

"There's been a murder," Matt said.

"What?" The older policeman sounded doubtful.

"A man called Tom Burgess. He's a farmer. He lives at Glendale Farm. I've just come from there." The sentences came out short and staccato. Matt was finding it hard to stitch the words together.

The two policemen looked doubtful.

"You saw him?" the older asked.

Matt nodded. "He was in the bedroom."

"What were you doing there?"

"I was meant to meet him."

"What's your name?"

Matt felt the impatience rising inside him. What was wrong with these men? He had just found a dead body. What did it matter what his name was? He forced himself to calm down. "I'm Matt," he said. "I'm staying with Jayne Deverill at Hive Hall. I met Tom Burgess. He asked me to visit him. I was there just now. And he's dead."

The older policeman looked more suspicious than ever, but the younger one shrugged. "We just passed Glendale Farm," he said. "Maybe we should take a look."

The other man thought for a moment, then nodded. "All right." He turned to Matt. "You'd better come with us."

"I don't want to go back there!" Matt exclaimed.

"You can wait in the car. You'll be all right."

Reluctantly Matt climbed into the backseat of the police car and allowed the two policemen to take him back the way he'd come. He gritted his teeth as they turned into the driveway. The police car slowed down, the wheels biting into the gravel.

"It seems quiet enough," the older policeman said. He twisted around to face Matt. "Where did you say you saw him?" he asked.

"Upstairs. In the bedroom."

"There's someone here," the second policeman said.

Matt looked out of the window. The policeman was right. A woman had appeared in the garden to one side of the house. She was tall and thin, with shapeless gray hair hanging to her shoulders. He recognized her. She was one of the women he had met in Lesser Malling. She had been pushing a pram. What was her name? Creasey. Or Creevy. She had come out of the house with a basket of washing and was hanging it on a line. Matt couldn't understand what was happening. She had been inside the house. She must have seen the state of the rooms. Hadn't she been upstairs?

The two policemen got out of the car. Feeling increasingly uneasy, Matt followed them. The woman saw them coming and stopped what she was doing.

"Good afternoon," she said. "How can I help you?"

"My name is Sergeant Rivers," the older policeman said. "This is Police Constable Reed. Who are you?"

"My name is Joanna Creevy. I help Tom Burgess with his housework. What's the matter?" She seemed to notice Matt for the first time. "Matthew? What are you doing here?" She scowled. "You haven't gotten yourself into trouble, have you?"

Matt ignored her.

"This is a little difficult," the sergeant began. "The fact is that we just met this young lad on the road."

"You left your bicycle here, Matthew," the woman said. "I thought you must have been visiting."

"Matthew claims that Tom Burgess may have been involved in some sort of accident," the sergeant went on.

"It wasn't an accident," Matt interrupted. "He's been killed. Cut to pieces. I saw him. . . ."

The woman stared at Matt, then broke into laughter. "That's impossible," she said. "I saw Tom ten minutes ago. You just missed him. He's gone to see to the sheep in the far paddock."

The policemen turned to Matt.

"She's lying," Matt said. "He didn't go anywhere ten minutes ago. I was here just a short while ago and he was dead."

"That's a terrible thing to say," Miss Creevy muttered. "Tom is fine. And here I am, hanging up his socks!"

"Go and look in the bedroom," Matt said.

"Yes. You do that." The woman nodded — and that was when Matt began to worry. She seemed confident — one step ahead of him.

"We'd better sort this out," Rivers said.

They all went into the house. Matt noticed at once that though it was still a mess, Miss Creevy — or someone — had tidied most of the evidence away. The books and papers had been cleared up. The shutters were folded back. And the knife had been taken out of the kitchen cupboard . . . although the gash it had left was still there. They went upstairs.

"You'll have to forgive the mess," Miss Creevy said. "Tom has been redecorating and I haven't had a chance to start work yet."

They reached the corridor. The door of the bedroom was closed, just as Matt had left it. He didn't want to go in. He didn't think he could bear to look at the body a second time. But he couldn't back out now.

Sergeant Rivers opened the door.

There was a man in the room, wearing a pair of white overalls that were flecked with green paint. Everything was different. The sheets and blankets had been removed from the bed. The bed itself was propped up on its side against the wall. The curtains had been hung up, and although one of the windows was still broken, there was no sign of any broken glass. The scattered clothes had disappeared. And so had the body of Tom Burgess.

The man saw the two policemen and stopped work.

"Good morning," he said.

"Who are you?" the police sergeant asked.

"I'm Ken," the man replied. "Ken Rampton." He was in his twenties, scrawny, with a sly, crumpled face and curly fair hair. He smiled and Matt saw that one of his front teeth had been chipped diagonally in half. "What do you want?"

"How long have you been here?"

"All morning. I got here about half past eight."

"You work for Tom Burgess?"

"I'm helping him out with the decorating."

"Have you seen him today?"

"I saw him about a quarter of an hour ago. He looked in to see how I was getting on. Then he went . . . something to do with his sheep."

"That's what I just told you," Miss Creevy said.

Matt felt the blood rush to his cheeks. "He's lying," he insisted. "They both are. I know what I saw." Suddenly he remembered. "Tom Burgess left a message," he said.

He swung around and pulled the door shut to reveal the wall behind it. But the wall, which had been off-white before, was now green. The words that the farmer had painted were gone.

"Be careful," Ken Rampton said. "Wet paint. . . ."

Sergeant Rivers came to a decision. He turned to the decorator. "We won't waste any more of your time, sir," he said. He grabbed hold of Matt, his hand tightening on his shoulder. "As for you, I think we should have a word outside."

Miss Creevy followed them back downstairs and out into the yard. Matt wondered if the policemen were going to arrest him. In fact, he suddenly realized, that was exactly what he hoped would happen. If they arrested him, maybe he would be taken back to London. Maybe this sort of behavior would mean that he could kiss the LEAF Project good-bye. But before anyone could say anything, Miss Creevy stepped forward. "I wonder if I could have a word with you, Officer," she said.

The sergeant left Matt with the other policeman and went over to the woman. They spoke for about two minutes. The sergeant glanced Matt's way a couple of times and nodded. The woman shrugged and spread her hands. The sergeant walked back over to them.

"You ought to know that wasting police time is a very serious business," he said.

"I'm telling the truth."

"Let's not have any more of that, thank you." The policeman wasn't going to budge. Matt could see that. He bit his tongue. "I understand you've been in trouble a few times before," Rivers continued. "You're with the LEAF Project, is that right? You ought to count yourself lucky. I don't personally believe in all this do-good stuff, if you want the truth. You're a thief and the best thing for you would be to be birched and locked up, where you can't do any more harm. But that's not my decision. The courts have sent you here, and if you had any sense, you'd be grateful and stop trying to draw attention to yourself. Now, we'll say no more about this nonsense. But I don't want to see or hear from you again."

The two policemen walked over to their car and got in. Matt watched them start the engine and leave. He turned around. The woman was smiling at him. Her long gray hair was flapping in the breeze. There was a movement at the door and Ken Rampton appeared, the paintbrush still clutched in his hand. He said nothing. But he, too, was smiling. The police car had gone.

"Go back to Hive Hall," the woman said. "Mrs. Deverill is waiting for you."

"I'm never going back!" Matt snatched up the bicycle.

"You can't escape from us, Matthew. There's nowhere you can go. Surely you can see that by now."

Matt ignored her. He picked up the bicycle.

"There's nowhere you can go." The woman echoed the words in a high-pitched voice.

Ken Rampton began to laugh.

Matt climbed onto the bicycle and pedaled away as fast as he could.

NINE
Local Affairs

Greater Malling was a small, attractive village that had grown into a large, unattractive town. There were still a few reminders of what it had once been: a pond, a row of almshouses, a lopsided sixteenth-century pub. But the roads had come, cutting in from every side and joining together at noisy intersections. New houses had elbowed out the old. Offices and car parks had sprung up, joined by cinemas, supermarkets, and a clattering bus station. Now it was very ordinary. Somewhere to pass through on the way to somewhere else.

It had taken Matt an hour to cycle here from Glendale Farm. Half the time he had been afraid that the road would play another trick on him and deposit him somewhere he didn't want to be. But he was still wearing the stone talisman that Tom Burgess had given him. Somehow the little golden key had unlocked the maze of country lanes and allowed him to arrive here. Matt parked outside a launderette. It occurred to him that someone might steal his bike, but he didn't care. He wouldn't be needing it again.

He was looking for a railway station and a train to London. There wasn't one. The line to Greater Malling had been closed down years ago. The nearest mainline station was at York. He found a traffic warden and asked about buses to York. There were two a day. The next one wouldn't be leaving until three o'clock. That left four hours to kill.

He walked aimlessly down the High Street and found himself facing a library — a modern building that already looked down-at-heel, with shabby pebble-dash walls and windows in rusting frames. Matt thought for a moment, then went in through a revolving door and up a staircase that was sign-posted REFERENCE. He found himself in a wide, brightly lit room with about a dozen bookcases arranged along the walls, a bank of computers, and an enquiry desk where a young man sat reading a paperback.

Something very dangerous was going on in the village of Lesser Malling. Somehow it involved many of the villagers, Mrs. Deverill, an abandoned nuclear power station, and something called Raven's Gate. It also involved Matt. That was what most unnerved him. He had been chosen. He was sure of it. Before he left Yorkshire, he was determined to find out why.

Raven's Gate. It was the only clue he had. That was where he decided to begin.

He started with the books in the local history section. The library had about a dozen books on Yorkshire, and half of them had brief references to Greater and Lesser Malling. But not one of them mentioned anything called Raven's Gate. There was one book that seemed more promising, so Matt carried it over to a table. It was called *Rambles Around Greater Malling* and had been written — some time ago to judge from the old-fashioned cover and yellowing pages — by a woman named Elizabeth Ashwood.

He opened the book and ran his eye down the contents page. He had found it. Chapter 6 was titled "*Raven's Gate.*"

He turned the pages and found chapter 7. He went back and found chapter 5. But chapter 6 wasn't there. A jagged edge and a gap in the binding told their own story. Someone had torn out the whole chapter. Was it just a random act of vandalism or had it been done deliberately? Matt thought he knew.

But the library offered more than books.

Matt went over to the man at the enquiry desk. "I need to use the Internet," he said.

"What for?" the man asked.

"It's a school project. We've been told to find out something about Raven's Gate."

"I've never heard of it."

"Nor have I. That's why I want to go on the Internet."

The man pointed and Matt went over to the nearest computer. There was a girl clicking away with the mouse at the next desk, but she ignored him. He called up a search engine, then typed in:

RAVEN'S GATE.

He remembered the words in green paint scrawled on the farmer's wall. Once again, he saw the dead man, his body torn apart, his eyes wide and empty.

He pressed ENTER.

There was a brief pause and then the screen came up with a list of results. Matt saw that his search had listed over twelve thousand possible sites relating to ravens and to gates, but none of them were even slightly relevant. There was an American football team, the Baltimore Ravens, whose players had walked out of the gate. There was a Golden Gate Park, also in America, where bird-watchers had spotted a variety of ravens. Ravens were also nesting, apparently, in the Kaleyard Gate in Chester. But there was no Raven's Gate . . . not on the first page, not on the second, not even on the third. Matt realized he would have to scroll through all twelve thousand entries. It would take him hours. There had to be another way.

He was about to give up when a pop-up screen suddenly appeared on the computer screen in front of him.

>Who are you?

Matt looked at the three words, floating in the white square. There was no way of knowing who they had come from.

He thought for a moment, then typed back:

>Who r u?

He entered the question. There was a pause. Then . . .

>Sanjay Dravid.

Matt waited a moment, wondering what would happen next.

>You have made an enquiry about Raven's Gate. What is your field of research?

Field of research? Matt didn't know how to reply. He leaned forward and typed again.

>I want to know what it is.

>Who are you?

>My name is Matt.

>Matt who?

>Can you help me?

There was a long pause and Matt wondered if the person on the other end — Sanjay Dravid — had gone away.

He was also puzzled. How had Dravid known that he was making the search to begin with? Had his enquiry triggered some sort of alarm on the Net?

Then the screen flickered again.

>Good-bye.

So that was it. Matt waited, but nothing more happened inside the pop-up screen. After a while he gave up. He went back to the enquiry desk.

"Yes?" The man looked up from his paperback.

"Is there a newspaper office in Greater Malling?"

"A newspaper . . . ?" the man considered. "There's the *Gazette*. I'd hardly call it a newspaper. They never print any news. Otherwise there's the *Yorkshire Post*."

"Where's the *Yorkshire Post*?"

"It's in York. If you want a local newspaper office, you'll have to try the *Gazette*. They're on Farrow Street. But I doubt they'll be able to help you with your school project."

It took Matt a moment to work out what the man was talking about. Then he remembered the lie he had told to get onto the computer. "I can try," he said.

• • •

Farrow Street was a leftover from medieval times. It was narrow and twisting, crammed with dustbins full of bottles and cans. As he turned off from the main road, Matt wondered if the man in the library had made a mistake. It seemed the last sort of place you'd want a newspaper office, cut off from the rest of the town in this dirty and forgotten corner. But about halfway down he came to a row of shops. First there was an undertaker. Then a travel agency. And finally a crumbling redbrick building on three floors that advertised itself with a plastic sign next to the door: THE GREATER MALLING GAZETTE.

The door led into an open-plan area with a young frizzy-haired girl sitting behind a desk, eating a sandwich, typing on a computer, and talking into a headset that was plugged into her telephone. She seemed to be both the receptionist and the secretary for the three journalists who were sitting at desks behind her. There were two women and a man — Matt was struck by how bored they all looked. One of the women was yawning continuously, scratching her head, and staring into space. The other woman was half-asleep. The man was fiddling with a pencil and gazing at his computer screen as if he hoped that whatever story he was working on would write itself.

"Can I help you?" It was the frizzy-haired girl who had spoken. Matt thought she was talking into the mouthpiece, but then he realized she was looking at him.

"Yes. I want to talk to someone who knows about local affairs."

"Do you live around here?"

"I'm staying in Lesser Malling."

The girl leaned back. "Richard!" she called. She had a nasal, rather whiny voice. "There's someone here for you."

The man who had been playing with the pencil looked up. "What?"

"This kid here — he wants to see you."

"Yeah. All right. . . ."

The man stood up and sauntered over to Matt. He was in his twenties, dressed in a striped shirt and loose, faded jeans. He had a serious, intelligent face . . . the sort of face Sherlock Holmes might have had when he was young. His hair was short, blond, and scruffy. He hadn't shaved for the last couple of days. Nor, from the look of it, had he changed his shirt. Everything about him was crumpled: his clothes, his hair, the very way he stood.

"What do you want?" he asked.

"I need help," Matt said.

"What sort of help?"

"I'm trying to find out something."

"Why?"

"It's for a school project."

"What school do you go to?"

That took Matt by surprise. "I go to school in Lesser Malling," he lied. He didn't even know the school's name.

"And you're doing a school project?"

"Yes."

"Try the library."

"I have tried the library. They sent me here."

"Well, I can't help you." The journalist shrugged. "I'm busy."

"You don't look busy," Matt said.

"Well, I was busy until you arrived."

"Busy doing what?"

"Busy being busy. All right?"

Matt forced himself to keep his temper. "Well, maybe I can help you," he said. "You're a journalist. Maybe I've got a story."

"You've got a story?"

"I might have."

"All right. Come upstairs."

The journalist led Matt through a door and up a staircase to the first floor. Here there was a conference room looking out onto Farrow Street. It wasn't much of a room, but it was already obvious to Matt that this wasn't much of a paper. There were eight seats arranged around a wooden table, a presentation board, and a water cooler.

"Thirsty?" the journalist asked.

Matt nodded

The journalist took out a plastic cup and filled it. Matt saw a single bubble of air rise up inside the water. He took the cup. The water was lukewarm.

"My name is Richard Cole," the journalist said, sitting down at the table. He produced a notepad and opened it to a blank page.

"I'm Matt," Matthew said.

"Just Matt?"

"That's right."

"You said you were staying in Lesser Malling."

"Yes. Do you know it?"

Richard smiled humorlessly. "I've been through it," he said. "I'm meant to cover it. Me, Kate, and Julia — they're the girls you saw downstairs — we all have our own territories. Lucky me! I got Lesser Malling."

"Why lucky you?"

"Because nothing ever happens. I'm twenty-five years old. I've been working in this dump for eighteen months. And do you know the biggest news event I've had to cover so far? 'BAD EYESIGHT KILLS OLD LADY.'"

"How can bad eyesight kill you?"

"She fell in the river. We had a dog show in Greater Malling last week. The fleas were more interesting than the dogs. I got a parking ticket once. I almost put that on the front page." He threw down the notepad and yawned. "You see, Matt, this is one of the most boring places in England . . . possibly the whole world. It's just a poxy little market town that doesn't even have a market. Nothing ever happens."

"So why are you here?"

"That's a good question." Richard sighed. "Three years at York University. All I ever wanted to be was a journalist. I did a course in London. I thought I'd get onto the *Mail* or the *Express* or maybe just freelance. But there are no jobs around. I couldn't afford to live in London, so I thought I'd come back north again. Maybe get a job on the *Yorkshire Post*. I live in York. I like York. But the *Yorkshire Post* wouldn't have me. I think I made a bad impression at my interview."

"What happened?"

"I ran over the editor. It wasn't my fault. I was late. I was reversing and I heard this thump. I didn't realize it was him until I met him ten minutes later." Richard shrugged. "Then I heard there was an opening here, and although Greater Malling was obviously a dump, I thought I'd take it. I mean, it was a job. But nobody reads the *Gazette*. That's because — apart from adverts — there's sod all in it. 'LOCAL VICAR OPENS FETE.' That's one week. Then, a week later . . . 'LOCAL SURGEON OPENS VICAR.' It's pathetic. And I'm stuck here until something else comes along, but nothing else has come along, so I'm . . . stuck!" Richard pulled himself together. "You said you had a story!"

He reached for the notepad and opened it. "That's the one thing that'll get me out of here. An old-fashioned scoop. Give me something I can put on the front page and I'll give you any help you need. You're staying in Lesser Malling?"

"I told you. . . ."

"Where?"

"A farm. A place called Hive Hall." Matt saw Richard scribble the name down.

"So what's the story?"

"I'm not sure you'll believe me."

"Try me." Richard had perked up. He was looking more interested and alert.

"All right." Matt wasn't sure about this. He had only come to the *Gazette* to ask about Raven's Gate. But there was something about the journalist that seemed trustworthy. He decided to go ahead.

And so he told Richard everything that had happened since his arrival in Lesser Malling. He described his first visit to the village and the chemist shop, his meeting with Tom Burgess, the lights and whispering in the forest, his time with Mrs. Deverill, his second meeting with the farmer, and his discovery of the dead body in the bedroom.

". . . and that's why," he concluded, "I'm trying to find out who or what this Raven's Gate is. It's obviously something important. Tom Burgess died trying to warn me."

"He died — but his body disappeared."

"Yes."

There was a brief silence and in that moment Matt knew that he had been wasting his time. The journalist had been making notes when he started talking but after a while he had stopped. Matt glanced at the notepad, at the

106

half-empty page with a doodle of a dog and a flea at the bottom. It was obvious that Richard hadn't believed a word he'd said.

"How old are you?" Richard asked.

"Fourteen."

"Do you watch a lot of TV?"

"There is no TV at Hive Hall."

Richard thought for a moment. "You never told me how you got there," he said. "You just said that this woman — Jayne Deverill — is looking after you."

That was the one part of the story that Matt had left out. The wounding of the security guard and his involvement with the LEAF Project. He knew that if he told the journalist who he was, he would end up on the front page of the *Gazette* . . . but for all the wrong reasons. It was the last thing he wanted.

"Where are your parents?" Richard asked.

"I don't have parents," Matt said. "They died six years ago."

"I'm sorry."

Matt shrugged. "I've gotten used to it," he said, although he never had.

"Well, look . . ." Richard was less certain now. Either he felt sorry for Matt and didn't want to say what he was about to say or he was simply trying to find a nicer way to say it. "I'm sorry, Matt. But everything you've told me is complete . . ."

"What?"

". . . crap. Lanes that loop round in circles. Strange looks from the villagers! Farmers that drop dead one minute and disappear the next! I mean, what do you expect me to say? I know I said I wanted a story. But I didn't mean a fantasy story!"

"What about the lights in the power station?"

"Okay. Yes. I've heard about Omega One. It was built about fifty years ago. It was a sort of prototype . . . before they built nuclear power stations in other parts of the country. But they shut it down before I was born. There's nothing there now. It's just an empty shell."

"An empty shell that Tom Burgess was guarding."

"That's what you say. But you don't know for sure."

"He knew something. And he was killed."

There was a long silence.

Richard threw down his pen. It rolled around the table and came to rest next to the notepad. "You seem like a nice kid, Matt," he said. "But the police came and there was nothing there, and maybe, just maybe, you sort of imagined the whole thing."

"I imagined a dead body? I imagined the words written on the wall?"

"*Raven's Gate*? I've never heard of Raven's Gate."

"Well, if you haven't heard of it, it obviously can't exist!" Matt snapped sarcastically. Suddenly he was angry. "All right, Mr. Cole. I can see I wasted my time coming here. It's like you say. Nothing ever happens in Lesser Malling. But I get the feeling that if it did happen, you wouldn't notice. I don't know what I've gotten myself involved in — but everything I've told you is true and, if you want the truth, I'm getting scared. So maybe one day when I turn up floating facedown in a local river, you might decide it's worth investigating. And I'm telling you now, I won't have died of bad eyesight."

Matt got up and stalked out of the office, slamming the door behind him. Coming to the newspaper had been a complete waste of time. He still had two hours until the bus left. It was time to work out how to get enough money to pay for the fare.

He burst out onto Farrow Street and stopped.

There was a car parked in front of him, blocking the entrance. A Land Rover. He recognized it even before he saw Noah sitting in the front seat, his hands resting on the wheel. The back door opened and Mrs. Deverill got out. She looked angry. Her eyes were ablaze and her skin seemed to have tightened. Although she was only two or three inches taller than Matt, she loomed over him as she stepped forward.

"What are you doing, Matthew?" she demanded.

"How did you know I was here?" Matt asked.

"I think you'd better come back with us, my dear. You've already caused quite enough trouble for one day."

"I don't want to come with you."

"I don't think you have any choice."

Matt thought of refusing. She couldn't force him into the car, not right in front of a newspaper office in a busy market town. But suddenly he was exhausted. Mrs. Deverill was right. He didn't even have enough money for a bus. He had nowhere to go. What else could he do?

He got into the car.

Mrs. Deverill climbed in after him, closing the door.

Noah rammed the car into gear and the three of them set off.

TEN

The Nexus

Mrs. Deverill had lit a fire. She was sitting in front of the burning logs with a knit shawl on her shoulders and Asmodeus curled up on her lap. To look at, she could have been anybody's grandmother. Even the portrait of her ancestor seemed more friendly than usual. The hair was neater. The eyes were perhaps a little less cruel. Matt was standing in the doorway. Outside, the sun had just dipped below the horizon and night had closed in once again.

"I think you and I need to have a talk, Matthew," she said. "Why don't you sit down?"

She gestured at the armchair opposite her. Matt hesitated, then sat down. Six hours had passed since she had found him in Greater Malling. There had been no work that afternoon. The two of them had eaten dinner together in silence. And now this.

"You and I don't seem to quite understand each other," Mrs. Deverill began. Her voice was soft and reasonable. "I get the feeling that you're against me. I don't know why. I haven't hurt you. You're living in my house. You're eating my food. What is it exactly that's wrong?"

"I don't like it here," Matt replied simply.

"You're not meant to like it. You were sent here as a

110

punishment, not because you deserved a holiday. Or maybe you've forgotten that."

"I want to go back to London," Matt said.

"Is that what you told the people in Greater Malling? The people at the newspaper? What did you tell them, exactly?"

"The truth."

A log collapsed in the hearth and a flurry of sparks leaped up. Asmodeus purred and Mrs. Deverill reached down, running a single finger down the animal's back.

"You shouldn't have gone there. I don't like journalists and I don't like newspapers. Busying themselves in other people's affairs. What were you thinking of, Matthew! Telling stories about me, about the village . . . it won't do you any good. Did they believe you?" Matt didn't answer. Mrs. Deverill drew a breath and tried to smile, but the hardness never left her eyes. "Did you tell them about Tom Burgess?" she asked.

"Yes." There was no point denying it.

"Well, that's exactly the point I'm trying to make. First you get the police involved. Yes . . . I heard what happened from Miss Creevy. And when that doesn't work, you go running to the press. And all the time you're completely mistaken. You actually have no idea what's going on."

"I know what I saw!"

"I don't think you do," Mrs. Deverill replied. "In a way, it's my own fault. I got you to clean out the pigs and I didn't realize . . . Some of the chemicals we use are very strong. They have a way of getting up your nose and into your brain. An adult like Noah can cope with it. Of course, he didn't have much brain to begin with. But a young boy like yourself . . ."

"What are you saying?" Matt demanded. "Are you saying I imagined what I saw?"

"That's exactly what I'm saying. I think you've probably been imagining all sorts of things since you arrived here. But don't worry. You're never going to have to clean out the pigs again. At least, not with disinfectant. From now on you're only going to use soap and water."

"You're lying!"

"I won't have that sort of language in my house if you don't mind, young man. It may have been allowed with your aunt in Ipswich, but it won't do with me!"

"I know what I saw! He was dead in his room and the whole place had been torn apart. I didn't imagine it. I was there!"

"What would it take to persuade you otherwise? What would it take to make you believe me?"

The telephone rang.

"Exactly on time," Mrs. Deverill said. She didn't move from her seat. She gestured with a single hand. "I think you'll find it's for you."

"For me?"

"Why don't you answer it?"

With a sinking feeling, Matt got up and went over to the telephone. He lifted the receiver. "Hello?" he said.

"Matthew — is that you?"

Matt recognized the voice instantly and felt a shiver work its way down his spine. He knew it was impossible. It had to be some sort of trick.

It was Tom Burgess.

"I wanted to say I'm sorry," the farmer said. No. It wasn't the farmer. It was the farmer's voice. Somehow it had been duplicated. "I'm afraid I missed you this morning. I had to go down to a market in Cirencester. I'm going to be away for a couple of weeks, but I'll come around and see you when I'm back. . . ."

Was it Matt's imagination or had it suddenly become very cold in the living room? The fire was still burning, but there was no warmth at all in the flames. He hadn't said a word to whoever — or whatever — it was at the other end of the line. He slammed down the phone.

"That wasn't very friendly," Mrs. Deverill said.

"That wasn't Tom Burgess."

"I asked him to call you." The firelight danced in her eyes. Matt glanced at the portrait and shivered. It was smiling at him, just like the woman in the chair below. "I thought it was best that he spoke to you himself."

"How did you . . . ?" Matt began.

But there was no point asking questions. He remembered the roads that led around in impossible circles, the cat that had been shot and come back to life. And now there was a farmer who had been dead one minute and who was somehow telephoning from Cirencester the next. Matt was in the grip of a power much stronger than himself. He was helpless.

"I hope this is the end of the matter, Matthew," Mrs. Deverill was saying. "And I think you should be careful before you tell any more of these stories. Anybody who knows anything about you is unlikely to believe you. And the last thing you need is to get into any more trouble with the police."

Matt didn't hear her. He had stopped listening. Silently he walked upstairs to his room. He was defeated — and he knew it. He undressed, slid under the covers, and fell into a troubled sleep.

● ● ●

The building was in Farringdon, close to the center of London. It was two stories high, Victorian, a survivor in a street that had been bombed in the Second World War and redeveloped ever since. It looked like a private house or perhaps a solicitor's office. There was a single black door with a letter box, but the only letters that were ever delivered here were junk mail. Once a month, the doormat was cleared, the letters taken away and burned. Lights came on and off inside the building, but they were all on time switches. Nobody lived here. Despite the high cost of property in London, for most of the year the building was empty.

At eight o'clock in the evening, a taxi drew up outside and a man got out. He was Indian, about fifty years old, dressed in a suit, with a light raincoat hanging loose. He paid the driver and waited until the taxi had driven away. Then he walked over to the door, taking a key out of his pocket. He turned it in the lock and the door opened. Briefly he glanced up and down the pavement. There was nobody in sight. He went in.

There was a narrow hallway, spotlessly clean and empty. Ahead, a flight of stairs led up to the second floor. The man had not been here for several months and he paused for a moment, remembering the details of the place: the wooden steps, the cream-colored walls, the old-fashioned light switch next to the banister. Nothing had changed. The man wished he hadn't come here. Every time he came, he hoped he would never have to return.

He went upstairs. The top corridor was more modern, expensively carpeted, with halogen lighting and, at every corner, a swiveling security camera. There was another door at the far end, this one made of darkened glass. It opened electronically as the man approached, then closed, quietly, behind him.

The Nexus had come together again.

There were twelve of them: eight men and four women. They had traveled here from all parts of the world. They only saw one another very occasionally, but they were always connected, communicating by telephone or over the Internet. All of them were influential. They were linked to government, to the secret service, to the various corridors of power, and to the church. They had told nobody that they would be here tonight. Very few people outside the room even knew that their organization existed.

Apart from the table and the twelve leather chairs, there was very little else. Three telephones and a computer sat on a long wooden console. Clocks showed the time in London, Paris, New York, Moscow, Beijing, and Lima, Peru. Various maps of the world hung on the walls. Although there was no way of knowing it, the walls were sound-proofed and filled with sophisticated surveillance equipment to prevent the room from being bugged.

The Indian man nodded and sat down in the last empty seat.

"Thank you for coming, Professor Dravid." The speaker was sitting at the head of the table. It was a woman in her late thirties, dressed in a severe black dress and a jacket fastened at the neck. She had a thin, chiseled face and black hair, cut short. Her eyes were strangely out of focus. She didn't look at the professor as she spoke. She couldn't look at anyone. The woman was blind.

"I'm very glad to see you, Miss Ashwood," Dravid replied. He spoke slowly. His voice was deep, his accent precise. "As a matter of fact, I was in England anyway. I'm working at the Natural History Museum. But I'm grateful to everyone else. This meeting was called at short notice and I know some of you have traveled a long way." He nodded at the man sitting next to him, who had flown in from Sydney, Australia. Dravid addressed the rest of the group. "As you are aware, Miss Ashwood called me three nights ago, requesting an emergency session of the Nexus. Having spoken with her, I agreed that it was critical we should meet straightaway. Again, I thank you for coming."

Dravid turned to Miss Ashwood. "Tell them what you told me," he said.

"Of course." Miss Ashwood took a sip of water from a glass in front of her. Her hand had to glide across the table to find it. "Seven months have passed since we last met," she began. "At that time I told you that I was aware of a growing danger, a sense that something was very wrong. We agreed that we would continue to monitor the situation, as we have always done. We are the eyes of the world. Although I, of course, have other ways of seeing."

116

She paused.

"The danger has become more acute," she continued. "For weeks now, I've been thinking I should call you, and I've spoken several times with Professor Dravid. Well, I can't leave it any longer. I am certain, in my heart, that our worst fears are about to be realized. Raven's Gate is about to open."

There was a stir around the table. But several of the men were looking doubtful.

"What evidence do you have, Miss Ashwood?" one of them asked. He was tall and dark-skinned, and had traveled from South America to be here.

"You know my evidence very well, Mr. Fabian. You know why I was invited to join the Nexus."

"Even so . . . what have you been told?"

"I haven't been told anything. I wish it was as simple as that. I can only tell you what I feel. And right now, it's as if there's poison in the air. I'm aware of it all the time and it's getting worse. The darkness is coming. It's taking shape. You have to trust me."

"I hope that isn't why you've brought us all here tonight," another man said. He was elderly, a bishop, dressed in a clerical collar, with a gold cross around his neck. He had been wearing spectacles, but he took them off and cleaned them as he continued. "I'm very well aware of your abilities, Miss Ashwood, and I have great respect for them. But can you really ask us to accept that something is the case just because you believe it to be so?"

"I thought that was what faith was all about," the blind woman retorted.

"The Christian faith is written down. Nobody has ever written a history of the Old Ones."

117

"That's not true," Dravid muttered. He raised a single finger. "You're forgetting the Spanish monk."

"Saint Joseph of Córdoba? His book has been lost and he himself was discredited centuries ago." The bishop sighed. "This is very difficult for me," he said. "You have to remember that, officially, the church does not believe in your Old Ones any more than we believe in demons or devils or all the rest of it. If it was known that I was part of the Nexus, I would have to resign. I am here only because you and I have the same aims. We are all afraid of the same thing, no matter what we choose to call it. But I cannot accept, will not accept, guesswork and superstition. I'm sorry, Miss Ashwood. You have to give us more."

"Maybe I can be of assistance," another man said. He was a policeman. He carried the rank of assistant commissioner and he was based at Scotland Yard. "I did notice something very recently that might be of interest. It was very minor and so I didn't report it to you. But in the light of what you are now saying . . ."

"Go on," Professor Dravid said.

"Well, it concerns a petty criminal, a drug addict by the name of Will Scott. He was last seen following a woman into an alleyway not very far from here, in Holborn. Presumably, she would have been his next victim. He had a knife. And a record of armed violence."

"What happened?"

"It wasn't the woman who ended up as the victim. She disappeared. It was Scott who was found dead. He killed himself. He pushed the knife into his own heart."

"What's so strange about that?" someone asked.

"He did it in broad daylight in the middle of London. But it wasn't just that. I saw his face. . . ." The policeman paused. "I knew at once that this was something completely abnormal. The look of terror! It was as if he tried to fight it. As if he didn't want to die. It was horrible."

"The power of the Old Ones," Miss Ashwood whispered.

"Why should one death in Holborn have anything to do with the Nexus?" the bishop insisted.

"I agree with you," Dravid said. "One isolated incident. A possible suicide. But there is something else and it happened only this morning. That in itself is rather strange, because of course I knew I was coming here tonight. But I was at my office, at the museum, and I was online. This was about eleven o'clock. And my computer picked up an enquiry into Raven's Gate." He paused a second time. "I have a program," he explained. "Whenever anybody, anywhere, puts those words into a search engine, I hear about it. It's only happened twice in the last year — both times academics. But this was different. I managed to instant-mail the person at the other end. And I have a feeling it was a teenager, or maybe even a child."

"Did he say so?" someone asked.

"No. But he used the letters r and u instead of writing 'are you.' That's very much the sign of a young person. He called himself Matt."

"Just Matt?"

"He gave no surname. But here's something else that's interesting. The enquiry came from a computer in the library at Greater Malling."

The statement caused another stir around the table. This time, even the bishop looked concerned.

"Shouldn't you have contacted us about this straight-away, Professor?" the South American asked.

"I hardly had time, Mr. Fabian. As I told you, this only happened today, and I knew we would all meet this evening anyway. On its own, it might not have been significant. A schoolboy might have stumbled onto Raven's Gate and made enquiries about it for no particular reason. But given Miss Ashwood's feelings and what we've just heard . . ." He let the sentence hang in the air. "Maybe we should try to find this 'Matt' and discover how much he knows."

"And how are we meant to do that?" another man asked. He was French, gray-haired, connected in some way to military intelligence. "Give me a full name and we could find him in seconds. But Matt? Short for Matthew? Or he could be from my country . . . Matthieu. Or he could even be a girl. Matilda."

"He'll find us," Miss Ashwood said.

"You think he'll just walk in here?" the bishop asked. He shook his head. "It seems obvious to me. If you really think something is happening in Lesser Malling, we should go there and try to prevent it. We should be there now."

"We can't," Dravid said. "It would be far too dangerous. We don't know what we're looking for. And anyway, we agreed from the start that we cannot become personally involved. That's not our role. We exist to watch, to share information, and — if and when the time comes — to fight back. That's when we'll be needed. We cannot do anything that will put us at risk."

"So we sit back and do nothing?"

"He will find his way to us," Miss Ashwood said. "You have to remember. It is *meant* to happen. Everything in the history of the world has been preparing itself for this moment, for the return of the five and the final struggle. There is no coincidence. Everything is planned. If we don't see that, we lose one of our greatest weapons."

"Matt." The bishop spoke the single word. He didn't sound too impressed.

Miss Ashwood nodded slowly. "Let's just pray he finds us soon."

ELEVEN
A Visitor

Matt was chopping wood again. There were blisters on his hands and the sweat was running down his back, but the pile never seemed to get any smaller. Noah was sitting a few paces away, watching him. Matt split another log apart and threw down the ax. He wiped his forehead with the back of his hand.

"How long have you been here, Noah?" he asked.

Noah shrugged.

"Where did Mrs. Deverill find you? Were you born here or did you escape from the local lunatic asylum?"

Noah glared at him. Matt knew he had difficulty understanding sentences with more than four or five words. "You shouldn't make fun of me." Noah scowled at last.

"Why not? It's the only fun I have." Matt picked up a handful of wood and dumped it in the wheelbarrow. "Why don't you go anywhere?" he asked. "You're always hanging around. Don't you have a girlfriend or anything?"

Noah sniffed. "I don't like girls."

"Do you prefer pigs? I think one or two of them fancy you."

Matt leaned forward to take the ax and at that moment Noah's hand shot out, grabbing hold of him. "You don't know," he rasped. He was so close that Matt could smell the rotten food on his breath. His fat lips twisted in an unpleasant smile. "Sometimes Mrs. Deverill lets me kill one," he said. "A pig. I put the knife in and I listen to it squeal. We'll do the same to you. . . ."

"Let me go!" Matt tried to pull away, but his arm was gripped as if in a vice. Noah was incredibly strong. His fingers were clamped onto Matt's arm.

"You laugh at Noah. But when the end comes, it'll be Noah who laughs at you."

"Get off me!" Matt was afraid his bone was going to break.

And then a car pulled into the yard. Noah released his grip and Matt fell back, cradling his arm. There were four welts where the fingers had held him. The car was a Honda Estate. As Matt watched, the door opened and a man got out, dressed in a suit and a white shirt but no tie. Matt recognized him at once. It was Stephen Mallory, the detective who had interrogated him after the Ipswich break-in.

Noah had seen him, too. As Mallory looked around him, the farmhand scurried away, disappearing behind the barn. Matt walked over to the detective. He could feel a sense of excitement stirring inside him but tried not to show it. Mallory was partly responsible for sending him here. But he was exactly the man Matt most wanted to see.

"Matthew!" The detective nodded. "How are you?"

"I'm fine."

"You don't look it. You've lost a lot of weight."

"What are you doing here?" Matt was in no mood to talk.

"I've been to a conference in Harrogate. It's not that far away, so I thought I'd look in and see how you were getting on." Mallory stretched. "I have to say, it wasn't an easy place to find."

"If you think it's hard getting in, you should try getting out."

"What?"

"Nothing." Matt glanced over Mallory's shoulder. Mrs. Deverill was somewhere inside the house. He knew she'd come into the yard any moment, and he wanted to talk before she arrived. "I was going to telephone you," he said.

"Why?"

"I don't want to stay here. You told me that the LEAF Project was voluntary. Well, I'm volunteering myself out. I don't care where you send me. You can lock me up in Alcatraz if you want to. But this place sucks and I want to go."

The detective looked at him curiously. "What were you doing when I arrived?" he asked.

"What does it look like?" Matt spread his hands, showing the red welts and blisters. "I was chopping wood."

"Have you started school yet?"

"No."

Mallory shook his head. "This is all wrong," he said. "This shouldn't be happening."

"Then do something about it. Get me out of here."

There was a movement in the doorway behind them. Mrs. Deverill had appeared, coming out of the farmhouse. Noah was with her. She had put on a brightly colored apron and was holding a basket of apples. Matt wondered if they were for Mallory's benefit, just like the suit she had worn when she went down to London.

124

"Don't say anything," Mallory muttered quietly. "Leave this to me."

Mrs. Deverill came over to them. She seemed surprised to see someone there. "Can I help you?" she asked.

"You don't remember me," Mallory said. "Detective Superintendent Mallory. We met in London. I'm with the LEAF Project."

Mrs. Deverill nodded. "Of course I remember you, Mr. Mallory," she said. "And it's a great pleasure to see you, although it might have been a courtesy to let me know you were coming. If I recall correctly, you were supposed to give me twenty-four hours' notice of any official visit."

"Do you have something to hide, Mrs. Deverill?"

"Of course not." The hard eyes blinked. "You're welcome anytime."

"The fact is that I picked up a report from the local police," Mallory said. "Something about a false alarm at a place called Glendale Farm. Matthew was involved."

"Oh yes." Mrs. Deverill rearranged her features into a look of concern. "Matthew and I have already spoken about that. I was very sorry that he wasted the policemen's time. But in the end, there was no harm done. I think we've both put it behind us."

Matt wanted to speak, but Mallory warned him against it with his eyes.

"Why isn't Matthew at school?" he asked.

"It's my feeling that it's too early," Mrs. Deverill replied. "I have discussed the matter with my sister. She happens to be the head teacher. We both agree that he would be a disruptive influence. We'll send him to school as soon as he's ready." Mrs. Deverill smiled. She was doing her best to appear friendly. "Why don't you come inside, Detective Superintendent? I'm not sure we should be discussing this in front of the child. Perhaps I could offer you a cup of tea?"

"No thank you, Mrs. Deverill." Mallory took a look around him. "I haven't seen very much," he went on, "but it seems obvious to me that living conditions on this farm are entirely inadequate to Matthew's needs —"

"We were examined before he came," Mrs. Deverill interrupted.

"— and I'm frankly appalled by Matthew's physical condition. He looks as if he's been worked to the bone. You've actually broken the law by keeping him out of school."

"The boy's been perfectly happy here. Haven't you, Matthew?"

"No." Matt was glad he'd been given a chance to speak. "I hate it here. I hate this farm. I hate you most of all."

"Well, that's gratitude!"

"I'm going back to London," Mallory said. "And I want you to know that I'll be contacting the LEAF committee the moment I arrive. I'll be recommending that Matthew is removed from your care with immediate effect."

Mrs. Deverill's face darkened. Her eyes were like razors. "I wouldn't do that if I were you," she said.

"Are you threatening me, Mrs. Deverill?"

There was a long pause.

"No." Mrs. Deverill nodded slowly. "Why would I want to do that? I'm a law-abiding person. And if you really think that Matthew would be better off locked up in some sort of juvenile institution, that's your business. But you aren't meant to be here, Mr. Mallory. You weren't invited and this visit of yours is a violation of our agreement. You make your report if you want to. But you'll be the one who ends up with the red face."

She turned on her heel and walked back into the farmhouse. Matt watched her go with a sense of elation. Mallory had defeated her. For the first time, he could see an end to his ordeal.

Mallory leaned toward him. "Listen to me, Matt," he said. "I'd put you in the car and take you with me if I could —"

"I wish you would," Matt said.

"— but I can't. I don't have any right and technically I'd be breaking the law. Mrs. Deverill could even say I'd abducted you and in the end I might be doing more harm than good. But give me twenty-four hours and I'll be back. And then we'll get you out of this dump. Okay?"

"Sure." Matt nodded. "Thanks."

Mallory sighed. "If you want the honest truth, I was always against the LEAF Project," he said. "It's just a gimmick . . . another bit of government spin. They don't really want to help kids like you. They're more interested in massaging the figures, reducing the number of children behind bars." He walked over to his car and opened the door. "Well, as soon as I've put in my report, they'll have to listen to what I say. And whatever happens, I promise you Mrs. Deverill will never get custody of anyone ever again."

He closed the door, started the engine, and drove out of the farm. Matt watched him go. Then he turned and looked at the farmhouse. Mrs. Deverill was standing in the doorway. She had taken off the apron. Now she was dressed all in black. She, too, had seen the detective leave. She said nothing. She stepped back, disappearing into the house. The door slammed shut behind her.

· · ·

It was dark by the time Stephen Mallory reached the motorway and the fast route back to Ipswich. He was deep in thought as he steered his Honda Estate onto the outside lane.

He hadn't told Matt the whole truth. There never had been any conference in Harrogate.

Stephen Mallory specialized in juvenile crime. He had met many young delinquents, some only ten or eleven years old, and it seemed to him that Matt, like so many of them, wasn't so much a criminal as a victim. He had already spoken to Kelvin, who was in a remand center, awaiting trial. He had met with Gwenda Davis and her boyfriend, Brian Conran. He had read all the reports. But even so, he felt that there was something missing.

And so, immediately after he had handed Matt over to Mrs. Deverill, he had decided to see if he could fill in the missing pieces. He was in London, anyway. Nobody would know or care how he spent the afternoon.

He had taken a taxi to a police records office in South London. Everything he needed was there in a cardboard box, one of about a hundred, filed away with a reference number and a name: FREEMAN, M. J. There were articles cut out of the local newspaper, reports from both the local and the metropolitan police, a postmortem report, and a psychiatric assessment from a doctor in Harley Street. The story was exactly as he had been told. A road accident. Two killed. An eight-year-old orphan left behind. Adoption by an aunt in Ipswich. Mallory had read all of it before. But then, at the very bottom of the box, he had stumbled on a witness report that he hadn't seen. It changed everything.

It was a signed statement by the woman who had been living next door to Matthew at the time of the accident, who had been looking after him when it happened. Her name was Rosemary Green. Mallory read it twice, then ordered a taxi to take him to Dulwich. It was four o'clock in the afternoon. He doubted she would be in.

But he was in luck. Rosemary Green was a schoolteacher and arrived home just as he stepped out of the cab. He talked to her outside her small Victorian house with pink and white honeysuckle trailing all the way up the front wall. It was strange to think that Matthew Freeman had once played in the garden next door. It couldn't have been a more different world from the one he would later inhabit in Ipswich.

Mrs. Green didn't have much to add to what she had already said. Yes, she agreed, her story didn't seem likely. But it was true. She had told the police at the time and she stood by it now.

Mallory had drunk two miniature bottles of whiskey on the train back to Ipswich. Copies of Matthew's file were on the table in front of him. So was the late edition of the *London Evening Standard*. It belonged to one of the passengers sitting opposite him. Mallory had almost snatched it out of the man's hand.

The story was on page 1.

A bizarre suicide in Holborn. A twenty-year-old criminal called Will Scott had been found dead in a street close to Lincoln's Inn Fields. The cause of death was a knife wound to the heart, which police believed to be self-inflicted. Scott had a record for aggravated burglary and assault and was a known drug dealer. Three witnesses had seen him following an elderly woman, dressed in gray with a silver brooch shaped like a salamander. Police were urging her to come forward.

A coincidence?

Mallory remembered the brooch Mrs. Deverill had been wearing. She had been late arriving at the meeting. And she might well have come through Lincoln's Inn Fields. He was certain she must be the woman referred to in the article, although he had no idea how she could have been involved in Will Scott's death. But from that moment on he had been worried. He had found himself thinking more and more about Matthew. He was certain that the boy shouldn't be in her care.

And then, three weeks later, he had intercepted a routine transmission from a police station in York. Something to do with another death, one that had been reported by a fourteen-year-old boy from the LEAF Project. It had been enough. Mallory had cleared a space in his schedule and headed for Lesser Malling.

He was very glad he'd gone. What he had seen had been a disgrace. The boy looked ill. More than that, he looked traumatized. And Mallory had quickly noticed the welts on his arm. Well, he would soon put a stop to it. He would hand in his own report the very next day.

He checked his speedometer. He was doing seventy miles per hour exactly. He had moved into the central lane and cars were speeding past him on both sides, all of them breaking the speed limit. He watched the red taillights blur in the distance. It was raining again, tiny drops splattering against the windscreen. Was it his imagination, or had it become very cold inside the car? He turned on the heater. Air pumped out of the ventilation grills in the dashboard, but it didn't seem to make any difference. He pressed another button and turned on the windscreen wipers. The road ahead shimmered and bent, broken apart by the rain.

He glanced at the clock. It was half past nine. He was at least another two hours from Ipswich. He wouldn't be home until nearly twelve. He turned on the radio. He would listen to the news. The voices would help keep him awake.

The radio was tuned to BBC Four, but there was no news. At first, Mallory thought there was nothing on the radio at all and he wondered if it had broken . . . like the heater. It really was very cold. Perhaps one of the fuses had blown. He would have to take the car in when he got back. But then the radio came on. There was a burst of static and, behind it, something else.

A faint whispering.

Puzzled, he leaned down and pressed the button that was preset to Classic FM. Mallory liked classical music. Maybe there would be a concert. But there was no music on Classic

FM. Instead, the whispering voices had somehow followed him across from BBC Four. They were definitely the same voices. He could even make out some of the words they were saying.

"EMANY . . . NEVAEH . . . NITRA . . . OH . . . WREHTAF . . ."

What was going on? Mallory pressed a third button, his eyes never leaving the road. The voices were on the next station, too. He tried a fourth button, then a fifth. It was impossible. The same voices were being transmitted on every station, louder now, more insistent. He turned the radio off. But the radio wouldn't turn off. The whispering continued. It seemed to be everywhere, all around him in the car.

The cold was more intense. It was like sitting in a fridge — or a freezer. Mallory realized he had to pull over onto the hard shoulder and stop. The rain was coming down harder. He could barely see out of the windscreen. Red lights overtook him and rushed past. White lights screamed toward him, blinding him.

He pressed his foot on the brake and signaled left. But the signal light had failed and the car wouldn't slow down. Mallory was beginning to panic. He had never been afraid in his life. It wasn't in his nature. But he was afraid now, knowing that the car was out of control. He stamped his foot down more urgently. Nothing happened. The car was picking up speed.

And then it was as if he had hit some sort of invisible ramp. He felt the tires leave the road, and the whole car rocketed into the air. His vision twisted 360 degrees. The whispering had somehow become a great clamor that filled his consciousness.

Mallory screamed.

His car, traveling at ninety miles per hour, flew up and somersaulted over the median. The last thing Mallory saw, upside down, was a gasoline tanker hurtling toward him, the driver's face frozen in horror. The Honda hit it and disintegrated. There was a screech of tires. An explosion. A single blare from the loudest horn in the world. Then silence.

• • •

Matt was sound asleep when the covers were torn off him. He woke up in the chill of the morning to find Mrs. Deverill in a black dressing gown, looming over his bed. He looked at his watch. It was ten past six in the morning. Outside, the sky was still gray. Rain pattered against the windows. The trees bent in the wind.

"What is it?" he demanded.

"I just heard it on the radio," Mrs. Deverill said. "I thought you ought to know. I'm afraid it's bad news, Matthew. It seems there was a multiple pileup on the motorway last night. Six people killed. Detective Superintendent Mallory was one of them. It's a terrible shame. Really terrible. It looks as if you won't be leaving after all."

TWELVE
Out of the Fire

The next few days were the worst Matt had experienced since he had arrived in Yorkshire.

Mrs. Deverill worked him harder than ever and Noah never left his side. The hours passed in a tedious procession of cleaning, painting, chopping, mending, and carrying. Matt was angry with himself. He had tried to escape to London and he had failed. He had gone looking for clues in the wood, but he had found almost nothing. Two people had tried to help him and they had both died. Nobody else cared. A sort of fog had descended on his mind. He had given in. He would remain at Hive Hall until Mrs. Deverill was finished with him. Maybe she planned to keep him there all his life and he would end up hollowed out and empty, like Noah, a dribbling slave.

And then, one evening — Matt thought it was a Saturday, although all days had become very much the same — Mrs. Deverill's sister came to dinner. He hadn't seen the teacher since his encounter with her in Lesser Malling. Sitting next to her at the kitchen table, he found it hard to keep his eyes off her birthmark, the discoloration that covered most of her face. He was drawn to it and repulsed at the same time.

"Jayne tells me that you have been missing school," she remarked in her strange high-pitched voice.

"I haven't been to school because she won't let me go," Matt replied. "I have to work here."

"And yet when you were at school, you regularly missed class. You played truant. You preferred shoplifting and smoking on motorway bridges. That's what I heard."

"I never smoked," Matt growled. But the rest of it was true and he felt his cheeks redden.

"Modern children have no real education," Jayne Deverill remarked. She was serving some sort of stew out of a pot. The meat was thick and fatty and came in a rich, blood-colored gravy. Roadkill in a primeval swamp. "You see them in the street in their shapeless clothes, listening to what they call music, but you or I would call a horrible noise. They have no respect, no intelligence, no taste. And they think the world belongs to them!"

"They'll soon find out . . ." the sister muttered.

There was a knock at the door and Noah appeared, dressed in what might have passed for a suit, except that it was about fifty years old, faded, and shapeless. He had a shirt buttoned to the neck but no tie. He reminded Matt of an out-of-work funeral director.

"The car's ready," Noah announced.

"We're still eating, Noah." Jayne Deverill scowled. "Wait for us outside."

"It's raining." Noah sniffed the food hopefully.

"Then wait in the car. We'll be out soon."

Matt waited until Noah had gone. "Are you going out?" he asked.

"We might be."

"Where?"

"When I was young, a child never asked questions of his elders," Claire Deverill said.

"Was that before or after the First World War?" Matt muttered.

"I'm sorry?"

"Forget it."

Matt fell silent and finished his meal. Jayne Deverill had also finished eating. She stood up and went over to the kettle. "I'm making a cup of herbal tea," she explained. "I want you to drink it all, Matthew. It has a restorative quality and it seems to me that you've been rather on edge ever since the death of that poor detective."

"Are you going to arrange for him to telephone me tomorrow?"

"Oh, no, Mr. Mallory won't be coming back." She poured steaming water into a squat black teapot, stirred it, and then poured a cup for Matthew. "Now you get that down you. It'll help you relax."

It'll help you relax.

Maybe it was the way she spoke the words. Or maybe it was the fact that Mrs. Deverill had never made tea like this before. But suddenly Matt was determined not to touch the liquid he was being offered. He cupped it in his hands and sniffed. Herbal tea, she had said. It was green and smelled bitter.

"What's in it?" he asked.

"Leaves."

"What sort of leaves?"

"Dandelion. Full of vitamin D."

"Not for me, thanks," Matt said. He tried to sound casual. "I've never been that crazy about dandelions."

"Nonetheless, you will try this. You're not leaving the table until you do."

Claire Deverill was watching him too carefully. Matt was certain now. If he drank the tea, the next thing he knew, it would be the morning of the next day.

"All right." Matt lifted the cup. "If you insist."

"I do."

The question was — how to get rid of it?

In the end, it was Asmodeus who helped him out. The cat must have crept into the kitchen while they were eating. It jumped up onto the sideboard and its tail caught a jug of milk. The jug toppled and broke, spilling milk. Both sisters turned around, their attention momentarily diverted. Instantly Matt reached out and upended his cup under the table. When the two women turned back again, he was cradling the cup in his hand as if nothing had happened. He just hoped they wouldn't notice the steam rising out of the damp carpet.

He pretended to drink until the cup was empty, then set it down on the table. He saw something stir in Jayne Deverill's eyes and knew she was pleased. Now he had to see if his theory was right. He yawned and stretched his arms.

"Tired, Matthew?" She spoke the words too quickly.

"Yes."

"No need to help with the dishes tonight then. Why don't you go up to bed?"

"Yes. I'll do that."

He stood up and went to the stairs, making his movements deliberately slow and heavy. He didn't turn the light on in his room. Instead he lay down on the bed and closed his eyes, wondering what would happen next.

He didn't have long to wait. The door opened and light spilled into the room from outside.

"Is he asleep?" It was Claire Deverill's voice.

"Of course. He'll sleep twelve hours and wake up with a chain saw of a headache. Are you ready?"

"Yes."

"Then let's go."

Matt heard the two leave. He listened to their footsteps on the stairs. The front door opened and closed. The engine of the car started and the headlights swung around as it turned in the yard and then set off up the drive. Only when he was sure that they weren't coming back did he sit up on the bed. Everything had happened just as he had imagined. He was alone at Hive Hall.

Half an hour later, the lights came back on at Omega One. Matt had been expecting that, too.

Dressed in black trousers and a dark shirt, he grabbed the bicycle and pedaled away from the farm.

It was time to go back into the wood.

● ● ●

It didn't take him long to find the entrance. The strip torn from his T-shirt was still there, tied around a branch. Grateful for the pine needles underfoot, he made his way along the corridor, making sure he didn't stray off the pavement that Tom Burgess had shown him the last time he was here. The moon was behind the clouds, but he used the glow from the power station to guide him on his way. When he looked back, the wood was pitch-black. An owl cried out. There was a scurry of leaves as some night creature batted its way up toward the sky.

Matt heard the villagers before he saw them. They were very close. There was the sound of crackling and the murmur of voices. He pulled aside a pair of low branches and realized that he was back at the fence that surrounded the power station. He knelt down and looked through the wire. An incredible sight met his eyes.

The flat square of land surrounding the power station was bustling with activity. A huge fire blazed outside the sphere, throwing out vivid snakes' tongues of flames. Thick black smoke curled into the air. Four or five people were throwing armfuls of twigs and shrubbery onto the fire, the damp wood hissing and snapping as it was consumed. Overhead, a line of arc lamps cast a brilliant glare over the field. It was a strange mixture. The building with its electric lights was modern, industrial. The bonfire with the shadowy figures of people grouped around reminded him of a scene from primitive history.

There was a car parked between the fire and the fence — Matt thought it might be a Saab or a Jaguar. The door opened and a man got out, but he was silhouetted against the light and Matt couldn't make out who he was. The man raised a hand and a gold signet ring on his finger momentarily flashed red, reflecting the light of the fire.

He had given a signal. There was a van parked on the other side of the clearing and at once it began to reverse right up to the corridor that joined the giant sphere of Omega One to the rest of the building. As Matt watched, the doors of the van were thrown open and several men dressed in strange, cumbersome clothes climbed out. They congregated together, then lifted something out: a large box about five meters long. It was obviously heavy. They took a lot of time lowering it to the ground.

Matt couldn't quite see what was going on. He had to get closer. He followed the fence back to the gap and waited there, making sure nobody was looking in his direction. But all the villagers were concentrating on the van. Matt chose his moment, then dived forward, headfirst. He felt the jagged edge of the wire tear his shirt and scrape his back, but he was lucky. It didn't draw blood. He landed facedown on the grass and lay still.

A large bearded man walked across the clearing, heading toward the van. Matt recognized the butcher. The ginger-haired chemist was there, too, as well as the woman — Joanna Creevy — who had been at Glendale Farm when Matt returned with the police. He looked back at the bonfire. The village children were standing around, poking sticks into the flames, making the sparks leap up. There were forty or fifty people at Omega One and suddenly Matt knew that he was spying on the entire village. Young and old, every one of the villagers had made the journey into the forest. They were all in it.

All his instincts screamed at him to slip away before he was spotted. But at the same time he knew that what he was seeing was important. He just had to work out what they were doing, why they were here. And what was inside the silver box? The two men had disappeared inside. The villagers were queuing up, about to follow them. The man with the signet ring was talking to Mrs. Deverill. Matt was desperate to hear what they were saying.

He crawled over the ground, keeping low, hardly daring to raise his head. The closer he got, the more chance he would have of being seen. He hoped the long grass would provide some sort of cover, but he could feel the light of the flames reaching out to him, eager to show that he was there. He could even feel the warmth of the fire on his shoulders and head. He heard laughter. The man with the ring had cracked a joke. Matt wriggled farther forward. His hand caught something and pulled it away. Too late, he saw the thin plastic wire that ran along the ground. Too late, he realized he should never have touched it.

The stillness of the night was shattered by a siren. The villagers spun around, staring out over the field. Three men ran forward, shotguns appearing in their hands. The children dropped their sticks into the fire and ran over to the van. The man with the ring stepped slowly forward, passing through the crowd, his eyes scanning the ground. Matt clutched the earth, burying his face in the grass. But it was too late to hide.

Mrs. Deverill was standing beside the bonfire. She shouted a brief sentence in a strange language and took something out of her pocket. Matt saw her wave a hand over the flames. It was trailing a cloud of white powder that hung for a moment in the air before falling.

The flames exploded, leaping almost as high as the power station itself, bright red light flooding the field. At the same time, something black began to take shape within them, molding itself out of the shadows. In seconds the blackness had solidified, and now it leaped — seemingly in slow motion — out of the fire and onto the ground beyond. It was some sort of animal, and moments later a second one appeared, bounding forward to join it. Behind them, the bonfire shrank back to its normal size. The wail of the alarm stopped abruptly.

They were dogs, but like no dogs Matt had ever seen.

They were huge, two or three times as big as Rottweilers . . . and more savage, too. The flames of the fire that had given birth to them still flickered in their black shark-like eyes. Their mouths hung open, teeth like two lines of kitchen knives jutting forward beyond their lips. Their heads were high and uneven, their bulging skulls topped by two tiny ears, like horns. Slowly, one of them turned its ugly snout up to the sky and uttered a ghastly howl. Then, as one, they padded forward, their heads slanting unnaturally to one side as if listening to the ground.

Matt had no choice. He had to get away. If the dogs found him, they would tear him apart. No longer caring if he was seen or not, he stumbled to his feet and began to run. His legs were as heavy as lead, but desperately he forced them to carry him forward. The fence was still twenty meters away. Arms outstretched, he raced toward it, not wanting to look behind him. But he couldn't stop himself. He had to know. Where were the dogs? How near were they? With a grimace, he looked back over his shoulder. And regretted it.

The first of the creatures had already halved the distance between itself and its prey. It didn't seem to be moving fast. It hovered in the air between each bound, barely touching the grass before leaping up again. There was something hideous about the way it ran. A panther or a leopard closing in for the kill has a certain majesty. But the dog was deformed, lopsided, ghastly. The flesh on one of its flanks had rotted. A glistening rib cage jutted out. As if to avoid the stench of the wound, the animal had turned away, its head hanging close to its front paws. Strings of saliva hung from its mouth. And every time its feet hit the ground its whole body quivered, threatening to collapse in on itself.

Matt reached the fence and clawed at it with his hands, crashing his fingers against the wire. He thought he had run in a straight line, following the way he had come, but it seemed he had gotten it wrong. He couldn't find the gap. He looked behind him. Two more bounds and the dogs would reach him. He had no doubt that they would tear him apart. He could almost feel the teeth tearing into him, ripping the flesh away from his bones. He had never seen anything so ferocious . . . not in a zoo, not in a film, not anywhere in the real world.

Where was the gap? In blind panic he threw his whole weight against the fence, almost crying with relief as the edge buckled and gave way, revealing the jagged hole. Without hesitating, he dived forward. His head and shoulders went through, but this time the wire hooked into his pants. Thrashing out with his arms, expecting to feel the jaws of the dog close on his leg at any moment, he struggled like a fish in a net. Out of the corner of his eye he saw a huge black shape plummeting toward him. He gave a last frantic heave. His jeans ripped and he fell through, rolling into a ball on the other side.

Blood oozed out of a gash in his leg, but he was safe . . . at least for the moment. Weakly he got to his feet, then staggered back as one of the dogs lunged at the fence, its mouth foaming, its teeth gnashing at the wire. The two creatures were trapped. The hole had barely been big enough to allow Matt to pass and they were bigger and more awkwardly built than him. But then, even as he watched, the dogs began pounding at the earth, raking the soft soil with their claws. They weren't going to allow the fence to stop them. They were going to burrow their way through.

Matt fled into the wood. Pine needles whipped into his body. Low-lying branches slashed his face and tried to take out his eyes. There was nowhere to hide, no way of knowing if he had taken the right path. He was trapped in a vast grid system where every direction looked exactly the same. The dogs had the advantage — they didn't need to see him. They would smell him out.

Matt didn't care where he was going. His only thought was to get away, to put as much space as he could between himself and the two dogs. How long did he have? Thirty seconds? A minute or two at most. And then they would emerge from the ground on the other side of the fence as if rising out of a grave. They would stalk him through the wood, outrun him, and rip him to shreds.

He crashed into the trunk of a tree and reeled away, spinning around. The lights from the power station were already a long way behind him, barely visible through the branches. Matt was exhausted, but he couldn't let himself rest. He needed to find a stretch of water, a river or a stream. Maybe he could throw the dogs off his scent. But there was nothing like that in this artificial wood. It stretched on endlessly. There was no water in sight.

He paused to catch his breath, his chest and throat rasping, his head pounding. At that moment, a terrible baying broke through the air. It was a howl of triumph. The dogs were through the fence. Matt almost gave up. He felt a shiver of despair travel through his body. It was all-consuming. He would just stand here and wait for them to come. All he could do was hope it would be quick.

He forced himself to snap out of it. He wasn't dead yet. Gathering up his last reserves of strength, he forced himself forward, desperately twisting between the trees.

Only the sudden stamping of his feet on hard pavement after the soft silence of the pine needles told him that he was out of the wood. Incredibly, he had broken out onto a road — but it wasn't the road to Lesser Malling. It was wider and there were white markings down the center. For a moment, Matt felt relief. He was back in the modern world. A car might come. He looked left and right. Nothing. And suddenly he knew that this was the worst place for him to be. He was out in the open, with no cover, nowhere to hide from the dogs.

Where could he go? The strip of pavement divided two worlds. Behind him was the wood. Ahead was some sort of moorland . . . wild and open. He remembered what he had been thinking. A river or a stream. He crossed the road and plunged into the wild grass. He could tell at once that the ground was damp. He could feel it, soft and sticky under his feet. He ran on and as he ran he became aware that the ground was getting wetter. Cold water slid over his sneakers and onto his feet.

He was only aware of the danger when it was too late. He staggered to a halt and at that same moment the ground gave way altogether and he found himself being sucked down, unable to move.

A bog. He had blundered right into it.

Matt screamed. He was being pulled under incredibly fast. He felt the mud and the slime rising up over his knees and thighs, then his waist and up his chest toward his arms. He flailed his arms, but the effort only sped things up. The bog gripped him around his stomach and he could already imagine what was about to happen next, the last, horrific moments of his life. The bog would rise over his face. One last scream. But there would be no sound. He would be silenced forever as stinking mud rushed into his mouth and down his throat.

Matt forced himself to stay calm. He knew that struggling would only make the end come faster. He almost smiled. At least he had cheated the dogs. He had found the one place where they could never reach him. And if he had to die, perhaps it would be better to go this way.

He relaxed and at that very moment he thought he could smell something . . . very close and yet, at the same time, distant. It was the smell of burning. A bonfire? Could there be someone out there on the moor? But no. His hopes were raised only to be dashed again. There was no one there. The smell disappeared. It had just been his imagination.

The bog bubbled around him and rose to his armpits. Its touch was cold, final. A stench of mud and rotting leaves reached his nostrils. Matt closed his eyes and waited for the end. But now the bog was toying with him, creeping up centimeter by centimeter, lovingly drawing him into its embrace.

The beam of light hit him before he even heard the noise of the engine. There was a car. It had come off the road, appearing out of nowhere. Now it was parked right on the edge of the bog. A man got out, barely visible behind the glare of the headlamps.

"Don't move!" a voice commanded. "I've got a rope."

But the bog, as if afraid it was going to lose its victim, tightened its hold. Greedily it clung to him, its hands spreading over his shoulders, pushing him down.

"Hurry!" Matt shouted.

The mud was touching his chin. He forced his head up despairingly, staring up at a pale moon that had at last come from behind the clouds. Only seconds remained.

The bog pulled. The stagnant water rose over his head, up his nose, into his eyes. But at the same moment, his hand was struck by the flying edge of a rope. Smothered, blind, he groped for it. And caught hold of it. Now only his hands remained above the surface. He held his breath and tightened his grip.

And then he was being carried up. His lungs were bursting. With a cry, he opened his mouth and sucked in. And breathed air. The man pulled on the rope and he felt himself being dragged forward. His waist cleared the edge of the bog with a loud sucking noise. He kicked out with his legs, still clinging onto the rope. A strong hand grabbed him and pulled him clear. Exhausted, he collapsed onto firm ground.

For a moment he lay there retching, getting the filthy water out of his system. Then he looked up. And recognized Richard Cole, the journalist from the *Greater Malling Gazette*.

"You!" he gasped.

"What the . . . ?" Richard was equally surprised.

"How . . ."

"What are you doing?"

The broken questions hung in the air.

Then Matt took control of the situation. "Not now," he said. He was thinking about the dogs. They might have lost his scent when he was in the bog, but they would find it again soon enough. "We have to go."

"All right. Can you get into the car?" Richard leaned down and helped Matt to his feet. Matt could feel the slime dripping off him. He wondered what he must look like.

The car was standing on the side of the road with its engine running. Richard rested Matt against the hood, then went around to open the passenger door. There were piles of old newspapers and magazines on the floor and he spread them quickly over the seat to protect the leather before Matt sat down. Matt was edging around to get in when he saw them.

The dogs had emerged from the wood. They were in the middle of the road. Watching. Waiting . . .

"There . . ." Matt whispered.

"What?"

Richard turned and saw them. The dogs were just ten meters away. Their tongues were hanging out. Their breath rose in white clouds. Their eyes flickered. Richard held up a hand. "Nice dogs! Stay!" he muttered. He reached back into the car, and when he straightened up again he was holding a can. "Get in," he said.

"What are you . . . ?"

"I'm going to put them down."

Painfully Matt eased himself into the front seat, his eyes fixed on the waiting dogs. Water oozed out underneath him and dripped onto the carpet. Richard fumbled in his pocket and produced a handkerchief. Slowly, forcing himself not to panic, he unscrewed the lid of the can and pushed the handkerchief into its neck. Matt smelled gasoline fumes. Richard leaned back in the car and found a lighter. The dogs padded forward, suddenly suspicious, and Matt knew they were preparing themselves for the final leap. Richard flicked the lighter against the handkerchief and hurled the can toward them.

The first dog had just left the ground when the can hit it and exploded into flame. Burning gasoline sprayed over the second dog, instantly setting it alight. The fire roared around them. With an unearthly howl, the dogs fell back, one curling itself into a ball, the other snapping at its own hide in a vain attempt to devour the cause of its agony. Fire had been their creator. Now fire destroyed them.

Richard slid over the hood and landed next to the driver's door. He got into the car, slammed the door, threw the gears into reverse, and stamped on the accelerator. The back wheels spun, then found a grip, rocketing the car backward. Matt felt a thump as they drove over the body of one of the dying creatures. But where was the other? He looked around, then yelled out as, still blazing, it slammed into the windscreen, having launched itself out of nowhere. For a few seconds it was in front of him, its dreadful teeth centimeters from his face. Then Richard changed into first gear and wrenched the wheel. The dog spun away. Matt looked out of the back window. The flickering remains of one carcass lay in the middle of the road. The second had gotten snarled up in the wheels, but as the car sped forward it fell free and was tossed to the side.

They drove through the night for half a mile without speaking. The car was filled with the smell of the bog. Water was dripping out of Matt's clothes, onto the seat and onto the floor. Richard pulled a face and opened the window. "So do you mind telling me what that was all about?" he demanded.

Matt didn't know where to begin. "I think something is happening in Lesser Malling," he said.

Richard nodded. "I think you could be right."

THIRTEEN
Matt's Story

Richard Cole lived in the very center of York. He had rented a flat in one of the city's most famous medieval streets: a pretty, cobbled passageway called The Shambles. The flat was arranged over three floors, a series of oddly shaped rooms piled on top of one another like children's building bricks. At ground level there was a shop selling souvenirs to tourists. Richard's home began on the first floor with a kitchen and a living room. Then there was a bedroom and a shower. And finally a twisting flight of steps led to a spare room built into the roof.

The place itself was a shambles. All the furniture looked as if it had been bought at a yard sale — as indeed much of it had. There were old clothes everywhere, unwashed plates piled high in the sink, CDs, books, magazines, and half-written articles shuffled together in a way that would surely make it impossible to find anything. The walls were covered with posters, mainly of old American films. Richard's laptop was on the kitchen table, next to a box of Cheerios, a half-eaten can of baked beans with the fork still sticking out, and two pieces of very cold toast.

Matt had felt awkward dripping on the stairs as they climbed to the first floor, and it was worse now that he was in the flat itself. He was very aware that he stank. Richard left him on his own in the kitchen and came back with a large towel.

"We can talk later," he said. "Right now you need a shower. And we'll have to get rid of those clothes."

"Have you got a washing machine?"

"Are you kidding? A washing machine hasn't been built that could handle all that muck. They can go in the bin. I'll find you some clothes of mine to wear in the meantime." Richard pointed upstairs. "You'll find the shower easily enough. Are you hungry?"

"Starving."

"Well, there's no food in the house. I'll go out and get something while you get changed. We can talk when I get back."

Half an hour later, the two of them were sitting in the living room, surrounded by Chinese food. Matt had spent twenty minutes in the shower, coming out only when he had washed away all traces of the bog. He was now wearing an old York University T-shirt with a towel wrapped round his waist and nothing on his feet. He hadn't realized how hungry he was until he had begun eating. Now he was feeling stuffed.

"Nice place," he said, looking around.

"I was lucky to get it," Richard said. "It's very cheap. Not that I'm here very much. I normally eat at the pub. . . ."

"Do you live on your own?"

"I had a girlfriend until about a week ago. Unfortunately, she took a liking to classical music."

"What's so bad about that?"

"Now she's going out with an opera singer." Richard

had finished eating. He went to the fridge and took out a can of beer. "You want anything to drink?"

Matt shook his head. "I'm all right." There was a brief silence while Richard sat down again. Matt realized that they both had a lot to explain. "How did you find me tonight?" he asked.

Richard shrugged. "There's not much to tell. After you left the newspaper office, I thought about some of the things you'd said. It all sounded pretty stupid, if you want the truth. But there were parts of your story . . . well, I couldn't get them out of my head. And I had nothing else to do."

"So you went to look at Omega One?"

"Well, let's just say I happened to be passing."

"You knew where it was?"

Richard nodded. "The man who built it still lives in York. He was a scientific adviser to the government back in the sixties, but he's retired now. Name of Michael Marsh."

"Did you meet him?"

"About six months ago. He got a knighthood from the Queen and I had to do a story about him. He was an unbelievably boring man. Lives in a big house near the river. He collects matchbox labels. I might give him a call and we can go and see him. He might be able to help."

"So you decided to visit Omega One in the middle of the night. . . ."

"It was on the way home from the pub. What's the big deal? I was nearby, so I thought I'd drive past. And then I heard someone shouting for help and that was how I found you."

"That's not possible." Matt shook his head. "I didn't shout for help."

"I heard you."

"I may have yelled once. But I didn't even hear your car. You were suddenly just there."

"Maybe you shouted without realizing it, Matt. I mean, you were panicking. You were probably out of your mind. I know I would have been."

"How fast were you driving?"

"About fifty. I don't know."

"Were the car windows open?"

"No."

"Then even if I had shouted, how could you have heard my voice? It's not possible."

"You have a point," Richard admitted. "But then how do you explain that I swerved off the road in exactly the right place and came straight to you?"

"I can't," Matt said in a quiet voice.

"Look . . . I heard someone. All right? I pulled over and there you were, up to your neck in . . ." He broke off. "You're just lucky I hadn't decided to stay for another pint. But now that you're here, maybe you should tell me a little bit more about yourself."

"Like what?"

"I don't even know your full name. You say your parents are dead, but you never told me how you ended up living with this woman . . . Mrs. Deverill." Matt looked away. "You might as well tell me now," Richard said. "It might help me work out what we're going to do."

"Are you going to put me in the newspaper?"

"That's the general idea."

Matt shook his head. "You can forget it. I don't want anyone writing about me. I don't want anyone to know about my life."

"I think you're forgetting something, Matt." Richard pointed out. "You were the one who came to me. You told me you had a story. . . ."

"I needed your help."

"Well, maybe we need each other."

"I don't want to be in the papers."

"Then maybe you shouldn't be in my flat." Richard put down his can of beer. "All right," he said. "That's not fair. I'm not going to throw you out. Not tonight, anyway. But to be honest with you, I don't really need a fourteen year old in my life. So I'll tell you what I'll do. Tell me your story and I promise I won't publish it until you say. Okay?"

"I never will say," Matt replied. But he nodded. "All right. . . ."

Richard reached for a notebook and a pen just as he had when they first met at the newspaper office. He sat, waiting.

"I don't really know where to start," Matt said. "But since you asked, my full name is Matthew Freeman. I was sent to stay with Mrs. Deverill because of something called the LEAF Project."

"The LEAF Project?" Richard had heard the name before. "Isn't that one of the government's big ideas? Some sort of crazy scheme for dealing with juvenile offenders."

"That's right. That's what I am. I was arrested for breaking into a warehouse. A man got stabbed."

"You stabbed him?"

"No. But I was there when it happened. I was to blame." Matt paused. "Maybe now you won't be so keen to help me."

"Why not? I don't give a damn what you've done. I just want to know why you did it." Richard sighed. "Why don't you try starting at the beginning? You may find it easier."

"All right." Matt didn't want to do this. His social worker, Jill Hughes, had always tried to make him talk about himself. *You have to take responsibility for who you are.* That was one of the things she had always said. But the more she had pressed him, the more reluctant he had become until their relationship had dissolved into a hostile silence. And now this journalist was asking him to do the same. Had he finally found an adult he could really trust? Matt hoped so, but he wasn't sure.

"I don't remember very much about my parents," he said. "I thought I would. They only died six years ago, but bit by bit they've just sort of . . . faded away. There's not much of them left.

"I think we were happy. We lived in a pretty ordinary sort of street in Dulwich. Do you know it? It's in South London. My dad was a doctor. I don't think my mum worked. We had a nice house, so I suppose there was a bit of money around. But we weren't that rich. The last time my parents took me on holiday we went camping in France. I must have been about seven years old then."

"Did you have any brothers or sisters?"

"No. There were just the three of us. And there wasn't much family. My dad was actually born in New Zealand and most of his family's still over there. My mum had a half sister called Gwenda who lived in Ipswich. She visited us once or twice, but they didn't get on. Gwenda was nothing like her. When I was small, I used to think she was really boring. I never dreamed . . ."

Matt drew a breath.

"Anyway, my mum and dad were killed. They were going to a wedding in Oxford, which was about a two-hour drive away. I was meant to go, too, but at the last minute I didn't feel well, so I stayed behind with a neighbor."

Matt stopped. Richard knew that he wasn't telling the whole truth about the wedding. He could see it. But he didn't interrupt.

"There was an accident," Matt said. "The car burst a tire while they were crossing a bridge. My dad lost control and they went over the side and into the river. They drowned." Matt paused. "The first time I knew about it was when the police came to the house. I was only eight years old, but I knew straightaway.

"After that it's all a bit jumbled. I spent quite a bit of time — it must have been three or four weeks — living in a sort of hostel. Everyone was trying to help, but there was nothing anyone could do. The real trouble was that there was nobody to look after me. They tried to get in touch with my dad's family out in New Zealand, but nobody wanted to help.

"And then my mum's one relation turned up. Gwenda Davis from Ipswich. She'd only ever seen me three or four times. But she was sort of my aunt. We met and she took me out for lunch. She took me to a McDonald's. I remember that because my dad never let me eat fast food. He used to say it was the worst thing anyone could eat. But she took me there and she bought me a burger and chips and there we were, sitting there with the noise and the plastic tables and a big clown looking down at us as she asked me if I wanted to move in with her. I said I didn't — but in the end what I wanted didn't make any difference because it had all been decided already. I moved in with her." He paused. "And Brian."

Matt sat down again. He looked Richard straight in the eye. "Promise me you won't write about this," he said.

"I've already said, I won't write about anything unless you let me."

"I won't let you. I don't want people to know."

"Go on, Matt. . . ."

"Gwenda's home was really gross. It was a terraced house and it was half falling down and it had a tiny garden that was full of bottles. Brian was a milkman. The whole place smelled. All the pipes leaked and the walls were damp and half the lights never worked. Gwenda and Brian had no money. At least, they had no money until I came along. But that's the point, you see. My mum and dad had left everything they had to me, and now Gwenda got control of the money. And of course she spent it. The whole lot of it."

Matt stopped. Richard could see him looking back into his own past. The hurt was right there, in his eyes.

"The money ran out pretty fast," he went on. "The two of them spent it on cars and holidays and that sort of thing. And when it was gone, that was when they turned nasty. Brian especially. He said it would have been better if I'd never come in the first place. He started finding fault with everything I did. He'd yell at me and I'd yell back. And then he started bashing me around a bit, too. He was always careful not to leave bruises. Not ones that showed.

"And then I met Kelvin, who lived down the road from me, and he became my mate. Kelvin was always in trouble at school. He had a brother who was in prison, and people were scared of him. But at least he was on my side . . . at least, that's what I thought. It felt good having him around.

"But in the end, he only made things worse. I started missing a lot of school, and even the teachers who'd been trying to help gave up on me. Kelvin and I used to go shoplifting together and of course we got caught, and that was when I had to start seeing a social worker. We used to nick stuff from supermarkets. It wasn't even things we needed. We just got a buzz off of doing it. Kelvin used to like scratching new cars. He'd run his key up the paint-work . . . just for the fun of it. We did all sorts of stuff together. And then one night we broke into this warehouse to nick some DVDs and we were caught by a security guard. It was Kelvin who stabbed him, but it was my fault as much as his. I shouldn't have gone there. I shouldn't have been there. I just wish I'd tried to talk him out of it."

Matt wiped his eyes with the back of his hand.

"Anyway, you know the rest. I got arrested and I thought I'd be sent to prison. But in the end I didn't even have to go to court. They sent me to Lesser Malling as part of this thing they called the LEAF Project. Liberty and Education . . . that is what it's meant to stand for. But since I arrived it's been more like Lunatics and Evil Freaks. Anyway, I've already told you about Mrs. Deverill and all the rest of it and you didn't believe me. I suppose that's fair enough. I wouldn't have believed any of it, either. Except I've had to live it. And what I told you, at the paper . . . it's all true."

"Why do you think she wants you?" Richard asked.

"I don't know. I haven't got the faintest idea. But I think I know what she is. I think I know what they all are."

"And what's that?"

"You'll laugh at me."

"No. I won't."

"I think they're witches," Matt said.

Richard laughed.

"You saw the dogs!" Matt protested. "You think they came out of Battersea Dogs Home? I saw how she made them. She sprinkled some sort of powder on the flames and they just appeared. It was like . . . magic!"

"It was an illusion," Richard said.

"Richard . . . this wasn't like something on TV. There wasn't a girl there in spangly sequins. I saw the dogs. They came out of the fire. And what about this?"

He was still wearing the stone talisman. He tore it off and threw it onto the table. The golden key lay faceup in the light.

Richard looked at it. "Yeah. All right," he said. "Witches! Yorkshire used to be full of witches, it's true. But that was five hundred years ago."

"I know. She's got a picture in her house. Some sort of ancestor who Mrs. Deverill said got burned. Maybe she was burned as a witch!" Matt thought for a moment. "If there were witches five hundred years ago, why can't there be witches now?"

160

"Because we've grown up. We don't believe in witches anymore."

"I don't believe in witches." Matt shrugged. "But the cat was killed and it came back. Tom Burgess died, but I heard his voice on the phone. And there was a detective from Ipswich . . ."

"What?"

"His name was Mallory. He said he was going to help me. He argued with Mrs. Deverill. And the next thing I knew, he was dead, too. He was killed on the M1."

There was a brief silence. Then Richard spoke again.

"They're not witches, Matt," he said. "They may think they're witches. They may act like witches. They may have made you believe they're witches. But whatever's going on at Lesser Malling, it's real. It has something to do with the power station. And that's science, not magic."

"What about the dogs?"

"Genetically modified. Mutants. I don't know. Maybe they'd been exposed to some sort of radiation."

"You don't believe in magic."

"I enjoyed Harry Potter like everyone else. But did I believe in it? No."

Matt stood up. "I'm tired," he said. "I want to go to bed."

Richard nodded. "You can have the spare room upstairs."

• • •

Ten minutes later, Matt lay in a sofa bed, looking at the ceiling that slanted above his head. The spare room was built into the roof of the house and was filled with junk. Richard used it as a dumping ground for anything that he no longer had a use for. Matt was still wearing the T-shirt. He was tucked under a duvet, feeling warm and drowsy.

The door opened. Richard was standing outside. "I just wanted to check if you were all right," he said.

"I'm fine." Matt twisted around. "What are you going to do?" he asked. "How long can I stay here?"

"I don't know. A couple of days, maybe." Matt's face fell. "I told you, Matt. You can't stay with me. It's just not right. I don't even know you. But I do want to help you." Richard sighed. "I must be crazy, because the last two people who tried to help seem to have ended up dead, and personally I have other plans. But at least we can take a look into Omega One. I mean, forget witches and all that stuff. The old power station seems to be at the heart of whatever's going on."

"You said you knew the man who built it."

"I'll call him tomorrow. All right?"

Matt nodded.

"Good night, then." Richard moved away.

"Wait!" Matt said. Richard stopped. "There was something I didn't tell you."

Richard hovered once again in the doorway.

"You said you wanted to know who I am, so you might as well know all of it. My mum always used to say I was strange. All my life, I've been involved in a lot of strange things. Mrs. Deverill and all the rest of it . . . I sometimes think it was *meant* to happen. I'm *meant* to be here. I don't know why.

"The night before my mum and dad were killed, I had a bad dream. I often had dreams, but this was something else. I saw the bridge. I saw the tire burst. I even saw the water flooding in through the windows, filling the car. It was like I was in the car with them, and it was horrible. I couldn't breathe." He stopped. He had never told anyone this before. "And when I woke up the next morning, I knew they would never get to the wedding. I knew the accident was going to happen exactly the way it did."

Matt drew a breath. This was the difficult part.

"My dad was like you. He didn't believe in stuff like witches and magic and things he couldn't understand. I suppose it was because he was a doctor. And I knew that if I told him about my dream, he'd just get angry. It had happened before . . . once or twice, when I was very young. Dad would say I was just being silly, letting my imagination run away with me. And maybe he was right. That's what I told myself. 'It's just a dream. It's just a dream. Everything's going to be all right. Don't get into trouble with Dad. . . .'

"So I said nothing.

"But I was too scared to get in the car. I pretended I was ill. I threw a tantrum and made them leave me with Mrs. Green, next door. I was only eight years old. I didn't know what was going on. I still don't. But I know that I'm different. Sometimes I seem to be able to do things that are impossible. You won't believe me, Richard. But I can break a glass just by looking at it. I can do it! I did it! I know when something bad is going to happen before it does. When I was in the warehouse, I *knew* the guard was there. And tonight. Maybe I managed to call to you — when I was in the bog — without opening my mouth. I don't know. It's like I have some sort of power, but I can't control it. It just flickers on and off, by itself."

Matt yawned. Suddenly he was exhausted. He'd had enough.

"I told Mrs. Green," he said. "I told her that my mum and dad weren't going to come back from the wedding. I told her about the bridge. The sides were weak. It was being repaired. I even got that right. She got very angry with me. She didn't want to hear it. And what was she meant to do? She couldn't ring my parents and tell them not to go to the wedding. In the end, she told me to go out and play in the garden. She didn't want to hear any more.

"I was still out in the garden when the police arrived. And I'll never forget the look on her face. She was horrified. More than that. She was actually sick. And it wasn't just because of what had happened to my parents. She was horrified and sick because of me.

"And the thing is, Richard — I was like you. I didn't believe in magic. I didn't believe in myself. And every day since then, almost every hour of every day, I've asked myself why I didn't try to warn my mum and dad. I could have saved their lives. But I said nothing. I just let them drive off by themselves. Every day I've woken up knowing that I'm to blame. It's my fault they're no longer here."

Matt turned over on the mattress and lay still.

Richard looked at the sleeping boy for a long time. Then he turned out the lights and crept quietly downstairs.

FOURTEEN
Science and Magic

Matt woke up slowly and with a sense of reluctance. It had been the best sleep he'd had for weeks — and for once there had been no dreams.

It took him a few moments to get used to the unfamiliar surroundings and remember where he was. His eyes took in a slanting roof, a narrow window with the sun already shining brightly behind, a box of old paperbacks, and an alarm clock showing ten o'clock. Then he remembered the events of the night. The power station, the dogs, the chase through the wood. He had told Richard Cole everything, even the truth about the way his parents had died. For six years he had managed to live with the knowledge of what he'd done.

I could have warned them. I didn't.

And finally he had unburdened himself to a journalist who probably hadn't believed him anyway. He wished now that he hadn't. He felt embarrassed. He remembered how Richard had dismissed his theories about witchcraft and magic. It wasn't surprising. If it had been the other way around, he wouldn't have believed it himself.

And yet . . .

He knew what had happened. He had lived through it.

The dogs *had* come out of the flames. Tom Burgess *had* died trying to warn him.

And then there was the question of his own powers.

He had seen the car accident that had killed his parents before it happened. It was the reason he was still alive. And there had been other things, too. The jug of water that had smashed in the detention center. And last night, the way he had somehow managed to get Richard to stop.

Suppose . . .

(Matt lay back against the pillows. His hands lay flat against the cover of the bed.)

. . . suppose he did have some sort of special ability. The police report that he had found in Mrs. Deverill's bedroom had mentioned his precognitive abilities. By that, they meant his ability to see the future. Somehow, Mrs. Deverill had gotten hold of a copy and that was why she wanted him. Not because of who he was. Because of what he was.

But that was ridiculous. Matt had seen the X-Men and Spider-Man movies. Superheroes. He even liked the comics. But was he really pretending that he had some sort of superpower, too? He had never been bitten by a radioactive spider or zapped by a mad scientist inside some sort of space machine. He was just an ordinary teenager who had gotten himself into trouble.

But he had broken the jug of water. He had gazed at it in the detention center and it had shattered.

There was a vase on the windowsill. It was plain glass, about fifteen centimeters high, filled with pens and pencils. Matt found himself gazing at it. All right. Why not? He began to concentrate. He breathed slowly and evenly. His back was supported by the pillows. Without moving, he focused all his attention on the vase. He could do it. If he ordered the vase to smash itself, it would explode then and there. He had done it before. He would do it now. And then he would do it again for Richard and after that the journalist would have to believe him.

He could feel the thought patterns emanating from his head. The vase filled his vision. Break. Go on . . . break! He tried to imagine the glass blowing itself apart, as if imagining it could make it happen. But it didn't move. Matt was gritting his teeth now, holding his breath, desperately trying to make it break.

He stopped. His chest fell and he turned his head aside. Who did he think he was kidding? He wasn't an X-Man. More like a zero kid.

There were fresh clothes in a pile at the bottom of the mattress: jeans and a sweatshirt. Richard must have come in at some time earlier that morning. And although he had threatened to throw them away, he had also washed Matt's sneakers. They were still damp, but at least they were clean. Matt got dressed and went downstairs. He found Richard in the kitchen, boiling eggs.

"I was wondering when you'd get up," Richard explained. "Did you sleep okay?"

"Yes. Thanks. Where did you get the clothes?"

"There's a shop down the road. I had to guess your size." He pointed at the bubbling saucepan. "I'm just making breakfast. Do you like your eggs hard or soft?"

"I don't mind."

"They've been in twenty minutes. I have a feeling they'll be hard."

They sat down at the table and ate together. "So what happens now?" Matt asked.

"Right now we have to be careful. Mrs. Deverill and her friends will be looking for you. They may even have called the police and reported you missing, so if they find you with me, we'll both be in trouble. You can't just pick up fourteen-year-old kids these days and hang out with them. Not that I intend to hang out with you. As soon as we've found out what's going on, it's good-bye. No offense, but there's only room in this place for one."

"That's fine by me."

"Anyway, I've been busy. While you were asleep, I made three calls. The first one was to take a day off work. No problem there. There's no news. They may even put the fact that I'm taking the day off on the front page. I wouldn't be surprised. Then I called Sir Michael Marsh."

"The scientist."

"He's agreed to see us at half past eleven. After that, we're going to Manchester."

"Why?"

"When you came to the newspaper office, you told me about a book you'd found in the library. Written by someone called Elizabeth Ashwood. She's quite well known. This will probably grab you, Matt. She writes about black magic and witchcraft . . . that sort of thing. We've got a file on her at the *Gazette* and I managed to pull up an address for her. No telephone number. We can drive over and see what she has to say."

"That's great," Matt said. "Thank you."

"Don't thank me. If this leads me to a story, I'll be the one thanking you."

"And if it doesn't?"

Richard thought for a moment. "I'll throw you back in the bog."

• • •

Sir Michael Marsh looked very much like the government scientist he had once been. He was elderly now, well into his seventies, but his eyes had lost none of their intelligence and seemed to demand respect. Although it was a Sunday morning, he was formally dressed in a gray suit with a white shirt and dark blue tie. His shoes were highly polished and his fingers manicured. His hair had long ago turned silver, but it was thick and well-groomed. He was sitting with his legs crossed, one hand resting on his knee, listening to what his visitors had to say.

It was Richard who was talking. He was more smartly dressed than usual. He had shaved and put on a clean shirt and a jacket. Matt was next to him. The three of them were in a second-floor living room with large windows giving an uninterrupted view of the river Ouse. The house was Georgian, built to impress. There was something almost stagelike about the room, with its polished wooden desk, shelves of leather-bound books, marble fireplace, and antique chairs. And Richard had been right about the matchbox collection. There were hundreds of matchboxes on the walls, displayed in narrow glass cases. They had come from every country in the world.

Richard had given a very cut-down version of Matt's

story. He hadn't told Sir Michael who Matt was or how he had arrived at Lesser Malling but had concentrated instead on the things Matt had seen at Omega One. At last he came to a halt. Matt waited to hear what Sir Michael would say.

"You say that there were electric lights at the power station," he began. "And the boy heard a humming sound."

"Yes, sir."

"He saw a van. Unloading some sort of box."

"Yes."

"And what conclusion have you drawn from all this, Mr. Cole?"

"Matt couldn't see very much in the darkness, Sir Michael. But he said that the people carrying the box were wearing strange, bulky clothes. I wondered if they might have been radiation suits."

"You think that somebody is trying to start up Omega One?"

"It is a possibility."

"An impossibility, I'm afraid." Sir Michael turned to Matt. "How much do you know about nuclear power, young man?" he asked.

"Not a lot," Matt answered.

"Well, let me tell you a bit about it. I'm sure you don't want a physics lesson, but you have to understand." Sir Michael thought for a moment. "We'll start with the nuclear bomb. You know, of course, what that is."

"Yes."

"A nuclear bomb contains devastating power. It can destroy an entire city as it did, in the last war, at Hiroshima. In tests in the Nevada desert, a small nuclear bomb blew out a crater so deep you could have fit the Empire State Building into it. The power of the bomb is the energy released in the explosion. And that energy comes from splitting the atom. Are you with me so far?"

Matt nodded. If he had been at school, his attention would have already wandered, but this time he was determined to keep up.

"A nuclear power station works in much the same way. It splits the atom in a metal called uranium, but instead of producing an explosion, which is uncontrolled, the energy is released gradually, in the form of heat. The heat is fantastic. It turns water into steam. The steam drives the turbines of an electricity generator and out comes electricity. That's all a nuclear power station does. It turns heat into electricity."

"What's wrong with coal?" Matt asked.

"Coal, gas, oil . . . they're all too expensive. And one day they'll run out. But uranium is incredible stuff. One tiny piece of it, a piece you could hold in your hand, has enough power in it to keep a million electric heaters running nonstop for twenty-four hours."

"Except it would kill you if you held it in your hand," Richard said.

"Yes, Mr. Cole. The radiation would indeed kill you. Which is why, when uranium is moved, it is carried in heavy, lead-lined boxes."

"Like the box I saw!" Matt said.

Sir Michael ignored him. "At the heart of any nuclear power station is a nuclear reactor," he continued. "The reactor is basically a massive concrete box — and it is in here that our controlled explosion takes place. The uranium is surrounded by long sticks called control rods. When you lift up the control rods, the explosion starts. And the higher you lift them, the more powerful the explosion becomes.

"The reactor is the most dangerous part of the station. You have to remember what happened at Chernobyl, in Russia. One mistake here and you risk what is known as an excursion, an explosion that might kill hundreds or even thousands of people and that would destroy a vast area of land for years."

Matt wondered if that was what they were planning. Did Mrs. Deverill and the other villagers want to commit some sort of act of terrorism? No. It made no sense. If that was the case, what did they want with him?

Sir Michael Marsh had continued. "When the government began to think about building nuclear stations fifty years ago, they set up a number of experimental stations where they could study reactors in action and make sure they were safe. Omega One was the first of these experiments and I helped design and build it. It ran for less than eighteen months. And after we were finished with it, we shut it down and left it to rot in the pine forest that surrounds it."

"Maybe someone wants to get it running again," Richard said.

"They couldn't — for all sorts of reasons." Sir Michael sighed. "Let's start with the uranium. As I'm sure you know, you can't just buy uranium. Even dictators in countries like Iraq have found it impossible to get supplies. Let's suppose these villagers of yours owned a uranium mine. It still wouldn't help. How would they process the stuff? Where would they get the technical know-how and the resources?"

"But Matt saw something. . . ."

"He saw a box. For all we know, it could have contained a picnic." Sir Michael glanced at his watch. "I last visited Omega One about twenty years ago," he said. "And there's nothing left inside. We removed anything that could possibly be dangerous when we dismantled the place. It was quite a job, I can tell you, transporting everything out of the wood."

"Why did you build it there?" Richard asked.

The scientist seemed momentarily thrown. "I'm sorry?"

"Why did you build it in the middle of a wood?"

"Well, it had to be somewhere out of the way. And there's an underground river. A nuclear power station requires a constant supply of water. There's a river that runs through the wood, under the ground."

There was nothing more to be said.

"I'm sorry, Sir Michael." Richard got to his feet. "It seems that we've been wasting your time."

"Not at all. I've found what you and your young friend had to tell me most disturbing. At the very least it would seem that somebody is trespassing on what is still government property, and I shall certainly contact the appropriate authorities." He stood up. "Personally, I wanted to knock the building down when we'd finished with it — but it was too expensive. As the minister put it, nature is the best demolition expert. But let me assure you, you couldn't spark a decent fire in that damp old place, let alone a nuclear reaction."

He showed them to the door. But before he opened it,

he turned again to Matt. "Are you interested in phillu-meny?" he asked.

"I'm sorry?" Matt didn't know what he was talking about.

"The collecting of matchbox labels. I have almost a thousand of them." He pointed at a case on the wall. "The Tekka brand, made in India. And those are Russian. I think it rather wonderful that anything so ordinary can be so beautiful."

He opened the door.

"Do let me know how you get on," he said. "And I'll call you when I've spoken to the police and will let you know if there's any news."

• • •

Elizabeth Ashwood, the author of *Rambles Around Greater Malling,* lived in Didsbury, a suburb of Manchester. The address that Richard had been given led him to a detached house in a wide, leafy street. A gate and a path led through a garden that was perfectly neat, with an array of spring flowers. There was a knocker on the front door, shaped like a hand. Richard lifted it and let it fall. A hollow boom echoed through the house, and a minute later the door opened.

A thin, dark-haired woman stood there, not looking at him but past him, her eyes covered by two circles of black glass. Matt guessed she must be about thirty-five. He had never met a blind person before. He wondered what it must be like, living in perpetual night.

"Yes?" she asked impatiently.

"Are you Elizabeth Ashwood?" Richard asked.

"I am Susan Ashwood. Elizabeth was my mother."

"Was?" Richard couldn't keep the disappointment out of his voice.

"She died a year ago."

So that was it. They had come all this way for nothing. Matt was ready to turn around and go back to the car, but suddenly the woman spoke again. "Who are you?"

"My name is Richard Cole," Richard said. "I'm a journalist from the *Greater Malling Gazette*."

"There are two of you."

"Yes."

How had she known? Matt hadn't made any sound.

"A boy. . . ." Her hand reached out and somehow it caught hold of Matt's arm. "Where have you come from?" she demanded. "Why are you here?"

Matt squirmed, embarrassed to be held by her. "I've come from Lesser Malling," he said. "We wanted to know about a book your mother wrote."

"Come into the house," the woman said. "I can help you. But you must come in."

Matt glanced at Richard, who shrugged. The two of them went in.

Miss Ashwood led them into a wide, airy corridor. The house was Victorian but had been carefully modernized with oak floors, concealed lighting, and floor-to-ceiling windows. There were paintings on the walls — mainly expensive abstracts. Matt couldn't help wondering who they were for, since the owner couldn't see them. Of course, it was always possible that the woman had a husband and a family. And yet, at the front door, he had gotten the impression that this was someone who was always alone.

She led them into a living room with low leather sofas and gestured at them to sit down. A polished grand piano, brilliant black, stood in the corner.

"Which of my mother's books brought you all this way?" she asked.

"It was a book about Greater Malling," Richard said.

Matt decided to cut straight to the point. "We want to know about Raven's Gate."

The woman became very still. It was hard to read her emotions behind the black glasses, but Matt could sense her excitement. "So you've found me," she whispered.

"Do you know what it is?"

Susan Ashwood made no reply. The two black circles were fixed on Matt and he felt uncomfortable, wanting to move. He knew she could see nothing at all and wished she wouldn't stare at him this way. "Is your name Matt?" she enquired.

"Yes."

"How did you know that?" Richard asked.

"I knew you would come," the woman said. She was ignoring Richard. All her attention was focused on Matt. "I knew you would find me. It was meant to happen this way. I'm just glad you've arrived in time."

"What are you talking about?" Suddenly Richard was angry. "I think we're wasting everyone's time here," he went on. "We came to see your mother. . . ."

"I know. She told me you'd seen her book."

"I thought you said she was dead."

For the first time, she turned to Richard. "You don't know who I am?"

"Sure." Richard shrugged at Matt. "You're Susan Ashwood."

"You haven't heard of me?"

"Are you famous? What do you do? Do you play the piano?"

By way of an answer, the woman fumbled on a table beside the sofa. She picked up a business card and handed it to Richard. He turned it over and read:

Susan Ashwood
Psychic and spiritualist
A link with the other side

"You're a medium," Richard said.

"What?" Matt asks.

"Miss Ashwood talks to ghosts," Richard told him. "Or that's what she believes."

"I talk to the dead in just the same way that I am talking to you now. And if you could hear them, you would know that there is a great upheaval in the spirit world. Terrible things are about to happen. They are already happening. That is what brought you here to my house."

"What brought me to your house," Richard said, "was the M62 motorway from Leeds. And it looks to me like I was wasting my time." He stood up. "Let's go!" he said to Matt.

"If you leave this room without hearing what I have to say, you will be making the mistake of your life."

"That's what you say!"

"You are involved in something bigger and more incredible than anything you could imagine. Like it or not, you have begun a journey without knowing it, and there can be no going back."

"I'm going back right now," Richard said.

"You can make light of it, but you have no idea what is happening. I feel sorry for you, Mr. Cole. Because, you see, there are two worlds. The world you understand and the world that you don't. These worlds exist side by side, sometimes only centimeters apart, and the great majority of people spend their entire lives in one without being aware of the other. It's like living on one side of a mirror. You think there is nothing on the other side until one day a switch is thrown and suddenly the mirror is transparent. You see the other side. That was what happened to you the day that you heard about Raven's Gate. Nothing can be the same for you anymore. It's as I say. You have begun a journey. You must continue to the end."

"What is Raven's Gate?" Matt asked.

"I can't tell you. I'm not allowed to. You must come with me to London. There is a man you have to meet. His name is Professor Sanjay Dravid."

"Dravid!" Matt whispered the name. He recognized it.

"Why do we have to go to London?" Richard said. "Why can't you tell us here and now?"

"Because the knowledge is too secret. We have all taken an oath. Professor Dravid and the other members of the Nexus will be the ones who decide. But I can assure you that if you'll make the journey with me to London, every-thing will be made clear."

"This is crazy!"

"No, Mr. Cole. There are forces you don't understand. But the boy does." Her head swiveled around. "You know. Don't you, Matt? Your friend here thinks that I'm a con artist who sits in this house and tries to frighten people, to cheat them out of their money. I call myself a psychic, so I must be a fraud. I tell stories about ghosts and spirits, and weak, gullible people believe me. But you know it's true. You know about magic. I felt your power the moment you came here. I have never felt such strength before."

"Where will we find Professor Dravid?" Matt asked.

"Give me your phone number. He'll call you."

"No." Richard shook his head. "We're not doing that. I don't care what you say, Miss Ashwood. We came here with a simple question. If you're not going to give us an answer, we might as well go."

"Professor Dravid is at the Natural History Museum in South Kensington. That's where you'll find him."

"Sure. We'll send you a postcard." Richard stood up and more or less dragged Matt out of the room.

The car was parked opposite the house. They got in and Richard searched in his pockets for the keys. Matt could see that he was rattled.

"A man called Dravid contacted me," Matt said.

"What?"

"When I was at the library in Greater Malling. I was on the Internet and he popped up. You know . . . in a pop-up screen."

"What did he say?"

"I was doing a search on Raven's Gate and he wanted to know why."

"What did you tell him?"

"I didn't tell him anything."

"Well, you can forget about seeing him." Richard had found the key. He put it into the ignition and turned it, then slammed the car into first gear, and they drove off. "We're not going to London, Matt. I can't believe I drove all the way here from York just to talk to a woman who was obviously out of her tree. You're not going to tell me you believed her, are you?"

Matt looked back and watched as the house disappeared behind them. "I wonder . . ." he said.

FIFTEEN
Unnatural History

The taxi dropped them off at the Natural History Museum in the west of London. Richard paid the fare.

"I don't know how I let you talk me into this," he said.

"I didn't say anything," Matt protested.

"You were the one who wanted to see Dravid."

"You were the one who called him."

It was true. When they had gotten back to York, Richard had checked Dravid out on the Internet. It turned out that the professor had an international reputation. Born in the Indian city of Madras, he had become a world expert on anthrolopogy, ethnology, prehistory, and a dozen other related areas. He had written books and hosted television programs. His name had led to over a hundred Web sites, the most recent of which concerned an exhibition about dinosaurs. It was opening at the museum in less than a week's time. Dravid had put it together and written the catalog.

In the end, Richard had decided to call him. He'd expected to be given the brush-off. Perhaps he'd even hoped that would happen. But Dravid had been eager to meet with him. They'd made an appointment for the following day — at six o'clock, after the museum closed.

Matt examined the famous building. It looked like something out of a fairy tale with its orange and blue bricks, its twin towers, and its menagerie of stone animals poking out of every nook and corner. There was a stream of people pouring out of the main entrance, down the curved walkways, past the line of wrought-iron lamps, and onto the lawns on either side.

"Let's do it then," Richard said.

They went up to the gate where a security guard stood, blocking their way. "I'm very sorry," he said. "You're too late for today. . . ."

"We have an appointment with Professor Dravid," Richard told him.

"Professor Dravid? Yes, sir. Of course. You can ask at the enquiries desk."

They climbed the steps and went in. There were certainly plenty of dinosaurs. As Matt entered the museum, he was greeted by the black skull of a huge creature. The skull was at the end of an elongated neck, suspended from an arch that swept over the entrance. He looked around. The dinosaur skeleton was the centerpiece in a vast hall that — with its many arches, its glass and steel roof, its broad staircase and mosaic floor — looked like a cross between a church and a railway station.

They went to the enquiry desk, which, like the rest of the museum, was just closing.

"My name is Richard Cole. I'm here to see Professor Dravid."

"Yes. The professor is expecting you. He has an office on the second floor."

A second guard pointed at a flight of stone steps that led up to a balcony overlooking the main entrance hall. They walked toward it, passing many other dinosaur skeletons, some in glass cases, others standing free. A few people went by, on their way out. The museum seemed bigger and somehow more mysterious now that it was empty. They climbed the stairs and continued along a corridor that led to a solid wooden door. Richard knocked and they went in.

Professor Sanjay Dravid was sitting in the middle of a room piled high with books, magazines, files, and loose bundles of paper. The walls were covered with charts, graphs, and maps. He was typing something into a laptop computer, working at a desk that was itself crowded with more papers, dozens of specimens in glass cases, bits of bone, and pieces of crystal and stone. He was a man in his late forties, Matt thought. His hair was black and well-groomed and he had very dark skin. His suit jacket hung over the back of his chair.

"Professor Dravid?" Richard asked.

The man looked up. "You're Richard Cole?" He finished typing his sentence, pressed ENTER, and closed the lid of the laptop. "Susan Ashwood telephoned me after she met you." His voice was warm and very cultured. "I'm glad you decided to get in touch."

"How do you know Miss Ashwood?"

"We've known each other for many years." Dravid turned to Matt, and Matt felt the dark brown eyes examining him minutely. "And you must be Matt. Nobody's told me your full name."

"I'm just Matt."

"Well, please sit down. I'm sorry I can't offer you any refreshment. There is a café here, but of course it's closed now. Perhaps you ate on the train. . . ."

Richard and Matt sat down in front of the desk. "What's the exhibition about?" Richard asked.

"It is without question the most remarkable exhibition of dinosaur fossils ever assembled in London," Dravid said. "You saw the diplodocus as you came in?" He spoke very quickly and all the time his eyes never once left Matt. Matt could feel himself being weighed up, assessed. "Very hard to miss it. It's about one hundred and fifty million years old and is probably the longest animal that ever lived. Shipped all the way from the United States, bone by bone, just for the exhibition. And then there's a first-rate ceratosaurus — a recent find. It would tear you apart in seconds if it were still alive. And then there are the museum's own specimens. A virtually intact paracyclotosaurus skeleton. It resembles a crocodile although in fact it's no relation."

He stopped suddenly.

"But of course that's not why you're here," he said.

"We want to know about Raven's Gate," Richard said.

"So Miss Ashwood told me."

"She wouldn't tell us anything. She mentioned something called the Nexus. And she said we had to meet you."

"Do you know what it is?" Matt asked.

"The Nexus? Yes, I do."

"Can you tell us?"

"That depends. I'm not entirely sure. . . ."

Matt lost his temper. "Why is it that nobody wants to help me?" he demanded. "You sit here, tapping away at your laptop and talking about dinosaurs. You don't know what I've been through. I've been dumped in Yorkshire. I've been jerked around and terrorized and the only people who have tried to help have ended up dead. Richard doesn't want me hanging around with him and now we've come all the way down here and you're not saying anything, either. You were the one who wanted to see us. Why won't you tell us what we want to know?"

"He's right," Richard agreed. "Three and a half hours on a train to King's Cross, not to mention the price of the tickets. You've got to make it worth our while."

Dravid had sat silently through all this. Now he looked at Matt more carefully. "Matt," he said, "I take it you were the boy on the Internet."

"In the library at Greater Malling. Yes." Matt nodded. "How did you know I was searching for Raven's Gate?"

"It's a simple enough piece of software. Whenever anyone, anywhere in the world, enters those two words, I am informed at once."

"Why?"

"I can't tell you that. Yet. And I apologize for mistrusting you, Matt. We live in a world with so many dangers that we have to be careful who we trust. Please bear with me for a moment. There are things I need to ask you." He paused. "You were in Greater Malling. Is that where you live?"

"No. I'm living in Lesser Malling. It's a village —"

"I know Lesser Malling," Dravid interrupted. "How long have you been there?"

"I don't know. About three weeks."

Dravid pressed his hands together underneath his

chin. "You must tell me everything," he said. "I want to know everything that has happened to you. I need to know exactly what brought you to me here today." He leaned back in his chair. "Start at the beginning and don't leave anything out."

•   •   •

There was only one guard at the museum. There should have been four, but as at many of London's institutions, a shortage of funds had led to cutbacks. Two of the men had been laid off and one was sick. The one remaining guard was in his twenties. He had only recently come to England from Bulgaria. He didn't speak much of the language, but he was learning. He liked London. It was only the job he could have done without.

He found it creepy patrolling the museum. There were all the dinosaur bones . . . they were bad enough. But the creatures in the glass cases were worse. Stuffed rats and leopards and eagles and owls. Spiders and scorpions and huge winged beetles. He could feel their eyes following him as he did his rounds. He should have gotten a job at McDonald's or KFC. The pay would have been only fractionally worse.

He had just passed the main gate when he heard a soft sound like the breaking of a twig. What now? It was getting dark and there was no moon tonight.

"Who is it?" he called out.

He looked up and smiled to himself, turning the flashlight off again. One of the ornate lamps, illuminated for the night, had blown a bulb. That was what he had heard.

"I am scared," he muttered to himself. It was a phrase he had learned in his English class only the day before. "You are scared. He is scared."

A second bulb blinked out. Then a third, then a fourth. Rapidly the darkness made its way along the whole line, squeezing the life out of the bulbs until none of them remained alight. The guard shivered. Was it his imagination or had the temperature fallen in the last few minutes? He breathed out and saw his own breath frost. It was crazy. It was almost the end of April, but it seemed that winter had just returned.

He pressed the switch of his flashlight. The bulb exploded in his hand, gray smoke curling beneath the glass. That was when the guard decided to call it a night. The museum had its own sophisticated alarm system. It could look after itself. And if he was fired, what did he care? He could always get that job at KFC.

The guard unlocked the gate and scurried through, then crossed the road, dodging the traffic through to South Kensington Station. He didn't see the shadows reaching out to enclose the museum or the soft white mist that trickled over the grass. All that he knew was that he wanted to get away. He didn't once look back.

•   •   •

Matt finished his story. He shivered in the sudden cold, but neither Richard nor the professor seemed to notice it.

"Well, what do you think?" Richard asked.

Professor Dravid turned on his desk lamp. "If I had sent

187

you out of here without listening to you," he said, "I would never have forgiven myself. I owe you an apology. But that's not what matters now. You're here. You've been dragged into something that is way beyond your comprehension. But somehow you've managed to find your way to me. You are *meant* to be here, Matt. That's the first thing you have to understand. There are no coincidences. It's all happening the way it was meant to be."

"But what is happening?" Matt asked. "What are Mrs. Deverill and the rest of them doing in Lesser Malling? What is Raven's Gate?"

"We're not leaving until you tell us," Richard added.

"Of course I will tell you." Dravid looked at Matt and there was something strange in his eyes, a sense of puzzlement and wonder. It was as if Dravid had been waiting to meet him all his life.

"If I told anybody else what I'm about to tell you now," he began, "my reputation — everything I've worked for — would disappear overnight. It makes no sense. Not in the real world. Susan Ashwood may seem eccentric to you. You may have thought she was a fraud. I'm telling you she was right. There *is* another world. We are surrounded by it. There is an alternative history as alive in the streets of twenty-first-century London as it was, many thousands of years ago, when it all began. But only cranks and lunatics are meant to believe in it, because, you see, that way everyone feels safer. . . .

"Raven's Gate is at the very heart of that alternative history. Few people have even heard of it. Look for it on the Internet — as you did — and you won't find anything. But that doesn't make it any less real. It is the reason why you are here now. It may even be the reason why you were born."

Dravid stopped. It seemed to be getting darker and darker in the room. The desk lamp had only pushed back the shadows a little way. They were still there, waiting.

"Raven's Gate was the name given to a strange circle of stones that stood — until the Middle Ages — outside Lesser Malling. It was mentioned by name in Elizabeth Ashwood's book . . . the only occasion, to my knowledge, that it has ever appeared in print. Standing stones are by no means unique to Lesser Malling. There are at least six hundred examples in Britain. The most famous of them is Stonehenge.

"You have to remember how mysterious all these stone circles are. Consider Stonehenge. No one is quite certain why it was built. There must have been a purpose. After all, it took a million and a half man-hours to construct. The stones, some of them weighing up to fifty tons, were carried all the way across England. Constructing the circle required a fantastic knowledge of engineering. Obviously, it wasn't put there just for decoration.

"Some say that Stonehenge is a temple. Some say it's a sort of stone computer or even a magical tape recorder. Some believe it's an observatory and that it can calculate the exact time of a solar eclipse. There are dozens of different theories. But the thing is, even in the twenty-first century, with all our knowledge and science, nobody knows for sure."

"But you know," Richard said.

Dravid nodded gravely. "Yes." He leaned forward. "Stonehenge is four or five thousand years old. But it wasn't by any means the first stone circle ever built. In fact it was nothing more than a copy of one that had been around a lot longer. Raven's Gate was the first stone circle and all the others, all the later ones, were nothing more than imitations."

"But where is it?" Matt asked. "What happened to it?"

"A great many of the stone circles in Britain have been destroyed over the years. Some were pulled down by farmers who needed the land for agriculture. The spread of towns and cities finished off others. A few simply collapsed or crumbled away over the years.

"But something very strange happened to Raven's Gate. At some time in the Middle Ages, it was deliberately taken down and smashed. More than that, each and every one of its stones was ground down to powder. The powder was loaded onto carts and carried to the four corners of Britain: north, south, east, and west. Then it was poured into the sea. Something about the circle was so frightening, so evil, that the people who set about this fantastic task were determined that every grain should be separated. Nobody ever spoke of it again. It was as if Raven's Gate had never existed."

"So, how did you hear of it?" Richard asked. It seemed to Matt that he still sounded doubtful.

"You're a journalist, Mr. Cole. You obviously think that if something hasn't been written down, then it can't possibly be true. Well, there have been some written records. The diary of a Spanish monk. A carving on a temple. A few letters and other documents. And of course, there has always been a strong oral tradition. How did I hear of it?" Dravid half-smiled, but his eyes were dark and serious. "I belong to an organization — you might call it a secret society — and we have kept the story alive for centuries. We have passed it from generation to generation.

"The society is called the Nexus."

There was a jug of water on the desk. Dravid reached out and poured himself a glass. He drank half of it, then continued.

"There are twelve members of the Nexus, as there have always been. Incidentally, a nexus means a connection — and we are, I suppose, connected by what we know. Susan Ashwood is a member, and there are ten others from all over the world. You will meet them, Matt. They will certainly want to meet you. The whole purpose of the Nexus, the reason it exists, is to help you with what you have to do."

"What do I have to do?" Matt asked. "Why should I do anything?"

"That's what I have to explain to you now."

Professor Dravid finished his water while he collected his thoughts.

"There are some who believe that a great civilization existed on this planet long before the Greek empire of 600 B.C. Even before the Egyptians, who had flourished two thousand years earlier. I'm talking about the time of Atlantis, perhaps as much as ten thousand years ago. In a way, I suppose, I'm talking about the beginning of the world as we know it today.

"This first civilization was destroyed . . . slowly and deliberately. Creatures of unimaginable power and evil

191

arrived in the world. They were called the Old Ones and their only desire was to create pain and misery all around them. The Christian church talks about Satan, Lucifer, and all the other devils. But these are just memories of the greatest, the original evil. The Old Ones. They thrived on chaos. Once they arrived on the planet, they started a war. Torturing, killing, causing pain and misery. That was their only pleasure. If they'd had their way, they would have reduced the whole world to an empty swamp.

"But according to the stories, there was a miracle, and it arrived in the shape of five young people: four boys and a girl.

"Nobody knows where they came from. They have no names. They have never been described. But together they organized the resistance against the Old Ones. What was left of humanity joined together behind the five and there was a single, final battle in which the future of the world would be decided.

"The five children won that battle. The Old Ones were expelled, sent to another dimension, and a barrier, a magical gate, was built to make sure they could never come back. This gate took the form of a stone circle and later on it came to be known as Raven's Gate."

"Wait a minute," Richard cut in. "You said Raven's Gate was destroyed because it was evil."

"I said it was destroyed because the people *thought* it was evil," Professor Dravid corrected him. "They were mistaken. They gave it a name, Raven's Gate, because the raven has always been associated with death. They had a memory that connected the stones with something horrible . . . but after all the years that had passed, they had forgotten what it was. And in the end they came to think that it was the stones themselves that were evil. So they tore down the stones."

"So the gate was destroyed!" Matt exclaimed.

Professor Dravid shook his head. "The *stones* were destroyed, not the gate," he said. "How can I explain it to you? It's like an idea. If you write something down on a sheet of paper and then burn the paper, do you burn the idea? Of course not! The stones are gone, but the gate is still in place."

Richard shook his head. "Let me get this straight, Professor," he said. "A very long time ago, the world was ruled by evil creatures called the Old Ones. However, five kids appeared and threw them out. These kids then built a barrier, which came to be known as Raven's Gate. Unfortunately, the stones that marked the gate were knocked down by medieval peasants who didn't know any better. But it doesn't matter that much, because the gate is still there after all. Is that about it?"

"Your sarcasm does you no credit, Mr. Cole," Dravid replied. "But you have summed up what I said more or less accurately."

"Miss Ashwood knew about this," Matt said.

"Yes. As I explained to you, we share our knowledge. We have sworn not to reveal it. That's why she couldn't tell you anything when you met."

"But you've told us," Matt said. "You said that the main reason for the Nexus was to help me with something I've got to do. But what is that? And what's any of this got to do with me?"

"I think you know."

"No!" Matt shook his head. "You're wrong."

"Then you must meet the Nexus. The other members are on their way back to London. They'll be here tomorrow night. I'll look after you until then."

"Forget it," Richard said. "We've got return tickets. We're going back to York."

"That's the last thing you should do. You mustn't go anywhere near Lesser Malling." He turned again to Matt. "I don't want to frighten you any more than you already have been. But I believe you are in terrible danger."

"Why?"

"I've told you why Raven's Gate was built. It was a barrier between two worlds and it was closed and locked. But for many centuries there have been people who have been trying to open it again. Of course, they haven't found it easy. They've had to develop special knowledge . . . special powers."

"You mean magic," Matt said.

"We are just two days away from the start of Roodmas," Dravid said. "It begins at sundown on the thirtieth of April. It is one of the most important days in the witches' calendar. It is a day when dark powers are at their strongest. When Black Sabbath is celebrated and evil has its way."

"Mrs. Deverill . . ." Matt began.

"I have no doubt at all that she and the other villagers of Lesser Malling are involved in some sort of black magic. Of course, you will sneer, Mr. Cole. But black magic is still practiced today all over the world. Yorkshire has a long history of witchcraft, and although the witches of medieval times are gone, their descendants, the children of their children, live on.

"A Black Sabbath on Roodmas will require three ingredients, the same ingredients you will find in any such ritual. The first is ritual. Matt has already described the whispers that he heard. The second is fire. You saw the dogs rise out of the flames. But the third, of course, is blood. They must have a sacrifice and the best sacrifice of all would be that of a child."

Matt stood up. "They brought me there to kill me," he said.

"I'm afraid so."

"But why me?"

"You know the answer, I think." Professor Dravid rested a hand briefly on his shoulder. "I'm sorry," he said. "I know how hard it must be for you to accept all this. But you'll have time. I'll put you in a hotel tonight. The Nexus will take care of the cost. And from now on, we'll look after you."

"I wish it wasn't so cold," Matt said.

The three of them left the office. They went along the corridor past a row of glass cases. Wax figurines of primitive people stared out at them. The sound of their footsteps echoed against the ceiling, flapping about the air like invisible birds. Halfway down the main staircase, Dravid stopped. "The keys!" he said. "They'll have locked the doors. I need my keys to let us out."

Hastily he stumbled back up the staircase and along the corridor. Matt watched him. It was only now that he realized how vast the museum was. Professor Dravid was a tiny figure, crossing a balcony high above them. They watched the door of the study open and the light go on.

"Listen, Matt," Richard said. "This is all just a bad dream. Nothing can happen to you."

Matt broke away from him. "You still don't believe it!" he exclaimed.

"Yeah — sure I believe in it. Old Ones and gates and witches and blood sacrifice! Look around you, for heaven's sake! There are rockets going to Mars. We've got satellites beaming telephone conversations all around the world. They've unlocked the genetic code. And you've still got throwbacks like Dravid going on about devils and demons. Well, take it from me, Matt. These five kids saving the world with magical powers don't exist."

"Of course they exist," Matt said. And suddenly he knew. It was very simple. "I'm one of them."

There was a sound. Something invisible had been thrown — or had flown — through the air. Matt and Richard heard someone cry out and looked back at the stairs. Sanjay Dravid had appeared again. He was walking slowly, his footsteps uneven, as if he were drunk or drugged. His hand was clasped to his neck. He stopped and let the hand fall and, with a gasp of horror, Matt saw a terrible wound — a gaping horizontal line, perhaps cut with a sword — across Dravid's neck. Blood curtained down, soaking into his jacket and shirt. Dravid raised his hands feebly. He tried to speak. Then he toppled forward onto his face and lay still.

Richard swore. Matt tore his eyes away from the still figure and looked at the main doors on the other side of the gallery. It was colder than ever. Even without seeing it, he knew there was danger all around.

And the doors, of course, were locked.

SIXTEEN
Bones

For what seemed like an eternity Richard and Matt stood where they were, staring at the still figure lying at the top of the stairs. Blood was spreading around Dravid's head. But there was no sign of an attacker. The museum was as empty and silent as it had been when they first came down. Matt shivered. It was colder than ever and the air seemed to have thickened. It had a white, smoky quality, like a bad photograph.

Richard was the first to recover. "Wait here!" he said, then bounded forward toward the stairs.

"Where are you going?" Matt called after him.

"The keys!"

He took the steps two at a time, not wanting to get any closer to Dravid but knowing there was no other way. The blood had reached the edge of the first step and was already trickling down. Richard knelt down beside the body, trying not to look at the horrible wound. And then, suddenly, Dravid opened his eyes. Miraculously, he was still alive.

"The gatekeepers . . ." The two words were all he could manage.

"Don't say anything. I'll get help." Richard didn't know

what else to tell him. He was lying. The professor was far beyond help.

Dravid extended a trembling hand that clasped a ring of keys. Richard took them gently. For a moment the two of them looked into each other's eyes. Dravid tried to speak again, but it was too much for him. He coughed painfully. Then his head fell back and his eyes closed.

Holding the keys, Richard stood up. He could see Matt below him, some distance away, and knew what he was thinking. Right now there was a killer inside the museum. Someone — or something — had attacked Professor Dravid and they would surely be next. But what were they up against? Why couldn't they see anything? Moving slowly now, Richard went back down the stairs, every sense alert. The two of them were so small. The museum was so vast. He felt horribly exposed.

"Did you get them?" Matt asked.

"Yes." Richard held up the keys. "Let's get out of here."

"What about Professor Dravid?"

"He's dead. I'm sorry. There's nothing we can do."

"But what killed him?"

"I don't know." Richard gazed upward, his eyes sweeping across the vaulted ceiling. "But let's not stay to find out."

He turned and at that moment there was a sudden whirl in the air. Matt threw a protective arm across his face and staggered into Richard.

"What's wrong?" Richard demanded.

"There was something . . ." Matt looked around him, but there was nothing there. "Something flew near my head," he insisted.

"Flew?"

"Yes."

"Did you see what it was?"

"No. But I felt it. It came so close . . . I felt it go past."

"I can't see anything."

But then it soared toward them again, sweeping down out of the mist, and this time there could be no mistaking it even if it took Matt precious seconds to work out what it was that he was seeing. It was triangular and white. A creature that was neither living nor dead, coming at them like something out of a hideous dream. It had sockets but no eyes, wings but no feathers, an empty rib cage with nothing inside. Moving faster than ever, almost a blur, it shot down. Its claws were stretching out and its teeth — stretched in an evil grimace — were needle sharp. Matt fell back. He felt one of the wings shudder past his face and knew that if he had waited a second longer he would have been decapitated. Now he understood what had happened to Professor Dravid.

Richard reached down and helped him up. "Did you see it?" he muttered.

"Of course I saw it."

"You saw what it was?"

"Yes!"

"What was it?"

"I don't know." Matt knew what it was, but he couldn't put it into words.

"It's a trick," Richard said. "It's got to be a trick. It wasn't real."

They had been attacked by something that couldn't fly,

that couldn't even exist. It was a creature that hadn't been seen on the planet for many millions of years. A pterodactyl. Except that it wasn't quite a pterodactyl. It was the fossilized skeleton of a pterodactyl, an x-ray version, wired together and put on display at the Natural History Museum. Something had brought it to life. It was somewhere above them now.

"Look out!"

Matt shouted the warning as the pterodactyl swooped down a second time, plummeting out of the gloomy heights of the hall and hurtling toward them. He had no doubt that the claws would rip his flesh away if he allowed them to make contact. The creature was as vicious as it had been when it had flown over the prehistoric world. But now someone or something was guiding it, using it as an impossible weapon. Its head and claws missed him by centimeters and he thought he had escaped. But as it went past, one of its wing tips brushed his face and he felt a searing pain as the bone cut into him. He gasped and put a hand to his cheek. There was blood on his palm. The pterodactyl performed an aerial somersault and soared back the way it had come. There had been no noise, no warning. Nothing. The museum was utterly silent.

"Matt . . ." Richard began. There was panic in his eyes.

"I'm okay," Matt said. His hand was pressed against his cheek.

"You've been cut."

"I don't think it's deep."

Richard craned his neck, staring up at the ceiling. "We've got to go."

Matt grimaced. "I wasn't thinking of staying."

He had barely spoken the words before the pterodactyl was back. This time, Richard was the target. The outstretched wing slashed through the air. It was as sharp as a sword. Richard swore.

"Richard!" For a dreadful moment, Matt thought he'd been hit.

"It's okay. It missed me. It's gone."

"Yes. But what about the others?"

"What . . . ?"

Professor Dravid had called it the most remarkable exhibition of dinosaur fossils ever seen in London. The pterodactyl was only one of them. There were dozens more all around them. The two of them were standing in the middle of an x-ray version of Jurassic Park.

Even as Richard realized the true nature of the danger, there was an explosion and one of the cases, just a few meters away from them, burst apart. There had been a skeleton inside it, held up by a steel frame, but now it broke free and came lumbering out. It was hard to see anything in the mist and the darkness, but Matt could just about make out something that resembled a crocodile, long and narrow, with short, squat legs holding it just above the floor. It had thrown itself forward, smashing through the glass in a sudden, silent frenzy. The one thing it couldn't do was roar. It had no lungs. But its feet — bones without flesh — made a bizarre sound as they clacked against the mosaic floor. It was charging them, its mouth gaping, its black teeth snapping at the air. Its tail thrashed behind it, scattering the fragments of what had once been its home.

The pterodactyl dived for a third time, its pointed beak aimed at Matt's head. With a cry, the boy threw himself onto the floor, then rolled over and over again, avoiding the crocodile creature that had accelerated toward him, its jaws snapping. How could it even see, Matt wondered, with eye sockets that were completely empty? But it didn't hesitate. It turned around and came at him again. Matt was on his back. In seconds the creature would be on top of him.

Then Richard acted. He had grabbed a chair and, holding it like a baseball bat, swung it at the crocodile, using all his strength. The heavy wood and upholstery slammed into the creature, knocking it off course. One side of its rib cage collapsed. It lay on the ground, twitching and rattling, still trying to get back onto its feet. Its mouth opened and snapped shut. Its head thrashed from side to side.

"Move!" Richard shouted.

A second display case blew itself apart. Glass crashed down. One by one, the dinosaur skeletons were coming to life. Bone rattled against marble. Matt got to his feet, wondering how many exhibits there were in the museum. And what about the one they had seen when they came in . . . ?

The diplodocus.

Even as Matt turned toward the huge creature, he saw the bones twitch and knew that it, too, was coming to life. The diplodocus stood twenty meters high. It was the longest creature that had ever lived. Its dreadful tail was coiling and uncoiling, animated by whatever energy was flowing through it. One of its legs moved, each of the black joints shuddering. Its head swiveled around, searching for its prey.

"The door!" Richard shouted, then cried out as something crashed into him. It was a giant lizard skeleton, walking on its two hind legs, its arms outstretched. It was made up of at least a hundred bones suspended from a long, curving spine, with vicious teeth jutting forward, snapping at his throat. Richard fell back, his arms flailing. Matt saw the keys leave his hands and arc into the darkness. The lizard leaped into the air. Richard hurled himself sideways. The lizard crashed down. If he had waited one more second, it would have landed on top of him. "The door!" He shouted the words again. "See if you can find a way out."

The mist was getting thicker. Matt could no longer see from one end of the museum to the other. There were more explosions, a series of them, one after another. More exhibit cases were being destroyed from within and more shapes were appearing, half-visible — flying, strutting, or crawling toward them. Richard was trying to find the keys. But perhaps the doors would open another way. Surely there would be a fire exit, some way out if there was an emergency.

Matt ran the full length of the hall and reached the front door. Sliding to a halt, he grabbed the handle and pulled. The door was locked. Frantically he tried a second. That was locked, too. Looking out through the glass, he could see offices and apartments across the main road. The traffic was moving as usual. Ordinary life . . . but it could have been a thousand miles away. Both sets of doors had been locked for the evening. There was no emergency lever. They were trapped.

"Richard!" Matt called out. There was no sign of the journalist.

"Stay quiet!" Richard's voice came out of the mist. "They can't see you. Stay where you are and don't make a sound."

Was it true? Another lizard thing — an iguanadon — was stumbling toward him, towering over him. Matt froze. The dinosaur skeleton had stopped right in front of him. He could see into its eye sockets, all the way into its skull. Its mouth was open. Its teeth were ugly and vicious. It wasn't breathing — it couldn't breathe — but even so Matt could smell its breath. It stank of sewage and decay. In the far distance he heard the clattering of feet, the rattling of bones. There was no sound from Richard. The dinosaur craned forward. It seemed to be scenting him, or perhaps sensing the pulse in the side of his neck. Now it was only centimeters away. Matt wanted to run. He wanted to scream. He was certain the creature was about to attack. Was he just going to stand there while it ripped out his throat?

"Matt? Where are you? Are you all right?" Richard's voice echoed from the other side of the museum and the lizard creature twisted away and lumbered off in that direction. So Richard had been right. The dinosaurs were blind. They needed sound and movement to find their victims.

"I'm okay!" Matt shouted back. He didn't dare add more.

"Can you get out?"

"No! I need the keys!"

The keys were lying on the floor beside the stairs. Richard saw them and lunged for them. At the same time, a squat, solid-looking creature charged toward him, a single horn protruding from its misshapen snout. Somewhere in the back of his mind, Richard remembered the creature's name. It was a triceratops. Fortunately, it was slower than the others. It was moving clumsily, slipping on the marble floor. Richard snatched up the keys before it could reach them. Overhead, a second pterodactyl had joined the first. The two of them were performing a ghostly dance, wheeling over each other, high in the air.

Matt was still by the door. Richard could just make him out behind the wall of mist. There were shapes moving everywhere. At least a dozen of the creatures had come to life. But the diplodocus was the worst of them. It was huge. There was no way Richard could get past it. Nor could he stay. The creatures were closing in on him from all sides. He couldn't see in every direction at once. If he stayed where he was, he would die.

And then the diplodocus swung its tail. It moved almost lazily. The great mass of bones whipped through the air and Richard gasped as it crashed into one of the columns. Broken marble and masonry rained down in a billowing cloud of dust. It was only now that he realized the full horror of his situation. Although they were only bone, the dinosaurs were as strong as they had been when they were alive. If they wanted to, they could bring the whole museum crashing down.

"Richard!" Matt called out, and the diplodocus turned, searching for him. The pterodactyls peeled apart and joined the hunt.

"Take the keys!" Richard shouted. "Just get out of here!"

He raised his arm and threw the key ring with all his strength at Matt. The keys flew over the diplodocus and landed on the other side. They hit the ground and skidded the rest of the way. Matt leaned down and picked them up.

"Come on!" Matt shouted.

"Get out!"

"I'm not leaving without you!"

"Just open the door!"

Matt knew Richard was right. Maybe opening the museum would in some way short-circuit the magic that had brought the dinosaurs back from extinction. Maybe he would be able to call for help. There were six keys on the ring. He picked them up and forced the first into the lock. It wouldn't turn. He jerked it out and tried the second, then the third. None of them worked. It was almost impossible to concentrate on what he was doing. His hands were shaking. Every nerve in his body screamed at him to watch out behind. He managed to insert the fourth key. But before he had time to turn it, the tail of the diplodocus brushed against his shoulder, enough to send him flying. It felt like he had been hit by a truck. Bruised and dazed, he staggered to his feet, lurched back to the door, and turned the key. The door swung open. He'd done it! But where was Richard?

Richard hadn't moved. He was still trying to work out how to get past the huge diplodocus. The way forward was blocked. Could he find a way out upstairs? A second later his ankle was gripped by a searing pain. A tiny crab-like thing only fifteen centimeters high had caught hold of him with teeth like thumbtacks. Swearing, he shook it free, then kicked at its head, smiling as the bone disintegrated. The smile was wiped away as its mother, ten times bigger, scuttled toward him.

He made his decision and began to run. Sure enough, the diplodocus heard the sound and its great neck twisted around. Other skeletons lumbered out of the shadows, closing in on him from all sides. But the door was open. The way ahead was clear.

"You can make it!" Matt shouted.

The diplodocus was still standing between the two of them, but with a shudder of excitement Matt realized what Richard was planning to do. As he watched, Richard ducked underneath the diplodocus, under its tail, between its legs, and beneath its belly. The dinosaur was too big and too cumbersome to stop him, and the other creatures — closing in from all sides — couldn't get anywhere near him. He would make it! A quick exit between the monster's front legs and he would be at the door. He would be safe!

Enraged, the diplodocus reared upward. Its powerful head pounded against the upper balcony.

A gust of cold wind touched the back of Matt's neck. Too late, he heard footsteps approaching.

Richard had come to a halt underneath the diplodocus. He was staring at Matt, his face twisted in shock and disbelief.

The balcony had been shattered by the impact. The great arch split open and with a deafening crash the whole massive pile of stone and mortar, glass and steel, plummeted down. Unable to bear the weight, the diplodocus itself collapsed, its legs buckling underneath it.

Matt began to run forward, back into the museum. But then a pair of hands reached out and seized him by the neck. He cried out and twisted around.

Richard was almost invisible behind the dust and the

falling stone. The curving rib cage of the dinosaur had become a cage of another sort for him. It was as if he had been swallowed alive. He was trapped inside it.

Matt couldn't move. Mrs. Deverill was glaring at him, her eyes aflame. Noah was holding on to him, his arm tight around Matt's throat. Matt lashed out, trying to break free. He felt his knee drive into Noah's stomach, but at the same time Mrs. Deverill had produced a damp cloth and pressed it against his face. The cloth smelled sweet and sickly. He choked, unable to breathe.

Richard saw Matt taken. Matt saw the journalist, his face streaked with blood, on his knees in the ghastly prison. Richard raised an arm, trying to brush away the curtain of dust and rubble that was smothering him. The curtain thickened and he was obliterated. A steel girder slammed down into the pile. Matt heard Richard cry out one last time.

And then, unable to fight anymore, Matt allowed the darkness to take him. The traffic rushed past. He heard the engines, saw a traffic light turn from green to red. Everything was suddenly far away.

The world twisted, turned upside down, and he remembered nothing more.

SEVENTEEN
Roodmas

The clouds had rolled in over Yorkshire, and the entire countryside seemed flat and colorless. Even the birds in the trees were strangely silent. It had rained all night and it was still raining now, the water spluttering out of the rusty drainpipes, trickling across the windows, falling into puddles that reflected a gray and hostile sky.

Matt woke up and shivered.

He was back at Hive Hall, lying on a rusty, sagging bed. He had been moved to a room next door to Noah on the upper floor of the barn. There was no heating and Matt only had one thin blanket. He looked at his watch. It was seven in the morning. He sat up very slowly. His neck ached and the bruise on his shoulder was so swollen that he could barely move his arm. There was a cut on his face where the wing of the pterodactyl had caught him. He could feel it, but he couldn't see it. There was no mirror in the room. His clothes were torn, dirty, and damp. He stretched his arms and rotated his shoulders, trying to work some warmth into his muscles. It was Saturday, April 30th. Professor Dravid had given the day a name. Roodmas. Some sort of witches' festival. This was what everything had been leading to. In twenty-four hours, it would all be over.

Matt got up and went over to the window. It looked out over the farmyard, and he could see a couple of pigs shuffling about in their sty. Otherwise, there was nobody in sight. This was his second day of captivity. He had only been let out of the room to use the toilet, with Noah standing guard outside the door. It was also Noah who brought him his meals on paper plates with plastic knives and forks. There had been no sign of Mrs. Deverill, but Matt had seen lights going on and off in the farmhouse during the night and knew she was close.

Richard had been killed. That thought hurt Matt more than anything. It seemed to him that anyone who had shown him any kindness had died, and now he was finally on his own. But he was determined to fight back. If Mrs. Deverill thought she could just drag him into the wood and stick a knife in him, she had a surprise coming her way.

He had already started. He was getting out.

Matt listened carefully for any sound in the barn. There was nothing, apart from the grunting of the pigs. It would be at least an hour before Noah brought his breakfast. He pulled back the mattress and removed a piece of iron about ten centimeters long, flattened at one end. Apart from the bed, there was no furniture in the room, nothing he could use to break out. But the bed itself had provided him with a clumsy tool. The metal bar had supported one of the legs. It had taken Matt most of the first day to work it free and another two hours to squeeze one end flat — using his own weight and the legs of the bed — so that it now resembled a crude chisel. His first intention had been to pry out the bars on the window, but he had soon realized they were too strong. Instead, he had turned his attention to the floor.

The bedroom floor was made up of a number of wooden planks, running parallel to the door. Each one was fixed in place with a dozen nails. Working during the night, Matt had managed to free nine of the nails on one plank. Three more and he would be able to lift it out. If he could make a hole big enough, he would be able to squeeze through and drop down to the level below. That was his plan.

He pulled back the old, colorless rug that covered the floor and set to work. The makeshift chisel was a clumsy tool and it was almost impossible to get it underneath the heads of the nails. It slipped several times and Matt's knuckles crashed into the floor. His skin was broken and bleeding. He had to be careful not to make any noise. That was the worst of it. Working quietly meant working slowly, and he was aware of time running out. He gritted his teeth and tried to concentrate on what he was doing. First one nail and then another came out. Almost an hour had passed since he had woken up, but at last the plank came free. He pried it out and looked through the narrow gap he had made.

He saw at once that his plan was hopeless. He was too high up. If he tried to drop down to ground level, he'd twist an ankle or even break a leg. He felt a wave of despair rise up inside him. Why did nothing ever seem to go his way? He fought it back. He wasn't going to give up now. Maybe there was another way.

His power.

The blind medium, Susan Ashwood, had told him what he already knew himself. *"I felt your power. . . . I have never felt such strength before."* That was what she had said just before he left her house. And he remembered the way Professor Dravid had looked at him at the museum. For a moment he had wondered if the professor was even, in some way, afraid of him.

Matt *was* different. He had known that all his life. He had seen the death of his parents the night before it happened. He had known all the details, right down to the bridge and the blown-out tire. He had known there was a security guard at the warehouse seconds before the man had actually appeared. He had smashed a jug at the detention center. He had called Richard into the wood without even opening his mouth. And then there had been the dreams that were somehow more than dreams. Three boys and a girl calling to him.

With him, that made five.

He sat down on the bed and concentrated on the door. If he could break a jug, why couldn't he turn a lock? It was just a question of finding the power inside him and activating it. He remembered the last time he had tried this. That had been the first morning when he woke up in Richard's flat. It hadn't worked that time — but perhaps he hadn't really been trying. This was a matter of life and death. Surely that would help.

He purposefully slowed down his breathing, staring straight ahead, trying to forget everything else. He focused on the keyhole, trying to visualize the metal bolts inside. He could move them. He could open the door with a key that existed only in his imagination. It was easy. He had the power.

He reached out with his hands, trying to make the energy flow through them. "Turn!" he whispered. "Turn!"

The handle turned.

The door opened.

Matt's spirits soared — but only for a second. He had been cruelly deceived. Noah was standing on the other side. He had unlocked the door to bring Matt his breakfast. He was holding a tray with a mug of tea and a single slice of bread. He had what looked like a sickle hanging from his belt. It had a wooden handle and a hooked blade that had been recently sharpened. The edge was raw silver and vicious.

"Breakfast," Noah said.

"Greasy and disgusting," Matt said.

"You don't want to eat it?" Noah asked.

"I wasn't talking about the breakfast."

There was a gap in the floor. Matt had been aware of it from the moment Noah came in. But the question was — would Noah notice it? Matt realized he had to keep Noah talking. Somehow he had to keep Noah's attention diverted.

Noah set the tray down on the bed.

"I'd like a bath," Matt said.

"No bath."

"How about a shower? Or maybe you don't know what that is. From the smell of you, I'd say you've probably never had one."

The taunt worked. Noah was gazing at him, his attention diverted from the rest of the room. For a moment he stood there, breathing heavily. He took the sickle out of his belt and held it up to his lips. Then he ran his tongue down the blade. "I'll enjoy watching you being killed," he breathed. "You'll scream like a pig. You'll scream and you'll cry and I'll be there!" He tucked the sickle back and walked over to the door. "No more food today," he announced. "You can die hungry." He slammed the door and locked it again from outside.

Matt waited until he was sure Noah had really left, then gulped down his breakfast. The tea was cold, the bread soggy. But he didn't care. Hot or cold, the food would give him strength, and that was one thing he needed. He was secretly glad that Noah wasn't going to bring him lunch. That gave him more time. It was obvious to him that he wasn't going to open the door by magic — or any other means. There was only one way out of here, and that was through the hole he had already made. It just had to be bigger, and now he could work uninterrupted all day.

When Matt next looked at his watch it was just after three o'clock in the afternoon. His knees were sore. His back was stiff. His fingers were covered in blisters and one of his thumbs was gashed. But two more floorboards were free and only seven nails remained before the hole would be large enough for his purpose. He couldn't jump down. He was too high up even to swing himself down at arm's length. But he had another plan — and he would only have one chance to make it work.

Six o'clock arrived and still the fourth plank refused to budge. Eight nails stood between him and success. Now he worked more feverishly, caring less about the noise. What would he do if this didn't turn out the way he hoped? He smiled grimly to himself. The chisel was hardly the most effective of weapons, but it would have to do. If he could at least give Noah something to remember him by, he would go more cheerfully. Picturing that moment, he stabbed down with the flattened bar of iron. Another nail came free. There were only seven left.

It was already dark when Noah returned. There was the familiar rattle of the key and the creak of the opening door. He stood on the threshold with the sickle tucked into his belt. There was no electricity in the room. He took out a flashlight and flicked it on.

"Time to go!" Noah sang out the words. "They're all waiting for you."

He was answered by complete silence.

"What's the matter?" he hissed. "Are you playing games?"

From the far side of the room, where the bed stood, there came a painful groan.

"What is it? Are you sick?"

Matt groaned again and coughed, a hard, rattling cough. Anxiously Noah held the flashlight at arm's length.

"If this is some sort of trick," he threatened, "I'll make you wish you'd never been born. I'll . . ."

He took two paces into the room and stepped onto the rug.

The rug was covering the hole that Matt had spent the whole day making. Noah dropped the flashlight and disappeared without a sound. The rug went with him, sucked down as if by an animal trap. At once, Matt sprang off the bed. The flashlight was lying on the floor and he snatched it up, then hurried out of the room, along the corridor, and downstairs. The sight that greeted him at the bottom was not a pretty one. He had hoped the laborer would knock himself out when he hit the ground. But somehow Noah had fallen on the sickle. It had gone through his stomach and out the other side. His face was twisted in an expression of pain and surprise. He was quite dead.

Matt ran out into the darkness. It was still raining and he felt needles of water slicing into his face. The road seemed to have been churned up into puddles and mud that threatened to drag him down. Twice he stumbled and fell, setting the bruise on his shoulder on fire. But he didn't hesitate. He ran headlong into the night, unaware of anything but the sound of his feet hitting the road, the drumming of his blood in his ears, and the gasping of his breath as it emerged in fierce white clouds from his mouth.

He ran until every step made him wince and his legs shouted at him to let him rest. His mind was dead. He was no more than a machine. Rainwater streaked across his face and trickled down the back of his neck. At last he came to the end of his strength. He had to stop. He saw a bank of grass and collapsed onto it. He had no idea how far he had come. A mile? It could have been ten.

The headlights of a car appeared in the distance. Matt lifted his head and, moving like an old man, began to get to his feet. He knew it was dangerous, but he had no choice. He had to stop the car and ask for a lift. Perhaps the driver would hand him to the police. But it didn't matter. It was Roodmas. Tomorrow he would be safe.

Staggering forward, he raised his arms. The car slowed down and stopped. Its headlamps lit up the rain, making it look like spilled ink. It was a sports car. A black Jaguar.

The front door opened and the driver got out. Matt tried to move toward him, lost his balance, and tumbled into a pair of outstretched arms.

"Good heavens!" Sir Michael Marsh said.

Matt recognized the government scientist he had visited with Richard. He tried to speak, but the words wouldn't come.

"What are you doing out here in the middle of the night?" Sir Michael demanded. Then: "No. Don't try to speak now. Let me get you into the car, out of this rain."

Matt allowed himself to be carried to the car and slumped gratefully into the front seat. Sir Michael shook off the rain and got in next to him. The engine of the car was still running, the windscreen wipers turning. But the car didn't move. Sir Michael was wearing a raincoat and hat. He looked completely perplexed.

"It's Matthew Freeman, isn't it?" he said. "What on earth are you doing in this dreadful state? Have you had an accident?"

"No . . . I . . ."

"You look as if you've just escaped from a pack of bears."

"I'm very cold."

"Then we must try to get you warm at once. Don't you worry. It's very lucky I ran into you. Everything's going to be all right now."

He put the car into gear and they moved off. Sir

Michael turned the heater on and Matt felt a cushion of hot air surround his legs. He was safe! Sir Michael Marsh would listen to his story. He had the power to see that Mrs. Deverill and the other villagers were defeated. Sir Michael would make sure that no more harm would come to him. The car sped on through the night. Matt relaxed in the soft leather seat. All he wanted to do was sleep. He had never been so tired.

But he couldn't. Something was wrong. Something was terribly wrong. What was it? He played back the words that Sir Michael had spoken just a few minutes ago.

"*It's Matthew Freeman, isn't it?*"

He knew Matt's last name.

When Richard had taken him to Sir Michael's house in York, he had introduced him only as Matt. Only Mrs. Deverill knew his last name. Sir Michael couldn't have known it.

Unless . . .

Matt scrambled for the door handle and tried to open it, but it was locked. He turned to Sir Michael just as a fist with a gold signet ring on one finger crashed into the side of his head, throwing him against the window, stunning him. The old man was unbelievably strong. Now Matt remembered seeing the car before, at Hive Hall.

"Please don't try to move," Sir Michael said. "The doors are locked and there's nowhere you can go. I don't enjoy hitting children and I don't want to do it again, but I will if you try anything."

There was nothing Matt could try. Every last ounce of his strength had deserted him.

"We'll be there very soon. It won't take long. And you

don't need to worry. It will all be over very quickly and it won't hurt as much as you think."

The car left the road. The wheels bumped over a muddy, stony track. They plunged into the forest. Pine trees sprang up on all sides. Ahead of them, the lights of Omega One shimmered in the rain. Matthew tried to throw himself at Sir Michael Marsh, but the old man easily pushed him back.

They reached the gates of the power station and stopped. The night was suddenly cut apart by an immense guillotine blade of lightning. The villagers were there. Mrs. Deverill was standing in front of them. Asmodeus was curled around her leg. They were all waiting for Matt.

"No!" he shouted.

"Take him!" Sir Michael ordered.

The door was pulled open. Gray, dripping hands reached in and clamped down on Matt. He lashed out, but it was too late. He was dragged out of the car and lifted into the air. A huge spotlight cut through the rain, blinding him. There was a crowd of people there . . . the entire village. This was the moment they had been waiting for, and now they had him.

Squirming and shouting, Matt was carried above their shoulders and into the heart of Omega One.

EIGHTEEN

Dark Powers

It was like being in a nightmare technological circus.

The reactor chamber was a great circle with a domed ceiling at least thirty meters high. Instead of sawdust, the floor was covered with black and white squares, and the roof was made of steel rather than canvas, with red and blue gantries crisscrossing high above the ground. The walls were silver. There was an observation window in front of what must have been a control room and a wide balcony that ran the whole way around. Seating for an audience?

A single wide corridor led out of the ring. If it had been a circus, this would have been the path along which the animals and the clown cars would come in. Two railway tracks ran parallel with each other and there was a massive tower — all platforms, railings, ladders, and dials, mounted on wheels so that it could move backward and forward. The tower dominated the chamber. For the moment, it was still.

The arena was lit by brilliant floodlights attached to brackets. Everything was spotlessly clean. The very air had a metallic, sterile taste to it as hidden ventilators sucked it in and filtered it with a constant hum.

This was the heart of Omega One. Matt knew that under the floor, protected by ten meters of reinforced concrete and steel, a dragon lay sleeping. Its every breath trembled with pent-up anger. When it awoke, its roar would have the force of an exploding sun. Such was the power contained in the fragile cage of the nuclear reactor.

Watched by the silent villagers, Matt examined his surroundings. For all its technology, the power station was not so different from any modern factory. What made it so fantastic was that in stark contrast to the machinery, it had been filled with the trappings of an almost forgotten age. The twenty-first century forced into an unholy marriage with the Dark Ages. Inside the nuclear power station, the ground had been prepared for a witches' Sabbath — for the celebration of Black Mass.

Despite the electric lights, the chamber was decorated with thousands of flickering candles, all of them black, their wicks spluttering. Smoke twisted up and was whisked away into the ventilation system. The candles surrounded a circle that had been painted on the chessboard floor with a series of words, written in capital letters, going all the way around. HEL . . . HELOYM . . . SOTHER. . . . They were foreign words that meant nothing to Matt and he gave up trying to read them. Inside the circle, there were various symbols — arrows, eyes, five-pointed stars, and spirals that could have been the doodles of some demented child, except that they had been drawn in gold paint, seemingly with care.

His eyes were drawn to a slab of black marble in the very center of the circle. The stone was the size of a coffin, with a single design engraved in gold at the foot.

A wooden cross hung from above. But it was upside down. Directly beneath it lay a knife, its blade a twisted tongue of dull silver, its handle fashioned from the horn of a goat.

Matt shuddered. He knew what all the preparations were for. This was where his life was meant to end. The knife, he knew, was for him.

The villagers closed in around him. They were all there — apart from a handful who were looking down on him from the window of the observation box. Mrs. Deverill and her sister were standing next to each other. Matt recognized the butcher, the chemist, the woman with the pram . . . even the schoolchildren had joined in the ring, their faces pale, their eyes hungry. Nobody spoke. Nobody tried to force him onto the slab. They knew he had no choice but to surrender. He had given them a run for their money. But he had lost and now it was time to pay.

"Matt . . ."

Somebody had called out to him. Matt looked past the villagers and saw a man standing outside the circle, his hands tied behind him to a metal railing. Matt ran over to him, everything else forgotten for a moment. It was the last thing he would have expected. Richard Cole was still alive. His clothes were ragged, his face smeared with blood. He was helpless, a prisoner. But somehow he had survived the destruction of the museum and had been brought here, too.

"Tell me I'm dreaming," Richard gasped as Matt reached him.

"I'm afraid not," Matt said. He was so surprised, he didn't know what to say. "I thought you were dead."

"Not quite." Richard managed a ghost of a smile. "It looks like Sir Michael Marsh is part of all this," he said.

"I know. He brought me here."

"Never trust anyone who works for the government."

Richard leaned forward and whispered suddenly, "My left hand is almost free. Hang in there!" Matt felt a surge of hope.

"So here we all are together!" The voice came from the one open door. The villagers turned toward Sir Michael Marsh as he entered the arena. "Shall we take our places? The end of the world is about to begin."

Two of the villagers had crept up behind Matt, and before he could react they pulled him away. He struggled, but it was hopeless. The two men were huge and handled him as if he were a sack of potatoes. They dragged him over to the sacrificial slab, threw him onto his back, and tied thick leather bands around his wrists and ankles. When they stepped back, he couldn't move. So this was where it ended. This was what it had all been for.

Richard was shouting, too. "Leave him alone! Why hurt him? He's just a kid. Let him go!"

Sir Michael held up a hand for silence. "Matthew is not *just* a kid," he replied. "He is a very special kid. He is a kid we have been watching for almost half his life."

Mrs. Deverill pushed her way forward. She was dressed in the same clothes she had worn in London, the lizard brooch in place, her eyes filled with hatred. "I want to be the one who cuts his throat," she rasped.

"You will do as you're told," Sir Michael replied. "I have to say, Jayne, you've disappointed me. You very nearly let him get away. A second time!"

"We should have locked him up from the start!"

"You're the ones who should be locked up," Richard shouted. "You're all mad —"

"We're not mad." Sir Michael turned to him. "You

know nothing. You live in your own cozy, mediocre world. You're completely blind to the greater things that are happening around you, like so many of your kind. But soon that will all change.

"I have dedicated my entire life to this moment. The preparations alone have taken more than twenty years, working night and day. Did Professor Dravid tell you about us? Did he tell you about the Old Ones?" Sir Michael paused, but Richard said nothing. "I will assume that he did, and you probably thought that he was mad, too.

"The Old Ones exist. They were the first great force of evil. At one time they ruled the world, until they were defeated — by a trick — and banished. And ever since then they have been waiting to return. That is what you are about to witness now. Your friend — Matthew — is tied down on the very mouth of Raven's Gate." Sir Michael spread his hands. "That is where we are now. And the gate is about to open."

The villagers shivered with pleasure. Even Mrs. Deverill forced a thin smile to her face.

"The forces that created Raven's Gate knew what they were doing," Sir Michael continued. "The gate is unbreakable. It is unopenable. It is unmovable. Or so it seemed for centuries. Our ancestors tried to break it as long ago as the Middle Ages. For hundreds of years they passed on their accumulated knowledge, their spells and rituals, from generation to generation. But nothing worked until now. We are the chosen generation.

"Because we live in the twenty-first century. We have new technology. And there is a power that we can harness.

The same power existed the day the world was created, but it only became available to us a short time ago. Nuclear power. The power of the atom."

He walked over to Matt, who strained upward, trying to break the leather bands. He forced his shoulders off the sacrificial block — but there was nothing else he could do. As Sir Michael approached, he slumped back.

"Do you really think it's so crazy to draw parallels between the power of the nuclear bomb and the power of black magic?" Sir Michael asked. "Do you really believe that a weapon capable of destroying cities and killing millions of people in a few seconds is so far removed from the devil's work? To me, it was obvious. I saw that the two different powers could be brought together and that together they could do what nothing had ever been able to do before.

"When Omega One was built, I used my influence to ensure that it was built here, on the very spot where the ring of stones — Raven's Gate — had stood. The ancient stone circle would be contained right here, in this reactor room, if it hadn't been destroyed. Beneath us, the reactor has almost reached critical. It is as if a gigantic bomb has been buried in the heart of the gate, waiting to blow it apart and allow the Old Ones through.

"I built Omega One. I was also in charge of closing it down once the government had finished with it. I managed to dissuade them from actually razing it to the ground, and as soon as everyone had gone away I set to work, quietly rebuilding it. It took me more than twenty years, working with the villagers, the sons and daughters of the sons and daughters of the warlocks and witches who have inhabited Lesser Malling for centuries."

"But how did you get the uranium?" Richard shouted. "It's impossible! You told us so yourself. You'd never get the uranium."

"There was a time when it would have been impossible," Sir Michael agreed. "And it was still extremely difficult. But the world has changed. The collapse of the Soviet Union. Events in Serbia and Yugoslavia. Wars in the Middle East. There are mercenaries and terrorists crawling all over the planet, and finding ones we could do business with was only a matter of time. They, too, serve the Old Ones in their own way. We're all on the same side.

"For six months now, we have kept the station going, feeding the reactor, priming it for tonight. Believe me when I tell you the reactor works. Soon I will give the order for the last control rods to be lifted. This will raise the heat to critical levels. And the gate will melt and open."

"You'll all be killed!" Richard said.

"Only you will be killed. Because only you are outside the circle."

"That's what *you* think. . . ."

"That's what I know." Sir Michael pointed to the symbols painted on the floor. "For centuries, magicians have painted circles like this for protection. And it will protect us right now. If the radiation leaks, we won't be touched by it. The heat, no matter how fantastic, won't burn us. Only you will die."

"What about Matt?" Richard demanded.

"Professor Dravid didn't tell you?" Sir Michael smiled.

"The three ingredients of the Black Sabbath. Ritual, fire, and blood. We have inherited the rituals. We have created the fire. Now Matthew will supply us with the blood."

He picked up the knife and ran a finger along the blade.

"Blood," he continued, "is the most powerful form of energy on the planet. It is the very life force itself. Sacrifice has always been part of magical ritual because it represents a release of that power. There, once again, is the connection. The medieval witch splits throats. The twenty-first-century witch splits atoms. Tonight we shall do both."

"But why him?" Richard insisted. "Why Matt?"

"Because of who he is."

"But he's nobody. He's just a kid!"

"That's what he thinks. But it had to be *his* blood. This is the moment that he was born for."

"That's enough!" Mrs. Deverill said. "Let's get on with it."

Sir Michael looked at his watch. "You're right," he said. "It's time."

Matt couldn't move. The slab was cold against his back. The leather bands held him tight.

Inside the observation room, a switch was thrown. Far beneath the ground, electromagnets gripped the control rods and began to pull them upward, centimeter by centimeter. The villagers joined hands, eyes closed. Slowly, the nuclear rods were sucked out of the nuclear pile. Sir Michael walked to the middle of the circle and stood above Matt, the knife in his hands.

It was midnight on the eve of Roodmas. It was time to open the gate.

NINETEEN

Raven's Gate

So it came to this.

Matt was tied down, surrounded, helpless. In a few moments, he would be killed. The ferocious heat of the nuclear reactor would weaken the gate, bringing it to the point when it could finally be smashed. And then the knife would plunge into his heart. Somehow, his blood hitting the floor would be enough. At that moment, Raven's Gate would open.

Richard Cole couldn't help him. Even if he managed to break free, he would never reach Matt in time.

But there was still the power.

Twice Matt had tried to find it inside himself. Twice he had failed to make it work. He had one more chance. But how?

The villagers had begun to whisper. It was a sound that Matt had heard before. They began with the same words that had haunted him when he was alone at Hive Hall.

"NODEB . . . TE MOCMOD . . . EMANY . . . NEVAEH . . . NITRA . . ."

Now that he was so close to them, Matt could make out the words that they were reciting. And suddenly he recognized them. He had assumed they were speaking in Latin or Greek, but it was much simpler than that. It was an old witches' ritual. They were reciting the Lord's Prayer backward.

Matt tried to ignore them. He was aware of the growing energy beneath him as the nuclear reactor reached critical mass. He knew he had to close his mind to all of it. Why hadn't he been able to break the vase in Richard's flat? Why couldn't he open the door when he was Mrs. Deverill's prisoner? What was he doing wrong?

The whispering filled the room, rising above the soft hum of the ventilation system. Sir Michael held the knife tightly in both hands, waiting for the moment when he would bring it down. Despite all his efforts, Matt found himself transfixed by the silver blade. This whole business had begun with a knife . . . the one that Kelvin had used to wound the security guard. It seemed that it would end with one, too.

Think about the knife. Concentrate on it. Make it stop. Lying on his back, unable to move, Matt tried to unlock the power that he knew was inside him. But it was no good. Sir Michael was in control. He was smiling to himself as he whispered the words of the invocation. Matt could see the sweat on his upper lip. He was going to enjoy this. His whole life had built up to it.

Far underneath the ground, the control rods moved slowly upward. As they left the core of the reactor, the neutrons rushed around the enclosed container, traveling at hundreds of miles per second, smashing into one another, releasing fantastic heat.

And as the control rods rose, so did Raven's Gate.

Richard had managed to free one hand, but the other was still trapped and he was fighting desperately with the rope. But seeing what was happening, he stopped, totally shocked.

The great stones, destroyed centuries ago, were rising out of the floor like monstrous plants. There were eighteen control rods. And there were eighteen stones, each one sliding up in the exact position that it had once occupied. They were ghosts, passing through the floor without touching it. But even as Richard watched, they shimmered, becoming more solid as they grew taller. Already they were towering above the villagers, forming a new circle behind them. In a few seconds they would be exactly as they had been. And he knew with a terrible certainty that it would be then that the knife would fall. At that moment, the Old Ones would break free.

Matt saw all this and closed his eyes. The more he was drawn into the events around him, the less control he would have. Was there nothing he could do? He had smashed the jug of water. It hadn't been a dream. He had done it. But how? Desperately he tried to remember how he had felt when he was in the detention center. What had made him different? Why had it worked then?

The whispers grew louder. Now something even more incredible was happening. The color of the floor inside the circle had changed. The black and white checks had been washed away by a glow of red that seemed to be shining through from underneath. The glow became brighter, the color more violent, until it was like a vast pool of blood. Suddenly a crack, deep and black, cut a jagged path across the reactor cap. The gate was breaking up.

Matt opened his eyes one last time. There was Richard, standing outside the circle, struggling again with the rope. There was Jayne Deverill with her sister, watching what was happening with something close to ecstasy. The ceiling — harsh industrial lamps and silver pipes. The observation room with the village children pressed forward, watching through the glass. The flames of the black candles, spluttering and swaying. And the floor . . .

A speck of darkness had appeared in the red. Matt forced himself up so that he was looking down the length of his body and beyond. The floor had become transparent. He was looking through it, into another world. The speck moved. It was climbing, flying, swimming upward, moving at an incredible speed. For a second he could make out a shape, some sort of creature. But it was too fast. The blackness welled up, blotting out the red, thrusting it aside in a chaos of swirling bubbles. A brilliant white streak seared across the surface of the pool. The black thing brushed it away and with a shudder Matt saw what it was. It was a huge hand. The monster that owned it must be as big as the reactor itself. He could see its fingernails, sharp and scaly. He could make out the wrinkled skin of its webbed fingers. It had placed its fist against the barrier and the crimson bubbles were exploding around it as it searched for the strength to punch its way through.

Matt closed his eyes. And suddenly, out of nowhere, the answer came.

The smell of burning.

That was what had triggered it. He had smelled burning when he was sinking into the bog. He had thought someone had lit a bonfire in the pine forest. The same

231

smell had been there in the detention center, when he broke the jug. And even before that, long before that. Now he remembered. His mother had burned the toast the morning of the accident that had killed her. Somehow, it was the burning toast that was the trigger. He had smelled burnt toast the moment before the security guard had appeared in the warehouse. He had known what was about to happen.

He stopped trying to influence the knife. He stopped trying to turn something on inside himself. Instead, he thought back six years. He was eight years old again, in a kitchen in a South London suburb. For just a second, a single frame in a film, he saw the yellow-painted walls. There was the kitchen cupboard. The teapot shaped like a teddy bear.

And his mother.

"Come on, Matthew. We're going to be late."

He heard her voice and at that instant he smelled it once again. The toast burning.

Inside the nuclear reactor, the whispering had stopped. The great stones of Raven's Gate had returned. They stood, almost touching the dome of the power station. Their worn, flinty surface — thousands of years old — contrasted insanely with the metal plates, the pipes and machinery that surrounded them. Sir Michael Marsh raised the knife. His fists, clutching the hilt, tightened.

"No!" Richard shouted.

The knife plunged down.

It had less than an arm's length to travel. It would slice easily into the boy's heart. The tip reached Matt's shirt. It pricked his skin. But that was as far as it went. Suddenly it stopped, as if caught in an invisible wire. Sir Michael uttered a strange, strangled moan, pushing down with all his might. He stared at Matt, knowing that the boy's power had finally awoken and with that knowledge came the first whispers of fear and defeat.

"No . . ." he muttered. And then, in a broken voice: "You can't! Not now! You can't stop me now!"

Matt looked at the knife and knew that he was in total control.

Sir Michael screamed. The blade was glowing molten red. The knife was burning the palms of his hand. His skin crackled and smoke rose, but he couldn't drop it. With a last effort he managed to bring his arms down, and the knife tumbled uselessly to the floor. Whimpering, he spit on his wounded hands. At the same time, the straps that had been holding Matt smoldered and snapped. Matt rolled off the altar and got to his feet.

He took a step forward and stood on the surface of the pit, daring the villagers to come close. Nobody moved. Even the creature beneath, although it was a thousand times his own size, cowered and backed away. A streak of poisonous green vapor rippled outward in a brilliant stain. Matt turned to face the villagers. Nobody tried to stop him. He broke through the circle and ran toward Richard. The metal railing behind him snapped. Instantly he was free.

"Follow me!" Matt ordered in a voice that was barely his own.

Too stunned to do anything but obey, Richard followed him. By the time the villagers had absorbed what was happening, Matt and Richard had disappeared through the one door of the chamber that was still open.

Mrs. Deverill recovered. With a howl of fury, she launched herself after them. The chemist — the man called Barker — tried to follow her. But he had left it too late. He had only taken three paces across the chamber when the ground in front of him broke apart, fragments of metal and concrete flying up. Orange flames roared all around him. A dense cloud of white smoke poured out, smothering him. Screaming, he collapsed to the floor and lay still.

A siren wailed and lights set all around the dome began to flash. A radiation warning. The levels were rising with every second that passed and already they were lethal. "Stay in the circle!" Sir Michael shouted. He was sobbing, still cradling his ruined hands. "The radiation has broken free. But we're protected in the circle!"

The orange flames climbed up, higher even than the stones, licking against the ceiling. The smoke belched out, forming a living carpet. A sprinkler system had come on automatically and thousands of gallons of water were showering down, soaking and blinding the villagers. But it wasn't enough to put out the fire . . . not this fire. The flames leaped through the water, hissing and crackling. The whole building began to shake.

Claire Deverill was the first to break. With a panic-stricken cry, she threw up her arms and ran between two of the stones, making for the same door that her sister had taken. But the moment Claire was outside the magic circle, she was no longer protected. The heat of the flames punched into her. Her clothes caught fire. The smoke grabbed at her legs, dragging her down. She screamed and tried to scream again. But there was no air in the room, only smoke and fire. Her face contorted and her eyes went white. She fell and lay there, jerking and convulsing on the floor.

"Stay in the circle," Sir Michael repeated. "The doors are locked. They can't escape."

Beneath the floor, the gigantic creature punched and punched again at the invisible barrier. But it couldn't break through. It had ritual. It had fire. But the blood of the child had been denied it and it didn't have the strength.

And that was when Sir Michael noticed the knife. The tip had penetrated Matt's shirt and skin. Matt's power had stopped it, but not before it had drawn blood. There was a single red drop at the very tip of the blade. Sir Michael saw it and his eyes widened. With a cry of pleasure he leaped forward and snatched the knife up. The blood was still wet. It glistened beneath the arc lamps.

Sir Michael laughed and brought the knife crashing down toward the gate.

•   •   •

The power was surging through Matt and nothing could stand in its way. Locked doors were torn from their hinges as if struck by a tornado. Steel plates bent and crumpled as he approached. Omega One was a labyrinth, but he seemed to know exactly where he was going. Down a flight of metal stairs, along a corridor, through an archway, and on to a set of automatic doors that hissed open as he approached. It was as if he had worked here all his life.

Richard was close behind him. The journalist no longer knew where they were going, but he could tell that their general direction was down. Already they had to be well below ground level. The warning sirens were still sounding all around them and lights flashed red and white at every corner. Steam hissed out of pipes. Water cascaded down from the sprinkler system. The whole power station seemed to be trembling, on the verge of breaking up, and he was worried that they were going to trap themselves. There couldn't be an exit under the ground. But he knew that this was no time to argue. He kept his mouth shut, following Matt in grim silence.

They passed through a room stacked from floor to ceiling with banks of machinery, then down another corridor. A door at the end flew open, beckoning them on.

The door led to a metal gantry above a tank of water. But it was like no water that Richard had ever seen. Pausing to catch his breath, he leaned over it. The water was blue — a fluorescent, unnatural blue. It was completely clear, without so much as a speck of dust on the surface. The tank was square in shape and about three meters deep. At the bottom, there was a row of metal containers, each one stamped with a series of numbers. Half of them were empty. Half of them contained twisted bars of metal, packed tightly together.

Richard knew what he was looking at. This was where the radioactive waste from the reactor was stored to cool. It wasn't water in the pool but acid. The boxes beneath the surface contained the deadliest substance in the world. With a shiver, he stepped back. Matt was waiting for him, his face set with a strange determination. It was hard to tell if he was asleep or awake.

"Okay. I'm coming," Richard said.

The blow took him completely unawares, crashing into the back of his head. If he hadn't been moving forward, it might have broken his neck. He fell to his knees. A woman brushed past him and stepped onto the middle of the gantry, facing Matt. It was Mrs. Deverill. Richard tried to get to his feet, but he was barely conscious. All the strength had drained away from him. He could only kneel there, helpless, as Mrs. Deverill walked toward Matt, an iron bar clasped in her hands.

"He didn't listen to me," she hissed. Her face was distorted by fury, her eyes livid, her mouth an inhuman grimace. "We should have locked you up, starved you, kept you weak. But it's over now, isn't it. The power's gone. You don't know how to control it. Now I can kill you and take you back."

She raised the iron bar. Matt looked around him. He had nowhere to run. On one side there was a wall. On the other, a low railing to stop him from falling into the tank of acid. The gantry was only two meters wide. Mrs. Deverill was standing between him and Richard. Even if Matt could have run away, he would have left his friend at her mercy, and he couldn't do that. He had no choice. He would have to fight.

The bar whistled through the air. As quick as a panther, he leaped aside, then lurched back as Mrs. Deverill thrust the pointed end at his stomach. He fell against the railing as the woman threw herself at him. She was taller than he was, and she was armed. Grunting with anger and exertion, she pressed the bar against his chest, pinning him against the side with such force that Matt thought she would crack his ribs.

He wished he could use his powers against her — but she had been right about that, too. The power was no longer there. He had exhausted himself getting this far. There was a faulty switch inside him and now it had turned itself off again. He was an ordinary boy again. And she was beating him.

Mrs. Deverill lifted the bar so that it slid over his chest and under his throat. Now she was using it to crush his windpipe. Her pinched face, with its jagged cheekbones, was very close to his. Her eyes were burning with hatred and indignation. Matt felt the floor slipping away beneath his feet. He was being forced over backward. The railing pressed into his spine and his neck bent back until he could see the pool behind him, upside down. With a gasp, he brought his knee up, crashing into the woman's stomach. Mrs. Deverill screeched and stepped back. Matt twisted to one side.

The bar slammed down again. Matt ducked. He felt the wind sweep past his cheek as the bar smashed into the railing. Sparks flew up. Then he leaped behind her, trying to take her by surprise. But she had been expecting the move. She lashed out with one foot, tripping him up. And then he was on his back, on the gantry, staring as Mrs. Deverill raised the bar in both hands. She was going to use it like a spear, crashing it down into his chest.

"You're still mine!" she gasped. "I'll have your blood. I'll tear out your heart and take it back with me."

Her fingers tightened. She took a breath.

And then she pitched forward, crying out. The steel bar missed. Matt looked past her and saw that Richard had recovered enough to make one last effort. With all his strength he had pushed her from behind. Jayne Deverill had lost her balance. For a moment she tottered; then, with a shriek, she fell over the railing and toppled into the tank.

She sank like a stone, plunging into one of the containers. With bubbles erupting from her mouth, she tried to reach the surface. But it was too late. The acid was eating into her. Richard leaned over and saw that already much of her face had gone.

"Don't look, Matt," he warned.

Mrs. Deverill was no longer recognizable. Her flesh was peeling away from her. Her hair had come out. Richard closed his eyes. Witches had been burned in the Middle Ages, he knew, but it could never have been as ghastly as this.

Matt got weakly to his feet. "This way," he said quietly.

There was another door at the end of the gantry, another flight of steps going ever farther down. The walls were suddenly different. The paint and smooth plaster of the upper corridors were absent. These walls were cut out of solid rock and they were covered with patches of damp moss. The iron steps were rusty, leading into pitch-darkness. Richard could hear the sound of rushing water. The underground river!

The steps ended. There was a small triangular platform. A couple of meters below them, the black river swept through miles of underground caverns, beneath the woods.

The cave system was like an underground pipe, filled almost to the roof with freezing water. There were no banks or towpath to walk on. There was no other way out.

"Hold on to me," Richard said. Matt passed his arms around the journalist. "Just hold on."

They jumped.

● ● ●

The reactor chamber of Omega One was breaking up. The flames had burst through almost everywhere. The heat was so intense that the heavy pipes and platforms were melting. The ground was buckling and breaking. A crack had appeared in one of the walls and the night air was feeding the flames, convulsing the smoke.

Sir Michael Marsh stood alone beside the altar, the wind and smoke twisting around him. The villagers, mad with fear, had attempted to flee. But outside the protection of the magic circle they had been incinerated instantly, swallowed up by the inferno. Now the observation box exploded, fragments of glass and metal splinters cascading into the chamber, a rain of death.

The metal tower at the far end of the ring wavered as a new spasm seized the floor. With a sickening screech and an eruption of sparks, it keeled over, tearing through a wall. Another window shattered, a fireball shooting out like a bullet from a gun.

The scientist leaned against the sacrificial slab. Beneath him, underneath the smoke and fire, the black hand of the creature he had summoned hammered one last time against the gate. The ancient stones had almost gone. They were crumbling away, dust pouring out of the gashes that had formed in them. Omega One was in the grip of an earthquake of its own making, the walls vibrating, the metal ladders and platforms shaking loose and crashing down.

But then with one last cry, a cry such as the world hadn't heard for a million years, the creature — king of the Old Ones — broke free. The gate shattered. A single drop of Matt's blood had been enough to weaken it. The hand stretched out.

"We've done it!" Sir Michael cried, his eyes widening. "You're here! You're free!"

The huge hand opened. All the light in the chamber was blotted out as the giant fingers stretched.

The hand was all around the scientist. He screamed a thin scream of delight that in an instant turned to terror as he realized what was about to happen. The hand closed on him and crushed him. Sir Michael Marsh died horribly, in the grip of the creature he had served all his life.

And then the reactor, pushed beyond its limits, disintegrated. A blinding, searing, fantastic light burst out. It was a light as bright as the sun itself. The light of an atomic explosion.

A huge mushroom cloud sprouted out of the ground. Man's most dreadful creation ran wild. Spiralling upward, it rushed into the night sky, carrying with it enough deadly radiation to destroy half of England.

But the gate was open.

The vacuum had to be filled.

The atomic energy recoiled, sucked back into the gate. The mushroom had risen a quarter of a mile above the ground, but now it was pulled down again. The smoke and deadly gases were dragged back into the hole that had been broken between the two worlds.

The light flooded into it. The creature itself was engulfed and dragged back. A torrent of pure light swirled around and around it, forming a whirlpool from which there could be no escape. The molten red flooded across like a curtain, then dimmed and died away. The black and white squares of the reactor floor shimmered and reappeared. The creature was gone. The gate had been resealed.

Two miles away, Richard and Matt, coughing and shivering, were spit out of an underground cavern and, reaching the bank, pulled themselves onto dry land. On the horizon, a ripple of pink spread through the night as the sun began its climb over the edge of the world.

At last, it was over.

TWENTY
The Man from Peru

"The *Times*?"

"Nothing."

"The *Telegraph*?"

"Nothing."

"The *Daily Mail*?"

"Nothing."

"The *Independent*?"

"Nothing."

"*Le Monde*?"

"I don't know. It's in French."

"There's got to be something, somewhere."

Matt and Richard were sitting at the kitchen table in the journalist's York flat. Each had a pair of scissors and a mug of tea. A week had passed since their escape from Omega One and both had changed. Matt carried a scar on the side of his face — a souvenir of the National History Museum. But he was looking a little less pinched and tired. A week spent with Richard, sleeping late, watching TV, and generally doing very little, had obviously been good for him. As for Richard, he was more optimistic, more organized. He still found it hard to believe that he had actually survived. And he was certain he was about to sell the greatest story ever written. It wasn't just a case of "hold the front page." His story would run on *every* page.

They were surrounded by newspapers and magazines that they had checked through, from first page to last. They had done the same every day for a week. And always it was the same.

"How many more do we have to read?" Matt asked.

"I can't believe this is happening," Richard said. "I mean, there must be a mention of it somewhere. You can't have a nuclear explosion in the middle of Yorkshire without somebody noticing."

"You've got that clipping from the *Yorkshire Post*."

"Oh, sure!" Richard plucked a scrap of newspaper off the fridge door where it had been held in place with a magnet. "Two column inches about a bright light seen over the wood near Lesser Malling. A bright light! That's what they call it — and they stick it on page three next to the weather reports."

For the past seven days, Richard had been monitoring the news in the press and on the radio and television. He was completely bewildered. It was as if nothing out of the ordinary had ever taken place. Structural engineers were still investigating the damage done to the Natural History Museum. Millions of pounds' worth of dinosaur fossils had been destroyed — but nobody had mentioned Professor Sanjay Dravid, who surely must have been found dead in the middle of it. Likewise the death or disappearance of Sir Michael Marsh. Here was a man who had once been an influential government scientist. He had been knighted at Buckingham Palace. But there were no obituaries, no comment, nothing. He might as well have never existed.

And what of Richard's story?

He had written it in the space of twenty-four hours. To start with, he had kept it simple, confining it to ten pages, outlining very broadly what had happened. Matt had insisted that his name be left out. He knew what he had done, but he still wasn't quite sure how he had done it . . . and the truth was, he didn't want to know. He had finally managed to find the power to stop the knife and to break out. But he remembered very little of it. One moment he was lying on the slab. The next he was fighting Mrs. Deverill over the acid baths. What had happened in between was like a dream. It was as if he had been taken over. As far as Matt was concerned, he never wanted to mention Jayne Deverill or Raven's Gate again. And he certainly didn't want to end up on the front pages of the world's newspapers. Some sort of superhero. Some sort of freak.

In the end, Richard had agreed to give him a false name. It was the easiest way. Richard hadn't mentioned the LEAF Project, either. It would have made it too easy to identify Matt — and anyway, it was something else Matt didn't want to see in print.

The ten-page story had gone to every newspaper in London. That had been three days ago. Since then, half of them had written back.

Dear Mr. Cole:

The editor wishes to thank you for your submission, received on 4th May. We regret, however, that we do not feel it is suitable for publication.

Yours sincerely . . .

All of them were more or less the same. Short and to the point. They didn't give any reason for turning him down. They simply didn't want to know.

Matt knew that Richard was frustrated and angry. He hadn't expected people to believe everything he had written. A lot of it was, after all, beyond belief. But at the same time, somebody must have been asking what had happened at the museum and at the power station. There was a giant crater in the wood where Omega One had once stood. Lesser Malling was now empty. How could an entire village simply disappear overnight? There were a hundred questions hanging in the air — and Richard's article provided at least some of the answers. Why did nobody want to publish it?

There was also an unspoken worry between the two.

Matt knew that he was living on borrowed time. Mrs. Deverill was dead and any minute now the authorities in London would take note of the fact that she had disappeared and wonder what had happened to him. The LEAF Project would reclaim him and he would be sent somewhere else. It was obvious that he couldn't stay with Richard much longer. There was enough room in the flat for the two of them, but anyway, a fourteen-year-old boy couldn't move in with a twenty-five-year-old man he'd only known for a matter of weeks. Worse still, Richard was out of cash. He hadn't shown up for work for a fortnight and as a result he'd lost his job on the *Gazette*. The editor hadn't even sent him a letter. It was simply there on the front page: JOURNALIST FIRED. Richard couldn't help being gloomy. If he wasn't going to have an award-winning scoop, he would need to find work. He had mentioned, briefly, that he might go back to London.

"You know what I think?" Richard said suddenly.

"What?"

"I think somebody is doing all this on purpose. I think somebody's put a D-Notice on the story."

"What's a D-Notice?"

"It's a government thing. Censorship. When they don't want a story to get into the papers."

"You think they know what happened?"

"Maybe. I don't know." Richard crumpled a newspaper into a ball. "All I know is that somebody should have said something, and I can't believe that nobody has."

The doorbell rang. Richard went over to the window and looked down.

"Postman?" Matt suggested.

"No. It looks like a tourist. He's probably lost." A lot of tourists went past the flat, but it was unusual for one to ring the bell. Richard stood up. "I'll go down and get rid of him."

He left the room. Matt finished his tea and rinsed his mug in the sink. He hadn't slept well the night before . . . or indeed any night since their escape from Omega One. He was afraid that if he slept, he would see the four children on the beach. Three boys and a girl. With him, that made five.

One of the Five.

That was what this had all been about. Four boys and a girl — who had saved the world once and who would return to do it again. At the museum, Matt had told Richard what he believed. That he was one of them.

But how could that be possible when they had lived thousands of years ago? Matt had some sort of power. That much was obvious. But it wasn't something he could control, and as far as he was concerned, he never wanted to see it or use it again. He sank his head into his hands. He had never been in control of his life . . . not for as long as he could remember. And right now he felt more out of control than ever.

Richard came back into the room. There was a man with him, dressed in a pale suit with a white shirt and a plain silk tie. He was certainly foreign, with very black hair, olive-colored skin, and dark eyes. But he didn't look like a tourist. He was carrying an expensive leather briefcase and looked more like a businessman — some sort of international lawyer, perhaps.

"This is Mr. Fabian," Richard said. "At least, that's what he says his name is."

"Good morning, Matt. I'm very glad to meet you." Fabian's voice was soft. He pronounced each word carefully, with a strong Spanish accent.

"Mr. Fabian has read my article," Richard continued. "He's from the Nexus."

The Nexus. Matt remembered the name. Professor Dravid had mentioned it before he was killed . . . some kind of secret organization, working all over the world. Susan Ashwood, the blind medium, was part of it, too.

"What do you want?" Matt demanded. He'd had enough. He just wanted to leave this all behind.

Fabian sighed. "Do you mind if I sit down?" he asked.

Richard gestured at a chair.

Fabian took it. "First of all let me say, Matthew, that I am very glad — very honored — to meet you. I know what you've been through. I hope you are fully recovered."

"You don't know the half of it," Richard growled.

Fabian turned to him. "You were, of course, at the Natural History Museum when Professor Dravid was killed," he said. "I would be interested to know how it was that you survived."

Richard shrugged. "It was the rib cage," he said. "I was trapped underneath a dinosaur. The rib cage protected me from the falling bricks and Mrs. Deverill dug me out." He stopped. "You say you've read my article. So maybe you can tell me something. How come nobody wants it?"

Fabian sighed apologetically. "As a matter of fact, that's the reason why I'm here, Mr. Cole. My organization has prevented your story from being published. It is our job to ensure that it never sees the light of day."

"What?" Richard stared at his visitor with anger and disbelief. "You're telling me that the Nexus —"

"I am very sorry. I know it must be extremely frustrating. . . ."

"Frustrating! Are you out of your mind?" Richard cast an eye over the table and Matt was glad there wasn't a kitchen knife at hand.

"We can't let you go to print, Mr. Cole."

"Why not? And how did you stop me?"

"As to your second question, I'm sure Sanjay Dravid already told you. We have a great deal of influence. We know people . . . in government, in the police, in the church. We advise them. And in this case, we advised them not to publish your material."

"Why not?" Richard thundered.

"Please, Mr. Cole." Fabian could see the fury in the journalist's eyes. "Let me try to explain." He waited a moment while Richard calmed down. "Let us start by admitting that your story is completely unbelievable. Witches and phantom dogs? Supernatural creatures called the Old Ones? A boy" — he pointed at Matt — "with some sort of magical power?"

"It happened exactly how Richard described it," Matt said, coming to his friend's defense.

"Did it? The police have been sniffing around for the last seven days and they have found precious little to support your version of events. It is true that the villagers seem to have packed their bags and gone. And Omega One is now in ruins. But, to give you just one example, if there really was an explosion there, how is it that no sign of radioactive fallout has been found anywhere in the area?"

"I said in the article," Richard explained wearily. "We reckon that all the radioactive particles must have gotten sucked back into the gate."

"Ah, yes. Raven's Gate. That's the most ridiculous part of all. You write that there was some sort of stone circle that nobody in the world had ever heard of. . . ."

"Professor Dravid had heard of it," Matt said.

"Sanjay Dravid has gone."

"Wait a minute." Richard slammed a hand down on the table. "You're part of the Nexus. You know I'm telling the truth. So why are you pretending otherwise?"

Fabian nodded. "You're right. We believe you."

Richard's head was spinning. "So why do you want to cover it up?"

"Because this is the twenty-first century and the one thing that people cannot live with is uncertainty. Where there is terrorism, people need to know that the police are in control. When new diseases appear, they expect science to find the cure. We live in an age where there is no longer any room for the impossible."

"But you believe in the impossible."

"Yes. But why do you think we have to keep our organization secret? Because people would think we were mad, Mr. Cole. That is why. One of our members is a Senator in the Democratic Party in America. He would be voted out immediately if he began speaking about the Old Ones. Another is a multibillionaire, working in the field of computer software. She supports us and believes in us. But her shares would plummet if that were known. I have a wife and children. But even they do not know why I am here."

He turned to Matt.

"Although you will not be aware of it," he said, "the LEAF Project knows that you are no longer in Mrs. Deverill's care. We could tell them where you are. One word from us and you would be back in their custody."

Matt's heart sank. So it had happened exactly as he feared.

But then Richard surprised him. "Nobody's taking Matt anywhere," he growled. "He's staying here with me."

"That is exactly what we have arranged." Fabian smiled for the first time. "You see? We have already spoken to the right people and it has all been dealt with. We can help you. And you can help us. We can work together."

"How can I help you?" Matt asked.

"I'm afraid your role in all this is not yet over," Fabian replied. "Sanjay Dravid spoke to me about you. He thought your appearance was the single most remarkable event of his lifetime."

"Why?"

"Because he believed you were one of the Five."

And there it was again. One of the Five.

Matt shook his head. "I don't think I can be."

"Five children saved the world. Five children will save it again. It's part of a prophecy, Matt. What happened here in Yorkshire was only the start. The Nexus will be called together again and you will have to meet us all. Until then, we ask only that you remain here. And tell no one. We must keep these matters to ourselves."

There was a long silence.

"That's all very well," Richard said. "But how am I supposed to look after him? Since the Nexus knows everything, you may have noticed that I'm out of a job. And shouldn't Matt be at school? He can't just sit here with me!"

"We can easily arrange a local school for Matt," Fabian replied. "Anything you need or want we can get for you." He produced a business card and slid it onto the table. "As for your living expenses, we can look after them, too." He clicked open the briefcase and took out a thick envelope that he handed to Richard. Richard glanced inside it and whistled. "That is five thousand pounds, Mr. Cole. Think of it as a first payment. When you need more, you only need to call."

Fabian stood up. He held out a hand to Matt. He shook it unwillingly.

"I cannot tell you what a great pleasure it is to meet you," Fabian said. "We will meet again in London, very soon." He seemed to be about to leave, but then he turned back and his eyes were troubled. "Perhaps I shouldn't tell you this," he said. "But you will have to know eventually, and I think my friend, Professor Dravid, would have wanted me to tell you." He took a breath. "We believe that there may be a second gate."

"What?" Matt was stunned.

"I live in Lima. In Peru. It is the reason why I was chosen to visit you today. There is evidence that another gate exists in my country. It may be that I have to invite you there."

"Forget it," Matt said. "I've had enough."

"I can understand that, Matt. Just remember — the Nexus is on your side. We exist only to be your friends." He nodded at Richard. "Please don't get up, Mr. Cole. I can show myself out."

· · ·

For ten minutes neither of them spoke.

"Well," Richard said at last. The cash was spread out on the table in front of him. "At least that solves the money problem."

"A second gate." Matt had gone pale. He suddenly looked tired.

"It's got nothing to do with you," Richard said.

"It's got everything to do with me, Richard. I know that now. I thought it was all over when the power station was destroyed. But I was wrong. It's like that man said. It was just the start."

Richard shook his head. "Forget it!" he said. "I mean, think about it for a minute. You really believe there's another circle of stones? And maybe some other crackpot has gone and built a nuclear power station in the middle of it? It's got nothing to do with you, Matt. He's talking about South America. Thousands of miles away!"

"They'll make me go there."

"They can't make you do anything you don't want to do. And if they try, they'll have to get past me."

Matt couldn't help smiling. "Thanks for sticking your neck out for me," he said.

"That was nothing. Actually, I didn't even mean to. It just sort of happened."

"Well, now it looks as if you're stuck with me."

Richard nodded. "I suppose so. It's a pain in the neck. On the other hand, I haven't got a job. I might as well play babysitter for you."

"I don't need a babysitter."

"Yes, you do. And I still need a story. So what it really boils down to is, we're stuck with each other."

"A second gate."

"Forget about that, Matt. Just put it out of your mind. I haven't got the faintest idea what's going on anymore, but I'll tell you one thing for certain. We're not going to Peru."

**The story continues
in EVIL STAR.**

AFTER WORDS™

ANTHONY HOROWITZ'S

Raven's Gate: Book One of The Gatekeepers

CONTENTS

About the Author

Q&A with Anthony Horowitz

The Mystery of Stonehenge

A Sneak Peek at *Evil Star: Book Two of The Gatekeepers*

After Words™ guide by Lucas Klauss

About the Author

Anthony Horowitz was born in 1955 in Stanmore, Middlesex, in the United Kingdom. He was raised in North London, where he also attended boarding school.

Horowitz's favorite book is *Great Expectations* by Charles Dickens, and he has described the people from his own childhood as being very much like characters out of Dickens's novels. Horowitz grew up in a very wealthy Victorian-style home with butlers, cooks, and maids, but his childhood was fraught with troubles. His father was emotionally distant, his grandmother was "evil," and his boarding school was "really horrible." Mr. Horowitz escaped the pressures of a difficult family and school life by writing and telling stories.

When he became older, Horowitz continued to use his troubled childhood as a source of inspiration, and he was first published when he was twenty-two years old. He has also written for numerous British television shows, including *Poirot*, *Foyle's War*, and *Murder Most Horrid*.

In 2000 he created the character Alex Rider, a fourteen-year-old secret agent for British spy service MI6, who appears in *Stormbreaker*, *Point Blank*, *Skeleton Key*, *Eagle Strike*, *Scorpia*, and *Ark Angel*. He also wrote the screenplay for the movie version of the first book in the series, *Stormbreaker*, released in 2006.

Raven's Gate is the first book in his new series, The Gatekeepers. The next book in the series is *Evil Star*.

If you would like to contact Anthony Horowitz, please visit www.anthonyhorowitz.com.

Q & A with Anthony Horowitz

Q: *What's the story behind the origins of* Raven's Gate *and The Gatekeepers? What made you return to the idea after all this time?*

A: *Raven's Gate* is based on a series of books that I began — but never finished — almost twenty years ago. I'd always had the idea that it might be possible to write a story like *The Lord of the Rings* or *The Chronicles of Narnia* that took place here, in the real world. I loved the idea of demons and devils, monsters and ghosts battling it out in modern-day London or New York . . . but always round the corner, just out of eyesight.

Why return to it now? Part of the answer lies in 9/11 and the Iraq war. It seems to me that if ever a battle of good versus evil was taking place in the real world, it is happening now.

Q: *How do you approach the horror and suspense in this series? Obviously, there are thrills and chills, but it's not as graphic as an adult horror novel.*

A: If the Alex Rider series is James Bond aged fourteen, then in my mind, *Raven's Gate* is Stephen King for kids. My aim is to push the envelope as far as possible. I want these stories to be really scary, and as the series progresses, you'll find the sense of darkness and danger growing. The ending (if I ever get there) will be very shocking.

Q: *Is it difficult to write both Alex Rider and The Gatekeepers at the same time? What do you think the series have in common, and what's different?*

A: I can't write Alex Rider at the same time as The Gatekeepers — the two are just too different. Fortunately, I've now finished the sixth Alex adventure, *Ark Angel*, and don't plan to return to him until I've finished the second and third volumes of The Gatekeepers series.

What do the two series have in common? Pace, adventure, action, violence, and, I hope, readability. They're both fairly adult — not classic "children's books." But Matt Freeman is no Alex Rider. He's much less sure of himself, even more a victim than Alex. And there won't be quite so many happy endings in The Gatekeepers.

Q: *Where do you come up with story ideas?*
A: Story ideas come to me all the time, from every direction. I believe that everything and everyone on the planet has a story. It's just a question of looking for it. I get a lot of inspiration from the newspapers. And also from dreams.

Q: *Is there any difference between the way British fans react to your work and the way American fans respond to your work?*
A: I think I'm still better known in England. Perhaps because I'm English, I get more of a sense of belonging there. Also, I'm able to travel a lot in England and visit a lot of English schools. I've only done one USA tour so far and would like to come back, because when I meet American kids, I find their approach to my books is exactly the same as in England. I'm also getting piles of letters from America, which is great.

The Mystery of Stonehenge

It at first appears simple: a circle of stones in an out-of-the-way corner of the English countryside. But Stonehenge, its history, and its mysteries are far from simple. Located in the English county of Wiltshire in the United Kingdom, the stone circle at Stonehenge has fascinated both students and scientists for centuries. The questions raised — Who built the monument? Why? — are still shrouded in mystery, but modern archaeologists believe they have some answers.

Construction of Stonehenge began around 3100 BCE. The builders created a large circular ditch about 115 meters (320 feet) across. Inside the flat area in the middle, the builders dug holes around the outside of the circle that may have held large wooden posts. Later, these holes appear to have been used as burial sites for cremated bodies. At this point, Stonehenge did not look much like it does today. It didn't even have any stones!

About 2600 BCE, people building at the site began using stones. These stones (called "bluestones") weigh about four tons and stand as high as two meters. They were probably brought from the Preseli Hills, about 250 kilometers away in what is now Pembrokeshire in Wales in the United Kingdom. Many experts believe builders transported these large stones over land using sledges and ropes and then rafts to complete the journey. How ancient people completed this difficult journey is a source of wonder for many modern experts.

It wasn't until about 2400 BCE to 2100 BCE that Stonehenge became more like the monument we know today. Builders used even larger stones to build a ring that circled the center of the monument. Setting two stones upright, they then placed another stone across the top, making a sort of ring of doorways. These stones (called "Sarsen stones") each weighed about twenty-five tons. Inside this circle, the builders used even larger stones in the same way to build a horseshoe shape. Each stone is about twenty to twenty-four feet in height and weighs about *fifty* tons! Today, neither the ring nor the horseshoe are in their original shape, as age and destruction by people have caused them to fall apart.

The Sarsen stones were probably transported from Marlborough Downs, which is about twenty-four miles to the north. Though the distance was shorter than the route for the bluestones, the weight of each stone was six to twelve times as much, surely making the journey even more difficult.

The construction of Stonehenge must have been a very complicated and grueling process, especially the transportation of the Sarsen stones. Researchers estimate the total man-hours needed for construction at over *twenty million*, including the shaping and transportation of the stones and construction of the monument.

Considering it was so difficult to build Stonehenge, it must have been built by people who had important uses for it. But who were these people and what did they use Stonehenge for?

Early legend had it that Merlin the wizard forced a giant to build the monument. (This was one of many stories connecting Stonehenge with Merlin and King Arthur.) Some researchers in the seventeenth and eighteenth centuries said Romans or Druids had built it. In fact, the idea that Druids (who were early Celtic priests) built Stonehenge is still popular, though most experts believe it is incorrect, since the Druids arrived after the dates during which Stonehenge was probably constructed. Though researchers have identified the culture or cultures that built Stonehenge as being part of the Bronze Age, they remain very mysterious.

As for its function, many see Stonehenge's alignment with astronomical signs as an important clue. For example, Stonehenge is located to enclose the midsummer sun's first rays in the middle of its horseshoe design. Some believe the various ways in which Stonehenge is aligned show that ancient cultures used it as a sort of temple for sun worship.

Other experts believe human and animal remains suggest Stonehenge was more important as either a sacrifice or a burial site and that it served as a waypoint on long funeral processions.

Whether these explanations are correct or not remains uncertain. The case of who built Stonehenge and why may remain unsolved forever, and that, along with the feeling of awe visitors get from seeing it, will continue to make it famous worldwide.

Forrest Hill was a private school in the middle of nowhere, halfway between York and Harrogate. And although Matt hadn't said as much, it was the main reason he had begun to think about leaving the north of England. He hated it there, and although the summer holidays weren't far away, he wasn't sure he could wait that long.

From the outside, it was attractive enough. There was a quadrangle, an old courtyard with arches and outside staircases — and next to it a chapel complete with stained glass and gargoyles. Some parts of the school were three hundred years old and looked it, but in recent times the governors had managed to attract more money and had invested it in new buildings. There was a theater, a science department, and a barn-size library on two floors, as well as tennis courts, a swimming pool, and playing fields. Everything was situated, as Forrest Hill's name suggested, in what was a basin in the countryside with the roads sloping steeply down from all directions. The first time Matt had seen it, he had thought he was being driven into a university campus. It was only when he saw the boys, aged thirteen to eighteen, walking between classes in their fancy blue jackets and gray trousers that he realized that it was just a secondary school.

It was certainly a world apart from St. Edmund's, the comprehensive school he had gone to in Ipswich. Matt didn't know where to begin when he compared the two. Everything was so neat and tidy here. There was no graffiti, no smell of chips, no flaking paint and goalposts with the net hanging in rags. There must have been a thousand books in the library, and all the computers in the technology center were state-of-the-art. Even the uniform made a huge difference. Putting it on for the first time, Matt felt as if something had been taken away from him. The jacket weighed down on his shoulders and cut underneath his arms. The tie with its green and gray stripes was ridiculous. He didn't want to be a businessman, so why was he dressing up as one? When he looked in the mirror, it was as if he were seeing someone else.

It wasn't Richard who had come up with the idea of sending him here. The Nexus — the mysterious organization that had taken over his life — had suggested it. Matt had done almost no work for two years. He was behind in every subject. Sending him to a new school in the middle of the summer term would cause problems wherever he went. But a private school wouldn't ask too many questions and might be able to look after his special needs. The Nexus was paying.

It seemed like a good idea. But it had gone wrong almost from the start.

Most of the teachers at Forrest Hill were all right, but it was the ones who weren't who really made themselves felt. It seemed to take Matt only days to make permanent enemies with Mr. King, who taught English, and Mr. O'Shaughnessy, who doubled as French teacher and assistant headmaster. Both these men were in their thirties but behaved like they were much older. On the first day, Mr. King had given Matt a dressing-down for chewing gum in the quadrangle. On the second, it had been Mr. O'Shaughnessy who had given him a high-pitched, ten-minute lecture for an untucked shirt. After that, both of them seemed to have taken every opportunity they could to pick on him.

Still, the teachers were nothing compared to the other boys at the school. Matt was a survivor. There had been some real bullies at St. Edmund's, including one or two who seemed to take a real pleasure in picking on anyone who was small, hardworking, or just different from them. He had known it would take time to make friends in a new school, especially now that he was moving into the private sector. But even so, he had been surprised by how few of them had been prepared to give him a chance.

Of course, they all knew each other. The other fourteen-year-olds at Forrest Hill were at the end of their second year and they'd already made their friendships. A pattern of life had been established. As a newcomer, Matt knew that he was intruding. Worse than that, he had come from a completely different world. Very few of the boys were snobs, but they were still suspicious about him. One boy in particular seemed determined to give him a hard time.

His name was Gavin Taylor. He was in most of the same classes as Matt. And he controlled their entire grade.

Taylor wasn't physically big. He was slim with a turned-up nose and blond, slightly greasy hair that hung down to his collar. He made a point of ensuring that his tie was never straight, slouching around with his hands in his pockets and an attitude that warned everyone — staff or student — to keep their distance. There was an arrogance to him that Matt could feel a hundred yards away. It was said that he was one of the richest boys in the school. His father had a company selling second-hand cars on the Internet throughout Britain. And Taylor had four or five friends who *were* big. They followed him round the school like bit-part villains in a Quentin Tarantino film.

It was Taylor who had decided that Matt was bad news. It wasn't what he knew about the new arrival that offended him. It was what he didn't. Matt had come out of nowhere at the end of the school year. He hadn't been to a prep school and he wouldn't explain why he had left his comprehensive, what had happened to his parents, or what he had been doing for the past two months. Taylor had taunted and teased Matt for the first few weeks, trying to make him drop his guard. The fact that Matt wasn't scared of him and refused to tell him anything only angered him all the more.

But then something happened that made the whole situation infinitely worse. Somehow, Taylor overheard the school secretary talking on the phone in her office and learned that Matt had been in trouble with the police. He'd spent time in a Secure Children's Home or something similar. And he had no money. Some sort of charity, an organization in London, had picked up the tab to send him here. Within minutes, the story had spread all around the school, and from that moment, Matt had been doomed. He was the new boy. The charity case. A loser. He wasn't part of the school and never would be.

Maybe there were boys there who would have been more generous . . . but they were too scared of Gavin Taylor. So Matt found himself virtually friendless. He hadn't told Richard any of this — Matt had never been the sort of person to complain out loud. When his parents had died, when he had been sent to live with Gwenda Davis, even when he had been working as a virtual slave at Hive Hall, he had tried to build a wall around himself. But each day was becoming harder to endure. He was certain that sooner or later something would snap.

As usual, the bus dropped him off at half past eight. The day always began with an assembly in the chapel, a hymn sung tunelessly by six hundred and fifty schoolboys who were only half awake, and a brief address from the head or one of the teachers. Matt kept his head down. He thought about what he had said to Richard that morning. He really was determined to go. He'd had enough.

The first two lessons weren't too bad. The math and history teachers were young and sympathetic and didn't allow the other boys in the class to pick on him. Matt spent the morning break in the library, trying to catch up with his homework. After that, he had forty-five minutes with the special-needs teacher who was trying to help him with his spelling and grammar. The last lesson before lunch was English, and Mr. King was in a bad mood.

"Freeman, will you please stand up!"

Matt got warily to his feet. Out of the corner of his eye, he saw Taylor nudge another boy and grin. He made sure his own face gave nothing away.

Mr. King walked toward him. The English teacher was beginning to lose his hair. He combed the ginger strands from one side of his head to the other, but the bald curve of his skull still showed through. He was holding a dog-eared copy of *Oliver Twist*. This was the book they had been reading in class. He also had a pile of exercise books.

"Did you read the chapters that I set you in *Oliver Twist*?" he asked.

"I tried to," Matt said. He liked the characters in the story, but he found some of the language old-fashioned and difficult to follow. Why did Charles Dickens have to use so much description?

"You tried to?" Mr. King sneered at him. "I think what you mean is, you didn't."

"I did —" Matt began.

"Don't interrupt me, Freeman. Your essay was the worst in the class. You scored a pathetic two out of twenty. You can't even spell *Fagin* correctly! *F-A-Y-G-I-N!* There is no *Y* in *Fagin*, Freeman. If you'd read the chapters, you'd know that."

Taylor guffawed. Despite himself, Matt felt his cheeks glowing red.

"You will read the chapters again and you will do the test again, and in the future, I'd prefer it if you didn't lie to me. Now sit down." He threw Matt's exercise book onto the desk as if it were something he had found in the gutter.

The lesson dragged on until the lunchtime bell. There were games that afternoon and at least Matt should have enjoyed that. He was fit and fast on his feet. But he was never part of the team on the sports field, either. They were playing cricket this term and Matt hadn't been surprised when he was sent to field at deep cover, as far away from everyone else as possible.

The school ate lunch in one of the school's modern buildings. There was a self-service buffet with a choice of hot or cold food, and fifty long tables arranged in lines beneath an ugly, modern chandelier. The boys were allowed to sit where they wanted to, but normally each year stuck together. The clatter of knives and forks and the clamor of so many voices echoed all around.

Matt was hungry. He had been late for the school bus and hadn't had time to buy anything at McDonald's. And there hadn't been much to eat in Richard's flat the night before. The food was the one thing at Forrest Hill that he did like, and he helped himself to a healthy lunch of ham, salad, ice cream, and fruit juice. Carrying his tray, he looked for somewhere to sit. After five weeks at the school, he had lost hope of anyone inviting him to join them.

He saw an empty space and made for it. With the tray in front of him, he didn't see the foot that was stretched out in his path. The next thing he knew, he had been tripped. Helplessly, he pitched forward. The tray, two plates, a glass, his knife, fork, and spoon left his hands and hit the floor with a deafening crash. Matt followed them. Unable to stop himself, he fell on top of what was meant to be his lunch. The entire room fell silent. Even before he looked up, Matt knew that everyone was staring.

It hadn't been Taylor who had tripped him up. It was one of Taylor's friends. But Matt had no doubt that it had been Taylor's idea. He could see him, a few tables away, standing up with a glass in one hand, a stupid smile spreading across his face. Matt got to his knees. Ice cream was dripping from his shirt. He was surrounded by pieces of salad, kneeling in a puddle of fruit juice.

And then Taylor laughed.

It was a cue for the rest of the school to join in. It seemed to Matt that just about the entire room — the entire school — was laughing at him. He saw Mr. O'Shaughnessy making his way toward him. Why did the assistant headmaster have to be on lunch duty that day?

"Why do you have to be so clumsy, Freeman?" Mr. O'Shaughnessy asked. The words seemed to be coming from a long way away. They echoed in Matt's ears. "Are you all right?"

Taylor was pointing at him.

Matt looked up. He could feel the anger coursing through him — and not just anger. Something else. He couldn't have stopped it, even if he had tried to. It was as if he had become a channel. There were flames flowing through him. He could actually smell the burning.

The chandelier exploded.

It was an ugly thing, a tangle of steel arms and lightbulbs that some architect must have thought would suit the room. And it was directly over Gavin Taylor. Now, as Matt stared, the bulbs shattered, one after another, each bursting apart with the sound of a pistol shot. Glass showered down, smashing onto the tables. Taylor looked up and cried out as a piece of glass hit him in the face. More glass rained down on him. A few wisps of smoke rose up to the ceiling. Nobody was laughing anymore. The entire room was silent.

Then the glass that Taylor was holding exploded, too. It simply blew itself apart in his hand. Taylor cried out. His palm had been cut open. He looked at Matt, then at his hand. His mouth opened but it seemed to take him forever to find the words.

"It was him!" he screamed. "He did it!"

He was pointing at Matt. His whole body was trembling.

The assistant headmaster stared helplessly. He looked bewildered, unsure what to do. This sort of thing had never happened before. It was way outside his experience.

"It was him!" Taylor insisted.

"Don't be ridiculous," Mr. O'Shaughnessy said. "I saw what happened. Freeman was nowhere near you."

Gavin Taylor had gone pale. It might have been the pain, the sight of his own blood welling out of the cut in his hand. But Matt knew that it was more than that. He was terrified.

Mr. O'Shaughnessy tried to take charge. "Someone get the matron," he snapped. "And we'd better clear the room. There's glass everywhere. . . ."

People were already moving. They didn't know what had happened. They just wanted to get out of the dining hall before the whole ceiling came down. They seemed to have forgotten Matt for the moment . . . but if any of them had looked for him, they would have seen that he was already gone.